Patricia Brooks Eldridge is a seasoned journalist, poet and novelist, and a lifelong civil rights activist. She has devoted decades to the research and site visitations for this four-book historical series, which follows its young protagonist from 19th-century London to America's slavery South and through its Civil War.

With limitless love for

my husband, Maurice Gray Eldridge,

the best case of/for Destiny of which I am aware.

Patricia Brooks Eldridge

Eagle and Child

Book One
The Old World

AUSTIN MACAULEY PUBLISHERS™

LONDON • CAMBRIDGE • NEW YORK • SHARJAH

A CIP catalogue record for this title is available from the British Library.

ISBN 9781786939227 (Paperback)
ISBN 9781786939234 (Hardback)
ISBN 9781786939241 (E-Book)

www.austinmacauley.com

First Published (2017)
Austin Macauley Publishers Ltd.
25 Canada Square
Canary Wharf
London
E14 5LQ

I know of no way of judging the future than by the past.
Patrick Henry, March 1775

We are, in fact, as Americans, the descendants of bound people, tied now by that binding in ways we have forgotten, which it would serve us well to remember.
John Van der Zee, **Bound Over**

BOOK ONE

THE OLD WORLD

Know you what it is to be a child? It is to believe in love, to believe in loveliness, to believe in belief.
Francis Thompson, on Shelley

In spite of illness, in spite of...sorrow, one can remain alive ...if one is unafraid of change, insatiable in curiosity, interested in big things, and happy in small ways.
Edith Wharton

Civilization is a movement and not a condition, a voyage and not a harbor.
Arnold Toynbee

Chapter 1
The Awakening

I shall not be a daughter anymore,

But through this final parting, all stripped down,

Launched on the tide of love, go out full grown.

May Sarton, *My Father's Death*

The first thing Devon's eyes saw when they opened was a single mote of dust. It hung suspended in the hot shaft of sun that slanted through the lone window of the loft. The sweet, thick, sickening odor of death filled her nostrils.

In the heat, Devon couldn't tell whether she still had the fever that had held them all in its grip for weeks. Her damp cotton shift clung to her, and the woolen shawl twisted about her arms was drenched with sweat. Devon untangled the shawl and lifted the limp fabric from her skin to let in whatever air was left between floor and roof.

With difficulty, she raised herself on one elbow. All the other shapes in the loft lay very still. Her older brother Boyle was sprawled on his back in the corner, bony bare feet tilted sideways toward each eave. The muslin drape that had provided him a bit of privacy from the younger children lay in a heap below its sagging clothesline; and the gray blanket Devon had kept over him to promote the sweating was wadded in a roll like a great spoiled sausage beside his face. At his feet, Dunny made only a small lump beneath the pale blue bit of worsted he had carried with him ever since he could crawl.

Devon turned her head, though the hope in her was vanishing. Under the far eave, her twin sisters, Carrie and Cavan, lay facing each other, their long brown hair spread about them like wet rushes from the River Thames, as though a girl and her reflection had been wrestling and had fallen finally, exhausted, into its waters.

Devon looked last for Annalee, the youngest, and found her lying near the attic's hatch, one small hand touching the ladder. Her pale feet protruded from the shift that served as both dress and nightgown, still white from the lye, though its starch was long since gone. Devon sank back and shut her eyes. There was nothing here she wished to know. She only wanted to go with them, beyond this misery.

But oblivion did not come. There was noise everywhere about her; it filled her ears. Only gradually did she realize that the roar was actually a great hollow absence of sound, in this room and the one downstairs, or in her parents' tailor shop at the front of the cottage. Even in the street. Normally, from the first glimmer of daylight, the alley would ring with the cries of the costers and peddlers — *Brass pots 'r iron... Hot sheep's feet... Or'nges, sixpence a pound...*

On both sides of the narrow alley, the second stories of the old wooden cottages overhung the first, reaching almost to touch, shutting out much of the light and air from the street below. The overhangs formed a kind of echo chamber with the cobblestones, in which the shrill penny whistles of the buskers and the falsetto calls of the shoeblacks rang with the deeper Cockney cries of the sellers – *Kitchen stuff, have you maids?... Four-a-pence mackerel.*

Devon's head was pounding, as though the fever, too, had left an echo. Her ears strained for any sound from downstairs – the clang of the iron stewpot on the stove or the sound of her mother humming some Irish song. All her children had been named for places from their mother's beloved Ireland. Devon's full name was Devonshire, the village that had been her home, in the county of Cavan. Carrick was the town from which her own mother had come, Boyle the birthplace of her father. Dunny was Dungannon, home of the wee folk of her tales, and Annalee the river of her lullaby. "My Irish children," she had called them, though their father was English and all had been born in this same cottage and alley. "Only Nathaniel Quail," she had been fond of saying, "could ever keep me from my home."

Now there was no sound of anyone. Oddly, the thought came to Devon that when she too joined her family in death, she would never have gotten to see even the length of Eagle and Childe Alley, let alone the maze of other twisting streets behind St. Andrews Church, all dead-ending at Fleet Ditch. Nathaniel Quail had been protective of his daughters, and had not allowed any of them beyond the doorstep of the tailor shop, to purchase

13

what was needed from the peddlers. And that only in daylight.

At night, Devon had sometimes knelt at the sealed window of the loft to peer down at the nightlife of the street, lit with the scarlet flames of the gas lamps outside the Two Roosters Tavern. Sometimes a traveling musician would come by with his wheezy hurdy-gurdy, stop outside the pub for a few tunes. And some street boy might join him with his mouth organ, cupping his hands about the instrument as though hiding its magic from her, then opening them to let the music out – open then closed, closed and open – sharing then keeping the magic to himself. Devon had wanted desperately to own one of those slender silver instruments. But they were very dear. And as she grew older, she'd had little time for such idle dreams. With her parents in the shop and her brother out with his barrow collecting rags that would transform into stout clothing under her parents' hands, it fell to Devon as the eldest girl to tend the younger children.

It was demanding, but essentially lonely work. While she was seldom without one or another of them pulling at her skirts, she had felt set apart for most of her twelve and a half years. Her mother had miscarried three children in the four years after Devon's birth; and her belly had grown so great carrying the twins, Devon had been certain that the child had been there all along and would emerge nearly her own size and age, a perfect playmate for her lonely days.

Instead, two tiny red things had been born, who had each other and needed Devon only to change their nappies, put bites of apple mash and ground kidneys into their mouths, and wipe the coal smudges from their cheeks when they played too near the stove. By the time Dunny and Annalee had come along, Devon had been resigned to her place as second mother in the family and scarcely thought of herself as a child at all. She had loved them all dearly, but still longed to leave the confines of her life, and dreamed of where she might go. To her mother's green Ireland, or the new colonies of America written of in Boyle's schoolbooks, where there was sun and air and people working the land.

Now it was too late for everyone. When the fever'd struck, Devon's mother had been the first hit, then her father. Devon had cared for them both, mixing the sweat-producing potions of contrayerva root and sage and ginger, wrapping blister-plasters about their necks while their bodies shook beneath the pile of blankets. And though she kept the drape drawn between their straw mattress and the rest of the room, all the other children she kept up in the loft, as far from the infection as possible. Even Devon did not go back and forth. Food was passed up through the hatchway on a rope tied to a basket, and their laundry was passed down, then up, the same way after Devon had boiled it and rubbed pitch into the fibers to help resist the disease.

Devon had slept on a quilt under the table, her eyes and nose burning from the fumes of vinegar and camphor which she periodically sprinkled on the coals as Doctor MacBride had instructed. She was so hot most of the time, she didn't know whether the fever was in her, too; the whole cottage seemed to drip with steam. Only Boyle came and went at first to buy foodstuffs or sell whatever was left in the shop, until their door, too, was marked with the red cross and no one could pass in or out anymore.

Then one by one, the children were stricken, Devon among them, and she was moved upstairs. Her father went back to work in the shop, though still carrying some fever; and her mother climbed up and down the ladder all day, tending to their needs. The last thing Devon remembered was her mother's face, glazed with sweat, as she removed Annalee's small arms from about her neck and lay the child's faintly protesting body beside the hatch, then disappeared below it. Now Devon squeezed her eyes shut and prayed for unconsciousness to claim her again.

But there came the sound of the front door to the shop opening, voices and footsteps coming through the drape into the room below. Then a deep, familiar voice said, "The both of them. Aye. And what of the children?" Doctor MacBride.

A thinner voice said something Devon couldn't make out, and then the doctor said, "No, leave it, dead is dead. Up with you, boy, my bones won't take the climb."

Devon tried to sit up, but she was very dizzy. Then the red-orange head of a boy, younger than she, rose out of the hatch and froze, gawking at her, his hand lifting to the rag that shielded his nose and mouth.

Devon reached for her shawl and wrapped it about her waist, then struggled to her knees. The boy backed down again as she crawled toward him, his eyes wide with alarm.

When she reached the hatch, she could see the solid frame and face of the old doctor below and turned, reaching behind her with one foot until it found the ladder and she climbed slowly down – foot then hand, foot and hand. As she neared the bottom, the doctor's strong hands grasped her around the waist. "Easy there, lass, ay've got you."

Devon let go, her weight nearly toppling them both to the floor. Eyes shut, she fumbled into the old doctor's embrace and buried her face against the rough wool of his vest, the staunch smell of Highland whiskey suffusing her body like a tonic. "Ya're all right now. There, set y'rself down." He pulled the bench out from the table and lowered her onto it. Devon was trembling nearly as violently as she had at the height of the fever. She made her chest breathe and her eyes open.

They took a moment to focus. When they did, it was upon the body of Belle, their pet rabbit, stretched beside the cold stove, its throat slit. The Searchers must have found her after all, Devon thought numbly. The order had been to kill all domestic pets in the infected households, to limit the spread of the disease from such animals running loose in the streets. So the children had kept Belle upstairs, and when the Searchers came, had thrust her under Boyle's blanket, Carrie and Cavan sitting on either side to hide its frantic movements. But the young Searcher had not stayed long, barely glancing about the loft, his feet still on the ladder. "It's my last," he said to someone below. "I'll not do it more. The few pence 'r not worth the risk of this bloody disease."

"No other?" the doctor now asked the red-haired boy as he came down the ladder the second time.

He shook his head.

"Come, child," the doctor said to Devon, grasping her elbow to lift her from the bench. "There's nothing more to be done here. Best get you to a clean bed and some broth in y'r belly."

17

Devon let herself be lifted, but she resisted the tug toward the doorway, turning instead toward that other drape, at the far end of the room.

"Gone child," the doctor said. But she moved toward it anyway, freeing her arm with more strength than she thought she still had. She couldn't just leave them there. The drape parted silently. They were lying close together, her father on his back, his honey-soft hair and beard glowing even in the dim light. Her mother lay face down beside him, her cheek resting on one hand, her other arm across his chest. *Only Nathaniel Quail could ever keep me from my home.* Maybe now, Devon thought, her mother had finally returned, and had taken her husband with her. Devon thought she should maybe feel glad for them, so peaceful now, together. But she only felt all the more alone.

Outside, the sun hit Devon's eyes and skin like boiling water. She stopped at the doorway, unwilling to go farther.

"Come now," the doctor's voice said. "Time to be gone from this wretched place, fast as our coach will take us."

Down a few houses, in the middle of the street, a tall fire burned. Beside it, a soldier in a wilted red uniform, open at the neck, laid juniper branches on the burning pile. The small blue-black berries burst as they hit the flames, like a hundred tiny guns going off in succession. The pungent smoke rose from the pile and billowed up, clouds of it flattening as they hit the second stories, then sliding back across the upper windows, all closed now, and down the blackening walls, curling in little wisps along the cobblestones like scuttling mice seeking exit. Every door bore the red cross.

As she was pulled toward the alley's entrance, Devon saw behind her an old man in a long shabby black coat, hunched over in the doorway to the shop down the street. He held a huge fiddle in his arms, like a great stout woman, the fingers of his left hand grasping the neck while the right sawed across the strings with an empty bottle. The mournful music the fiddle made seemed to come from much farther away, perhaps from Fleet Ditch itself, as the streets emptied into it. Above the fiddler, the sign *H. Ayers, Stonecutter* swayed slightly, as though set in motion by the sound. To Devon, the whole world was swaying, echoing with the hollow tones of the fiddle, as though they would be the last ever to be heard in Eagle and Childe Alley. As the doctor boosted her up the step into the musty, muffling interior of the coach, Devon leaned for one last look into the smoky tunnel, before the thuds of the horse's hooves and the rattle of the wheels overcame the fiddle's song, pulling her down Shoe Lane toward the infamous Fleet Street.

Chapter 2

To Pilgrim Street

*I have formerly lived by hearsay, and faith, but now I go where
I shall live by sight.*

John Bunyan, *The Pilgrim's Progress*

The sun-struck air beyond the open coach was unbearable
to Devon's eyes, accustomed as they were to the gloom of
the loft and the windowless interior of their small cottage.
She kept her eyelids tightly shut, huddled against the bulk
of the doctor's side as the coach jounced its way down
Shoe Lane, the wheels and horse's hooves making a
dreadful clatter against the bricks beneath them.

Soon their noise was joined by others – creaking
carriages, shuffling bodies, horses snorting, voices calling
– as though they were nearing a great mob, as dense as
that at the St. Bartholomew's Fair to which their father
had taken them once; and Devon peered out beyond the
doctor's ample girth, half fear, half curiosity pulling at her
senses.

It seemed a mob indeed, but one unlike any she had seen. Along the wide boulevard they had turned into, fine gentlemen and ladies strolled on smooth pavements to either side of the rough street, their garments a continuous flow of the fine silks and brocades Devon had encountered only as remnants in her parents' shop. These were the people they'd belonged to, their heads held high under wide bonnets and tall black hats that balanced off the full skirts of the ladies and the long, graceful cut of the men's waistcoats.

"It's a parade," Devon whispered aloud, and felt the doctor's belly jiggle against her cheek.

"'Tis that," his deep voice grumbled. "And it goes on the livelong day. See and be seen: it's what makes up their pathetic little lives."

"Where are they all going?" Devon asked.

"Where indeed. A few to work, I suppose, but the rest just out to show off their finery, rationalize the pounds they've spent on it would feed the whole of Clapton Orphanage for a week."

Devon felt a swift chill move through her, only half aware that the word *orphanage* had produced it. But already her fear was being distracted by the sight of the horses that pranced before the carriages, their noble heads and flowing tails held even higher than the people's heads, their painted hooves lifting one after the other as though dancing before the carriage rather than pulling it.

"What grand creatures!" Devon whispered.

"Nothing grand about them," the doctor's voice rumbled, "except perhaps the size of their pretensions."

Devon suspected he meant the people rather than the horses, but she was too busy staring to correct him. All the light that filled this wide street seemed to gather in the tossing plumes that bobbed on the heads of the ladies and the horses. Devon had a few such feathers, given to her on special occasions by her mother – ones she had especially admired in the basket in the corner of the shop, taken from the discarded hats Boyle salvaged from the trash in the finer streets along his route, waiting to become the centerpiece of some modest hat or patched-together bodice. But here they were in all their original glory, crowning the shining curls and soft felts of these ladies and the higher, even finer heads of the horses. It was hard to believe these feathers actually came from birds, as she'd been told; the few sooty pigeons she'd seen in Eagle and Childe Alley had certainly never dreamt of such grandeur.

The coach labored slowly through the crowd of carriages and carts until the street widened even further as it approached a hill. The broad panes of glass on the shop fronts glittered on either side like winking eyes, until beyond the hill rose an enormous dome topped by a crown – which seemed fitting, since it reigned over the whole elaborate scene. Devon had never known the likes of it; the highest edifice she'd ever seen was the steeple of St. Andrews Church, at the entrance to Eagle and Childe Alley.

"It watches over us," her mother had said about the constant presence of the church overshadowing their neighborhood. It had been one of the few instances Mary Quail had spoken of religion. It was an agreement they had, Devon had come to understand, her Irish Catholic mother and her English Quaker father: they avoided all talk of religious dogma, focusing instead on morality and character with their children.

"Just lead a good life. Care for everyone alike," Devon's father had said the once she'd asked, "and let the hereafter take care of the hereafter."

Devon felt a deep pang at the memory. She fervently hoped her father had been right, and that her parents and her sisters and brothers were now being cared for by whatever powers there might be in some hereafter.

Then the coach veered from the crowd, and the sun turned off as they pulled into a narrow court lined with small shops interspersed with tall houses. Halfway down, the coach stopped, and the doctor's reassuring bulk left her to climb stiffly down the coach's steep step, the coachman's hand at his elbow.

The same arm reached toward her, the man's face invisible in the shadow of his hat. Devon hesitated. But the doctor motioned to her impatiently from the curb, so she inched forward, and with the man's strong hand under her arm, let herself down to the step, then the pavement. She was glad for the shadows from the buildings on either side, feeling dreadfully exposed in her sweat-soaked shift, the limp shawl barely covering her naked arms and shoulders. She was relieved when a door above them opened and they could ascend the narrow steps, Devon gripping the iron railing, the doctor's bulk at her back, until they were through the tall door into the cool foyer beyond.

Devon scarcely noticed the woman who stood behind the open door, her gaze caught by the graceful staircase before her; until the woman's voice, nearly as deep as the doctor's, said, "So. What have we here? Another stray brought home to nurse?"

Devon started at the sound, and turned to look up into the wide, ruddy face of the woman, her features as stiff as the high white collar and barrel cuffs on her plain gray dress.

"Close the door and mind your business," the doctor's voice said from Devon's other side, gruff but without particular rancor, as though such exchanges were a commonplace between them.

"Did you fish this one out of the Thames then?" the woman said, though her voice sounded a little softer.

"Out of the fever. And for the love of God, woman, close the door, before she gets a chill as well."

"In this heat? Hardly," the woman said, but closed the door, then reached for Devon's tangled shawl. "Let's get rid of this," she said. "Everything," she added, looking at Devon's shift. "All contaminated with the influenza, is my guess."

Her words were cloaked in the same thick Scottish brogue as the doctor's, and seemed just as rough, but no more unkind. Devon trusted her immediately, and gave over the length of cloth she'd been clutching.

Holding it from her between two fingers, the woman dropped it into a covered basket by the door. She looked Devon over critically then, as though, after all, considering adding her to the basket.

"She needs a washing."

The doctor laid his hand on Devon's forehead. "Use the tub. And cool only. I don't want the fever returning."

"The 'tub'," the woman snorted as she started up the stairs. "As though every part of a person need be washed all at once. Then sit in their own dirt."

She looked back at Devon, still standing in the hallway. "Ar' ye comin' then?"

Devon started up, gripping the smooth bannister, holding her damp shift away from her legs, which didn't want to bend, and were trembling by midway, but made it to the top.

Without turning, the woman moved down the hall and opened the last door on the left, motioning toward its interior as she said, "Ye can take those rags off in there. Just drop 'em to the floor," then disappeared through a door across the hall.

Devon had scarcely reached the door indicated when she heard a sudden crash. She moved quickly across the hall to that room, to see water dropping from a great height into a huge white tub below. The oval tub was not metal, like the washtubs in which Devon had bathed both children and clothing at home, but a smooth, thick substance that stood on little feet in a room larger than their combined kitchen and sitting room. Yet it held only the tub and a ruffle-skirted dressing table and chair. Devon wanted to move closer, to see how so much water had been gotten into that great metal container above, from which a long funnel hung, reaching just short of the tub. But the woman was looking at her sternly, so Devon did as she'd been told and crossed the hall and through the other door.

This room was even more spacious and quite daintily furnished compared to the dark woodwork of the entrance hall and stairs. At its far end was the biggest bed she'd ever seen, its curly posts at each corner painted glossy white, shining in the sunlight through the single window. It stood a full foot off the floor, its headboard draped with a filmy white fabric that hung over it like a halo. Pillows with white lace coverings were piled at the top, and a plump, satiny white comforter was spread below them, with tiny red rosebuds scattered across its grand expanse.

A matching fabric was gathered in the skirt of another vanity in a bay to the left of the bed, with all manner and color of bottles arrayed across its top. Against the opposite wall, two great chests of drawers of a blond wood looked large enough to hold all the cloth that had passed through her parents' shop in a month.

Slowly, Devon moved across the thick rose rug to the bed and stroked the comforter lightly. Did people really sleep under such things? she wondered. It must feel like being inside a cloud in a clear white sky.

"Get y'r things off now," came the woman's voice behind her, making Devon start guiltily. "Y'r bath's near ready."

Devon quickly set to stripping off the filthy wet clothing that had clung to her skin for weeks, loading the stove with coals even in the sweltering heat to try to sweat away their sickness, then coming down with it herself. She was ashamed of her grimy things, their smell, and grabbed her shift and underthings in her hands before they could fall to the fine carpet, clutching them against her to hide her nakedness.

But the woman was at one of the chests of drawers, and pulled a long pink garment and underthings from its topmost drawer. With scarcely a glance at Devon, she dropped them on a nearby chair and went back out the door. "Ye can handle the bath, I take it?" she said over her shoulder. "Just pile y'r old things in the basket yonder" – she pointed to a corner – "then get some sleep. I'll bring up some broth f'r y'r insides."

Devon waited until she heard the heavy footsteps descending the stairs, then crept to the door and peered down the hall, empty now but for a row of high-backed chairs along the far wall, standing upright and to no apparent purpose.

Devon slipped back for the gown, dropped her wet things into the basket indicated, then peered out again to be sure no one was about before darting for the other door, shutting it tight behind her.

Across the room, the vanity took up much of the wall, trimmed in the same rosebud material as that in the bedroom, its marble top glistening with shell-like cups and boxes, gilt-backed combs and brushes of all shapes and sizes. The tub itself was fully large enough for both twins to sit in, with room for Annalee as well.

Another pang shot through Devon's chest, the sense of loss flushing her skin with its force. Carrie and Cavan had been just on the brink of being old enough to be real companions to her, Devon had been hoping. Now they were gone. Forever. All of them.

Devon leaned over the tub, her tears dropping into the deep water. She rubbed at her eyes and made herself climb over the tub's curved rim, alarmed when the water reached above her knee when her first foot hit bottom. Slowly, she planted the other leg, then lowered the rest of her body into the cool water. Halfway down, she feared that the water would be deep enough to reach over her nose. Fortunately, it stopped at her shoulders; but the sensation of so much water all around her quite took her breath away, and she held to the sides of the tub and opened her mouth for air.

But it quickly felt quite thrilling, really, rather like floating – an ability she'd always envied the faraway birds she'd seen riding the narrow strip of sky high above the overhanging second stories of the houses in her alley. Their long, gliding, motionless motion had seemed effortless – a skill Devon had imagined she could almost feel within her, a lift right at the hollow of her breastbone, then soaring on the air, weightless as a feather on a fine blue hat.

But this was almost better, being enclosed in all this coolness, feeling the sticky sweat and dirt lifted weightlessly from her skin, dissolving into the vast basin of clear, clean water. Devon stretched her arms forward, watched them almost float upon the water, then her legs, her toes appearing at the surface, where she curled them on the far lip of the tub.

A bright bottle caught her eye, resting on the tub's edge against the wall. It was filled with a creamy gold liquid and stoppered with a cork. Unable to resist, she reached for it, studied the changing patterns of the oily liquid as she tipped it this way and that, then carefully uncorked it and raised it to her nose. She was still thirsty after gulping down the glass of cool water the woman had left on the vanity for her; but clearly, this was not to be drunk. Its pungent perfume made her nostrils cringe and her eyes water. She dipped a cautious finger into the bottle's top, but its neck was too narrow for the finger to reach the liquid; so she tipped the bottle until the liquid hung briefly at the lip, then fell in thick golden drops past her fingers into the water, sinking in a slinky trail between her legs.

Devon scooted back from the stream, and as she did, churned the water enough to produce a burst of golden bubbles. This was some magical form of soap, she decided, going from oil to froth with the slightest stir. Devon raised a palm-full to her face and found the fragrance lighter now, most pleasing.

She thumped her arms in the water, producing more bubbles. This was a gift the twins would love – and with that thought, the ache returned, overriding the relaxation of her body since she'd sunk into this great vat of water. These pleasurable new experiences came at the cost of her family, and any joy she had felt vanished. But maybe, she thought then, wherever they were, their new world might have such luxuries, might be all soft and frothy and perfumed. She must hold to that thought. Wherever they were was beyond pain. She must move beyond it, too.

Chapter 3

Making Rounds

*Where wealth is created, there are grime and sordidness often
amounting to horror.
Where wealth is spent, there are light and colour and
sometimes even beauty.*
Sidney Dark, *London*

Devon wakened to the sound of voices – far away,
scarcely familiar. Where was she, lying so high,
enveloped in all this whiteness, this softness?

"Time she was up. Ay've got rounds to make."

"You let that girl sleep. She's near dead. Wouldn't
even wake f'r the broth."

"The sick don't wait on the sick. In any case, if she's
not pulled back into the land of the living, she'll be dead
as they are."

"Then you let me do the pulling. It needs a woman's
touch."

"And how would you know, pray tell?"

"You just keep yourself down here. I'll go check on the girl."

Instantly, Devon's legs were off the bed. How long had she slept? The light at the window that had been strong was now weak. Could she really have slept through a day and a night and into morning again? They would think her a lazy good-for-nothing and she'd be asked to leave. If even there were hope of her staying here where she had no real right to be.

But her legs, when she put weight on them, wouldn't hold her, and she experienced a kind of panic as the heavy footfalls of the woman finished mounting the stairs, then started down the hall. With her arm around the bedpost, Devon managed to be standing upright by the time the footsteps reached the door and it silently opened.

"I'm up," Devon said, before the woman's head had even rounded the opened door. "I'll be out straightaway."

"No need t' rush y'rself, girl. Y've been through enough."

Devon hurried to assure the woman that she would soon be ready to do whatever was expected of her, all holding fast to the bedpost to be sure her legs would not betray her and drop her to the floor.

"The doctor has qualities," the woman said then, apparently less in response to Devon's words than continuing some thought of her own. "But patience is not one of them." And she closed the door again.

Devon held to the bedpost, waiting for the dizziness to leave her, and looked about this room she found herself in. Why had the woman put her here, with all its elegant furnishings, instead of in some more plain servant's room? And who belonged to all this "feminine finery" as her father called such trappings. So far as she knew, Doctor MacBride was a widower. Often, when he'd stopped by, to check on one of the children after a bout of pox or fever, or just because he was "in the neighborhood" as he often said, Devon's mother had always insisted he stay to supper. "It's not much," she would say, "but with your missus gone, you'll be wanting something to warm you, after tending to all the rest of us the way you do."

The memory of her mother's voice weakened Devon's hold on the bedpost, and she dropped to the rug. There seemed to be an echoing noise around her; but as in the loft, she soon realized that it was only an unnatural silence. Her household had never been silent. At every moment, it seemed, one or another of the children was woefully wailing or shrieking with laughter. Restricted as they were to the two rooms behind the shop and the shallow loft, the family had kept growing, one after another child arriving, while the space had not expanded. The only silent moments Devon had found were when the family was all finally asleep, but her own head too full of thought to quickly join them. Now…this silence. It was unearthly. Unnatural. Where were all the people who belonged in this big house? Surely there were more than just the doctor and the woman who appeared to be a servant of some sort, yet too bold to be only that.

"Well?" came the doctor's voice from below. "And is she in the land of the living?"

"She's pale," was the woman's short reply.

"Well of course she's pale," the doctor said, sounding half angry. "The father never let the girls out of the house.

Thought the streets would soil them beyond cleaning, I suppose, and p'rhaps right to think it. But the girl has never seen the sun."

"Then don't give it her all in one dose," the woman's voice retorted, though coming from a greater distance this time. "She will be burned soon enough. Let her take her time."

But Devon thought time was probably not on her side, and forced herself to her feet. She must do whatever was needed of her, she told herself, to maintain the doctor's kindness in bringing her here.

She looked about and saw a multicolored pile of garments piled on the chair where the woman had put the nightdress the day before, and she stood, weaved her way over, and struggled into them.

Like the nightdress, the clothes were too big. The extravagant undergarments were pure silk, like the nightdress; Devon had learned enough about cloth in the shop to know that much. But they bagged on her thin frame. And the linen skirt proved so long, she had to pull it higher than her waist and fasten it there with its belt. The bodice was clearly cut for a woman with breasts grown longer than twelve and a half years, but luckily the fabric was stiff enough to stand on its own. All in all, the outfit felt quite strange on her skin, and she was sure it would look just as strange to others.

She saw no mirror about, but that was probably just as well; her father had not held with admiring one's image too much. The women who frequented the shop were servants mostly and needed to maintain modesty even on their days off. Still, Devon looked down at herself with a kind of wonder; never had she expected to wear such finery as these garments. Who, she wondered again, did they belong to. And where was she now?

Devon was not to get an answer to that question for the full balance of the day, which hurtled by at a giddy pace from house to house and neighborhood to neighborhood, as the doctor made his way among his patients with an alacrity surprising in one who seemed to move always in pain. Devon lost track of routes taken as they wound through narrow streets, leaving the boulevards behind, the coach's horse, now without coachman, seeming to seek out the darkest of streets and the shabbiest of hovels. Seldom did she see any shillings or pence, let alone pounds, change hands. "Next fortnight," some would say; and the doctor would wave his hand as though at some pesky insect.

But they did collect a fair assortment of goods as they went – a bucket of coal here, an embroidered handkerchief there. They supplemented the slices of mutton and bread provided by the woman at the doctor's house with such gifts. One grateful mother had thrust scones upon them, after the doctor had stopped her baby's convulsions. He had rubbed the infant's limbs with a pungent salve, then held him gently in a pail of cool water while Devon squeezed sponge- after sponge-full over his tiny body, until his squalling settled into a steady breathing and his wet lashes rested peacefully against his cheeks. He reminded Devon of Dunny as a babe, and her eyes brimmed with tears as she helped to soothe him.

"You're a saint," the woman said to the doctor as she handed him up four scones wrapped in a bit of cloth, after he'd settled heavily onto his seat on the coach bench and taken up the reins. "I'll be saying you a Hail Mary every night. You too, Miss."

The doctor smiled ruefully as he said, "Mary will probably be most shocked to hear it, having heard no word from me of late."

The woman batted her hand at him, as though the doctor must be jesting; but Devon doubted that he was. Though his face and belly would puff up into a chortle at times, there appeared to be an undertow of deep sorrow always in him that gave Devon a sense of someone in long-standing pain of the heart. It made her want to put her arms about his stout trunk to drain it from him, as her pain seemed to ease from the very presence of his bulk beside her. But his brusqueness, and a kind of distraction about him, as though it took all his concentration just to keep going, counseled her to keep a certain distance. So they said little as the coach jounced along the cobblestones or bumped through the rutted dirt from stop to stop.

But Devon could not help asking as the coach pulled away from this cottage, "Did that baby have the same sickness?"

The doctor did not ask her what sickness or turn to her, just shook his head. "He'll likely have those seizures the rest of his life. Or not. But we've shown her what to do if they come."

"Is it still out here, in the city? We haven't seen anyone with it." Only once she'd said it aloud did Devon realize the relief she'd been feeling that she didn't have to again tend to someone in the awful grip of the influenza that had killed her family. "Or the red crosses even." Just the memory of them made her shudder.

Again the doctor simply shook his head. "Mostly gone now. But as always, it hit the poor harder than the rich. Those who can afford to stay away from each other usually do, in my experience."

Then she asked what she hadn't been able to bring herself to at the time. The doctor had said as they pulled away from Eagle and Childe Alley that they could not return. "Have they been buried?"

"No," the doctor said, turning to glance at her only once, then looking forward again over the reins. "Everything had to be burned. The whole neighborhood. They will remain where they lived."

Devon began to cry, but kept her tears silent. Without turning, the doctor squeezed her hand tightly in his large one. "You did fine back there," was all he said.

Devon was kept as fully occupied, mind and body, for the rest of that day – from checking on newborns to helping a woman hold her husband's arm down while the doctor sewed up a near-severed finger with coarse thread.

"As good a chance of keeping as losing," the doctor answered when the wife asked anxiously if the finger could thereby be saved.

She was a little bit of a woman beside her husband, a burly factory worker. She had run into the street as the coach was crossing an alley where smoke streamed from the chimney of a big sooty building. They had stopped immediately, let her lead them to their rooms just beyond the building, where the man had stumbled after the accident.

"You make the bastards pay," the doctor had said to the man after he heard the circumstances of the event and that the foreman would not let the other workers stop to help him.

But when they left and Devon reminded the doctor that he had not left a bill of charges for the factory to pay, he only scowled and snorted. "That man'll grow a new finger before he ever sees a farthing from the likes of them. And he'll be back to risk the other four tomorrow to feed his family."

Devon remembered then the man's insistence that the doctor bind up only the one finger on that hand; and the cluster of children who'd watched from the door to the only other room in the quarters, dark as night though it was full daylight just outside the open door.

But the doctor did not alight from the coach for everyone, Devon found. As they approached an intersection of broad streets marked by a massive building with arches rippling along its front, a young man approached the coach, stalled in a tangle of carriages, carts, and the chairs carried by men instead of horses.

Devon had been distracted, studying the gray stone figures posed in each arch of the building, and startled when the man's voice spoke up so close to their coach.

"Doctor MacBride, isn't it?" the young man said, touching but not removing his hat. "We met at Lady Compton's, I believe? You and your charming wife."

"Yes?" The doctor's tone was none too gracious.

"Happened to notice you here," the young man went on, his bright eyes moving from the doctor to Devon on the far side of the bench. Then his expression grew more sober. "It's my wife, you see. She's rather delicate I'm afraid, and develops a dreadful rash when her nerves are running high. On the hands mostly. She's taken to wearing gloves the day around. I wondered when I might bring her to see you."

"Take her to the theater instead," the doctor said gruffly. "The gloves will be right in order there. Better, send her to Saint Giles – the sick will keep her hands too occupied for rashes."

The young man's face went blank, as though he didn't understand the language the doctor was using. Then the line of coaches began to move again, and the doctor did not look back, leaving the man standing in the street.

Devon stared at Doctor MacBride, unable to believe what she had just witnessed. Was this the man she had just seen holding that other hand so tenderly, taking such care cleansing the wound?

But the grin that then began to widen the doctor's mouth and wreathe his cheeks was infectious, and soon they both were laughing, the doctor's belly bouncing along with the coach. "If he ever took his wife with him on his gallivantings about," he said between chuckles, "he'd find the rash gone soon enough. 'Stead of chasing other men's wives."

Devon saw her opportunity. "I didn't know you had a wife," she said. "I mean, I thought your wife had died. But that room, that bed. Are they a new wife's? And where is she now?"

She had said that very badly, Devon knew. But she did not regret having the subject finally come up.

"That where she put you?" the doctor said, frowning.

"Oh, it is far too fine for me," Devon said hastily. "I would be happy to move to another. I don't know why I'm even there."

The doctor shrugged, still frowning. "No, it's all right. Better it be used. She'll likely never be back in it again."

Devon knew she should leave the conversation at that, as bungled as she'd made her query. But her curiosity had not been satisfied.

"Is she visiting then? Somewhere?"

"Somewhere," the doctor said, the roughness returning to his voice and face. The word had been spoken with such finality, Devon knew not to press the subject further. Maybe the woman in his household would be more forthcoming.

Your curiosity will be the death of you, her brother Boyle had said to her more than once. He just might be right, Devon thought, but what was there to do about it; it was her nature.

The sun was already low in the sky, and the coach had gone a good way down a cobblestoned street before the buildings dwindled to an irregular array of shops and tenements and a sign on a tilted pole announced their presence in *Hungerford Market.*

They turned onto a dirt path, and the horse picked its way among carts and great baskets, from which men without hats and women with bare arms sold tin pans, blue and yellow crockery, giant gourds and other assorted vegetables with the soil still on them. Dogs and children milled about the place as though oblivious to the passage of moving objects larger than themselves, the din even greater than that which had filled her days in Eagle and Childe Alley.

Devon's eyes filled until they could not see, and they closed, opening again only when the coach came to a full stop before a low house fronted by a roughly lettered sign that announced it as *The Dairy of T. Olley, Cowkeeper.*

The doctor was out his side of the coach already, and Devon climbed down wearily from hers. She stumbled as she touched down, still unused to the bulk of the skirt she'd been given to wear. The layers of fabric at her elbows and hips, too, restricted her movement in ways she wasn't used to; and the uncommon weakness of her limbs had grown greater as the day wore on. She clung to the edge of the coach and contemplated for a moment asking whether she might wait here this time. But already the doctor was disappearing through the door, beneath a smaller sign that read *Tho' Olley's Genuine Milk & Cream*, so Devon wearily followed.

Inside, the air was sour with stale milk and rotting cheese, and so dim after the late-slanting sun outside that Devon had to stop to get her bearings. When her vision cleared, she saw no one in the little anteroom in which she stood, only stacks of pails and buckets beside a huge wooden churn that took up half the room. She followed the sound of muffled voices through a drape, into a room darker still, in which the shapes of several people stood in

40

a rough circle, gazing down at what looked to be a pile of rags heaped on the bare dirt floor before them.

The doctor was bent over it, and straightened at last with the same single word Devon had heard him use – could it really have been only yesterday? – "Gone."

For a moment, no one moved. Then the woman who'd been on her knees beside the doctor gathered a small bundle of the rags into her arms and stood, rocking it slightly back and forth, while small, strangled sobs came from deep in her throat.

What was left, Devon saw now, was the body of an old woman, whose thin gray hair lay across her cheek and forehead like scattered ashes.

Then there was a clatter at the door and a large robust woman burst through the drape, a squalling baby draped over one arm. "Like a charm it worked," she crowed to the gathering, a pair of wooden crutches swinging freely from her other elbow, clacking together like dull cymbals.

"Doubled the alms. More." And she held out her hand toward the circle, the bright coins seeming to collect all the light of the room into her palm.

The woman's arm stayed stretched while she looked from one to another of the solemn faces in the circle, then down to the floor where the old woman lay. She handed the kicking baby to one of those gathered and stooped, laying the coins by the dead woman's head. "Goodbye, Mother," she said in barely a whisper.

Then, holding the crutches clear of the floor, she left as quickly as she had come.

Back in the coach, neither Devon nor the doctor spoke. But as the horse pulled the coach back onto the cobblestones from the dirt, Doctor MacBride muttered into his gray beard, "Should have come sooner. Could maybe have saved the babe at least."

Devon knew he was not speaking to her and kept her peace, her own load of sorrow weighting her lids and carrying her quickly into the merciful arms of sleep.

Chapter 4

Far and Wide

The world was to me a secret which I desired to divine.
Mary Shelley, in a letter to
Mrs. Saville.

Devon was unsure, that evening, just how she'd made it from the coach to the doctor's door. The first she could remember was standing in the front hall, thinking that she must be having some kind of frightful dream. The passageway ahead, now lit and down which the doctor had just vanished, was crowded with massive standing clocks and cabinets, looking ready to swallow her as well.

Then the woman appeared out of it. "I thought so. He wore you out. Well, come now, let's get something in y'r belly before we get y' to bed." And she was gone again into the threatening hallway.

Devon didn't know what else to do but follow. She crept forward between the looming shapes, themselves piled with objects – bowls and vases, and delicate little figurines of girls ornately dressed, complete with hats and gloves and dainty boots – until she came to a small parlor, lit only by the light seeping from the passageway.

The single side window in the room was curtained with layers of gauze, and the doors at its far side were both closed. She didn't know which of them might have swallowed the doctor.

Then the woman reappeared carrying a tray holding a silver teapot and a china plate. She set the tray on an end table beside one of the overstuffed chairs and lit a lamp beside it.

"Eat now," she said, and then was gone again.

Would the doctor not eat with her then? Nor the woman? Was she now thought to be higher than a housekeeper, which the woman appeared to be? Devon remembered that her parents' customer, Mrs. Galt, a housekeeper for the Barwicks in Shoe Lane, had said no servants ever ate with those they served. But it was hard to think of this woman as a servant. Herself more so, surely.

But she didn't think longer on the matter. The fragrant stew and bun on the delicate plate claimed all her attention until her hunger was satiated – as she had thought it never would be again.

Then, as she chewed slowly on the glazed bun, savoring its flavors of orange and vanilla, she pondered her place here once more. Apparently, the doctor planned to take her with him on his calls. That was good; it gave her back a little of the feeling of being needed that had defined her life up until now. And already she felt of use to him. Had he not praised her for her help with the baby? And she hadn't shrunk from helping to hold down the arm of the man with the chopped-off finger. Thankfully, she'd gotten past any queasiness at the sight or smell of blood long ago. Attending to childhood accidents had quickly cured her of that. And she was fascinated by the doctor's methods and remedies. Wouldn't it be grand if she could become a kind of doctor – or at least a nurse – someday? She must attend closely to all his practices.

On the other hand, maybe the doctor did not see her help as a continuing asset. Maybe he was only making use of her services until he could find a more suitable disposition of his unasked-for burden.

The sticky bun stuck in her throat. She remembered her father's words remarking on the many women, young and old, who walked the street alone past their tailor shop, nothing in their arms to sell. "They have no family," he'd said, "to protect them. Nothing to sell but themselves."

She wasn't sure what he'd meant at the time, but she hadn't liked the sound of it. And now she had no family either.

A gulp of tea hurt her throat with more than its heat, it was so strong. She was used to the tea at home, made from the used leaves Mrs. Galt sold for a few pence each Friday. The Barwicks never, she'd told them, used their tea leaves twice. This liquid was too rich for her insides, Devon decided, just as the tightly stuffed cushion and padded back of this chair felt unyielding against her body – made for show, most likely, rather than comfort.

Then the woman came back through the door, and Devon felt a pang of guilt, as though she might guess her ungrateful thoughts. She hurried to speak before the woman could disappear again. "Pardon me," she said, "but could you tell me your name?"

The woman laughed gruffly. "The doctor isn't much for the social graces," she said. "I'm Mrs. Dofferman, cook, housekeeper, and anything else needs doing around here."

"This is such a big house... Devon began. "Is it only yourself and the doctor live here?"

Devon waited to see if Mrs. Dofferman would find her curiosity too rude; but she only grumbled, not unlike the doctor. "Now it is. And why he keeps this elephant of a house is more than I can fathom. She's not coming back, that I can assure you."

"'She'? Would that be his new wife then?"

"Humph!" The woman made a thick snorting sound through her broad nose, the way Devon had heard donkeys do when they tired of standing in harness before their carts. "Not much of a wife, if you ask me. More like a mistress, going through his pockets till she'd emptied them all, then taking herself off to some other fool with deeper pockets. Doubt he ever saw the inside of her bedroom either."

Devon was surprised by how forthcoming the woman was, but hurried to make further use of her knowledge. "Is that her room I'm in then?"

"Oh, that's hers right enough. And every fancy piece of frufraw in it. Like everything else in this place. She threw out every blessed piece had been his first wife's. And she left just in time: one more of those oversized horrors and the house would have bust out its walls. Hopefully, she'll send for them one of these days, when she takes up with some another fool with an even bigger house, leave the poor man in peace."

As harshly as the woman spoke, Devon detected a note of something else in her voice – a sadness of some sort, more personal than pity. She suspected there was more soft feeling in this woman than she let on. She'd had the same sense the day before.

"Has she been gone long?" Devon asked.

She heard her mother's voice in her ear: *It's not polite to press a person so*, after she'd kept a customer in the shop or a guest at the supper table too long with her questions.

But I really wanted to know was all Devon could ever answer. There was no time in the day, with the children to tend and the chores to be done; but in the evening, when Boyle had fallen asleep and she could keep her eyes open just a little longer, Devon had pored over the books he brought home – most traded for something he'd collected in his barrow. She had long since exhausted her father's schoolbooks with reading and rereading –– history, geography, the tales of Chaucer and Shakespeare. He had read to the children every night of King Arthur and his knights, and stories from the Brothers Grimm. But she had wanted more.

She had pleaded with Boyle to teach her to read, but he had refused. "What does a girl need to know of books?" he'd said. So when her father read to them and it was her turn to sit on his lap, she had studied the words as he'd pronounced them, memorizing their look and sound, until she could practically recite the tales from memory.

But this woman hardly seemed to notice the persistence of her questions. She seemed as glad to talk as Devon was to listen. It must be lonely for her to be here by herself all day when the doctor is out, Devon realized, and felt a bond was forming between the two of them, just a little.

"In the early days of that damned epidemic," Mrs. Dofferman was saying, "that woman persuaded the doctor to go with her. To 'the continent'" – she spoke the words with disdain. "Whined and threatened until he went along. Then when he heard how many of his patients had died he thought he might have saved, he came back. Has been going day and night ever since. But her – she never did. Found she liked Paris shopping even better than Bond Street, I'd wager. Or else she'd bought out all of London and had to move on."

She gave that snort again, but then her voice softened. "He drives himself past all strength, determined to save every sick soul he can find. It's killing him, that's what it is." And the pained look on the woman's face showed Devon that she cared for the doctor beyond the role of a servant. She wondered if he knew that.

"Thank you, Mrs. Dofferman," she said sincerely. "Thank you very much."

The woman looked at her as though she might ask for what, but in the end said only, "Ye'd best get right t' bed now," as she picked up her empty plate. "Who knows what the old goat will have in store f'r ye tomorrow."

And indeed, Devon found much 'in store' for her in the long days and weeks that followed. From early morning, until the doctor fell asleep in the coach, as the coachman drove them more and more frequently, Devon found her days filled with the city's multitude of sights and sounds and people needing their attention. She felt guilty sometimes when she realized how much she was enjoying this life, being out and about, every day new things to learn and experience. She felt like a bird let out of a cage – however dear her 'cage' had been to her as a girl. But now she felt herself growing into a young woman, a woman of a wider world, and she welcomed it all.

Each street the coach came to was another name to be savored and remembered – St. Bride's Street just across Fleet, leading to that delicate church and courtyard; or up the hill to Ludgate Circus, where Bridge Street led off as far as the eye could see – all the way to the Thames and the Blackfriar's Bridge across it, though they'd not yet gone that far.

Or if the coach continued up Ludgate Hill, the dome she'd seen that first day would grow into the full awesome bulk of St. Paul's Cathedral, which, like St. Andrews, spun off its own little maze of streets, their names as odd as their angles: Ave Maria Street, Amen Court, Paternoster Row. The names all had religious significance, the doctor had told her, but wouldn't say what it was. "Enough mindless chanting in the world," he grumbled, "without adding your voice to it."

She never really heard any chanting; but what she did hear one morning, when the coach had stopped to visit a sick old man in Warwick Lane, was glorious music that seemed to issue from the cathedral's very walls. There were voices, but they were as unlike those of the bawdy street singers Devon had heard in her neighborhood as porridge was to plum pudding. These voices, and an instrument the doctor identified as an organ – "though a bit more finely tuned than the human sort," he'd said with

49

a gurgly chuckle – all blended into a song so magnificent, Devon felt it must swell the very sky it rose into with its grandeur.

She had pleaded with the doctor to go inside, nearer the music, to see what unimaginable surroundings must have inspired it. But he said they had no time. "Mrs. Tillson's baby won't wait for us to tour a church," he said, peering at the sky as though he might see the baby now, winging its way toward its new home.

The gesture reminded Devon of one of her childhood images. She had seen a picture of an angel in some religious book; and not only had it looked like a fat, smiling baby, it had wings sprouting from its back. After that, Devon had assumed for years that that was how babies came to be in their mother's tummy; they just flew there when they took a notion to be born. And the very confusing explanation her mother had given her later for how babies started growing in their mothers had not entirely erased that image, only attached to it the information that a man was somehow involved in the process. And that fact did, she was told, make it imperative that all men who were not your husband – and therefore naturally your baby's father – were to be strictly avoided.

But that morning, the doctor's coach left the churchyard and its marvelous music and clattered instead down the rough cobblestones toward the river, winding through streets with names like Godliman Street, Sermon Lane, and Little Divinity Lane, to Stew Lane, where Mrs. Tillson's baby had not yet arrived; and Devon had to content herself with peering over the rooftops and beyond the steeples to get a glimpse of the river and the great ships that sailed upon it. Someday, she told herself, shivering with the sheer thrill of the thought, she would herself be on one of those ships, sailing on the water as smooth as one of those imaginary babies about to be born sailed through the clouds, off to somewhere wondrous and brand new.

She just didn't expect it would be so soon and so far.

Chapter 5

Newgate

But Doctor MacBride did not only visit the sick in their homes; he went also to the hospitals – St. Giles, St. Bartholomew's – and made his way through the narrow beds crowded together more tightly than his wife's dark furniture, to examine the ailing bodies and listen to their complaints, for hours on end.

And he went to the prisons – the Fleet, a debtors' prison mostly; the Old Compter, so out of place in the prosperous Giltspur Street; and to the Newgate. It was there they met the barrister of the same name, Pierce Newgate.

He had come up to them and introduced himself with an air of such authority, in fact, that Devon had politely inquired, "Is this prison named for you then, sir?"

To which the man responded with a roar of laughter that would have shaken the walls, if anything could have shaken those gray, grim walls that extended so far on all sides, it seemed they could imprison every last soul in London.

"No," the man said when he'd regained his composure, "this is one place I would rather not be credited with. It's objectionable enough, the time I have to spend here."

The doctor was looking impatient, having been headed for his usual full day of attending to the inmates when the man had stopped their coach just after it passed through the inner gate. He had helped the doctor down, unasked, though he'd been looking at Devon all the while.

"We have met," he said to her finally, his tone so direct it seemed to her almost aggressive.

It was then she remembered. It had been a day some months before, when her mother had enlisted her help in the shop, to finish a gown a man was to pick up that afternoon. She'd asked Devon to put on the dress and stand on the usual box to hold it steady while she finished the hem. Devon remembered being surprised when the man arrived to claim it, for he was finely dressed and appeared to be a gentleman in all respects, while the dress was too low-cut and thick with ruffles to suit a lady of the upper classes. And there was something about the way he looked at her in the dress that had made her relieved when she could go behind the curtain to remove it and put back on her more modest frock, and disappear into the rooms in the back. Now she thought she saw that same look come into the man's eyes, though his smile and voice remained most cordial.

"My family had a tailor shop," she said, hoping that the information would be enough to end the topic.

"Ah, the tailor shop," he said. "Yes. Eagle Alley, I believe."

"Eagle and Childe," she said, sorry to have prolonged the encounter even so long as to correct him. She was now as eager as the doctor to get on with their mission here.

"Yes." That was all he said before he turned again to the doctor. "I was wondering, Doctor – MacBride, isn't it?"

"Yes? Be quick, man, I have much to do here this day."

"I have seen you around the yard. You used to treat the debtors without charge, I understand, before they were moved to Whitecross Street. Most commendable. I wish we could all afford to do that."

The doctor had already begun to edge away, fingering his watch chain.

The man moved forward with him, raising his voice just slightly. "What I'm needing – what *my client* is needing rather – is a little of your famous attention. There has been an accident, you see, a most unfortunate occurrence, and the man is now not only ill but finds himself in goal as well. He is in great need of treatment, and perhaps a kind word in his favor before the court. From what I've heard, I knew the generous Doctor MacBride would be just the man for the job."

The doctor hesitated. The man spoke with much earnestness, Devon thought. But there was something…

"And just what illness has the man?" the doctor asked, still an edge to his voice.

"If you could just come this way…" And Mr. Newgate started off in a direction far from their course, turning every few steps to be sure they were following. "It won't take but a moment of your time," he said to the doctor's clear reluctance. "And my client will be most grateful."

Huffing with impatience, Doctor MacBride altered his course and followed the man; and with some hesitation of her own she could hardly name, Devon followed as well. Perhaps at least, she thought, she would finally see more of the prison here and the situations of its prisoners. Until now, Doctor MacBride had let her attend him only to those few of his patients who could afford to pay for finer and more private accommodations in the gaols. The others apparently had to make do with conditions that, in Doctor MacBride's words, "aren't fit for any living soul, the innocent or the guilty."

Devon had suspected that his term "the innocent" referred to herself as well as those who might be imprisoned here unjustly. But she had been feeling the layers of innocence strip from her every day she'd spent with the doctor these past weeks. She had come face to face and skin to skin with people she had seen formerly only from a distance, through her loft window, or in books. From the poorest beggar in the street to the occasional member of the gentry who would show up at the doctor's door with some urgent petition for his attendance at a bedside, Devon was coming into intimate contact with them all – and in moments of crisis that tended to bring out their true natures, whether frantic or calm, broad or narrower of spirit. It had been a source of endless fascination to her, this carousel of humanity, revealing as many different facets to their natures as the surfaces that sparkled on the chandelier in the doctor's dining room that he evidently never entered.

She had come upon the room quite by accident, one of the many for which the doors were kept closed. But this door was ajar one afternoon, so of course she entered; and in the light streaming from a window, easily the widest in the house, the chandelier's sparkling facets quite took her breath away. Hanging gracefully above a long, dark table, the glittering piece cast rainbows all across the room.

Not that all the facets to people's natures that she'd been meeting resembled anything close to rainbows; many would be more accurately classed as one form or another of storm. But those had also been instructive, and she had welcomed each new venture among them as another opportunity to acquaint herself with all the human variety she'd been missing in the first twelve and a half years of her life.

Arriving now at a section of the prison Devon had not yet been to, Mr. Newgate gave a sharp rap at a massive door, which eventually produced only a face at a small window set high in the door. The man squinted at them, as though his eyes were unaccustomed to the light of day.

"Ah, Mister Newgate," the man said finally. And then brightening, "Come in, come in. Always good to see you, sir."

The door opened slowly, as though too heavy to pull; and as they passed inside, Devon noticed that Newgate pressed a coin into the man's hand, which caused him to brighten further.

"It's Mister Merdick we will see today, Henry," Newgate said. "The good doctor here will examine the poor man, see to his condition."

"Ah," the man said again, bobbing his head several times in what was either assent or understanding.

Doctor MacBride turned a sharp look on Devon then, and she was afraid he would instruct her to stay back while they went further. In fact, the gloom of the place – even darker and more oppressive than that she had experienced in other areas of the prison – almost made her wish he would. But in the end he simply turned and followed the other men down the dark corridor ahead, and she followed behind them.

They came to another door which required two keys to open, and then entered an even darker passageway. Lined with solid gray stone on either side, the hallway echoed with the sound of their footsteps, like mournful calls, which seemed to be answered by the shadowy forms Devon could barely see in the dim cells on either side. She was beginning to understand why the doctor had not taken her before this far into the bowels of the prison, and to agree it was not a fit place for her – or anyone. She was glad they progressed quickly down the passageway, before the prisoners could reach the bars of their cells.

The cell they finally stopped at was barely as deep or wide as a man's height, and not much taller. The only light came from a narrow window near the top, lined with a double grate. The turnkey took some time with the lock and then glanced at Devon as he swung open the barred gate. So, to forestall any argument about her being included in this interview, after coming all this way, Devon followed quickly on the doctor's heels as he went through.

"The man is not dangerous, Doctor," the turnkey was saying, making a little bow as the doctor moved past him into the cell. "He has killed only one person, and that his wife."

Oh, is that all, Devon thought hotly, but restrained herself from saying it aloud.

Even after the cell's gate had been shut again behind them, the turnkey lingered, until Newgate slipped him another coin through the bars, and the man bobbed his head twice and moved to stand back against the far wall.

Indeed, the prisoner hardly looked dangerous. With one foot shackled to the floor, he sat bent upon a pile of rugs in one corner, his hands clasped under his chin.

Newgate approached him first, and the man reached toward him with both hands.

"I've brought a doctor, Merdick," Newgate said to him. "He can examine your condition and then be able to tell the court of your suffering."

The man turned great watery eyes on the doctor.

"And just what is it seems to be your trouble?" the doctor said, his voice not as gentle as Devon was used to hearing it when he addressed his patients.

"It's these sores, sir," the man said quickly. "They come and go, and how am I to know what they are? It could be the pox only."

"Have you been told otherwise?" the doctor asked.

"Well, the ship's doctor, he said it might be the syphilis, but he couldn't say for sure, not so early. And then the woman who attended my wife – no more than a midwife she was – she said it must be, to take a baby so soon before its time. That's how she became so enraged, you see, my wife, that I had to put an end to it. But it could be the pox only, wouldn't you say so, sir? The sores went away the first time; they could go away again?" The man spoke rapidly, never taking his eyes off Doctor MacBride, as though the doctor's naming of his affliction would determine his ultimate fate.

Doctor MacBride reached for Devon then and called to the turnkey, "Unlock this door. The girl must not be here."

And before she could protest, Devon was hustled out of the cell and made to wait against the far wall with the turnkey. She could hear what was being said in the cell, however, and strained to catch every word.

After the doctor ordered the man to take down his pants, he said nothing more for some time, while the man's high-pitched voice prattled on. "Being on the sea, sir, a man gets lonely, don't you see, and needs a woman now and again, the ports so full of the wicked temptresses as they are. It must have been one of them done it to me, for the sores appeared not long after. I saw no sense to tell my wife, it might be nothing, and she'd just have made a fuss. But she saw it then and carried on something terrible. Her father died of the syphilis, you see, and she claimed she could tell it when she saw it. It took me quite some time to calm her down. But the apothecary said it could be either, might well be only the pox, such as many had at that time. So when it went away, I told her what a foolish woman she had been, and the sores that came later on her own skin must be only signs of her bad temper. Terrible temper the woman had, once she'd worked up to it."

"Most unfortunate." That was Newgate's voice. "Most unfortunate."

"She came at me like a madwoman, she did. Had the tongs in her hand they'd pulled the baby out with. It was a wonder she could move, with all the blood, and with such force. I knew she meant to kill me. What could I do? She just kept screaming, 'Five years I've waited for this child, and now you've killed it and me along with it.' But I never meant to kill her, don't you see? Only to stop her coming at me, make her stop her infernal noise."

There was a general space of silence then, except for another "most unfortunate" from the barrister; and Devon was tempted to move forward again, when the doctor's voice finally spoke up, more flat and dispassionate than she'd ever heard it. "Well, it's the syphilis all right. Tertiary stage, I'd say. Ye'll join y'r wife soon, and well y've earned it."

Shock propelled Devon forward – shock at the man's story and the doctor's response as well.

"We will get you out then," Newgate said to the man. "Never fear. Your sailor's pension should be enough to cover the costs. And you said your father had a little something put away for just such trying times as these?"

But the man continued to stare at the doctor.

"'Twill be in the muscles soon enough," the doctor's voice went on, putting away the tools of the examination in his bag, his tone as casual as though he were speaking of a passing ague. "Though it may start on the brain before it's through. That's the nasty part. Raving maniacs I've seen, once it gets to that stage."

"Is there not something you can do?" Newgate asked, his voice and face now reflecting some of the shock Devon felt at the coldness of the doctor's words.

"Well, there's the balsam. Mash of that might take the edge off the pain. Or a drink of columbine, they say, can help. Can't harm at least. But in the last stages, there's not much that will make a difference."

He closed his bag with a snap and turned to Newgate. "But then, I'm sure you'll get him clear soon enough of this bothersome business of killing his wife. Then he can rest more comfortably at home, with no one to bother him further in his last days."

Then Devon stepped back again as the two men came to the gate, and the turnkey hustled to let them out.

The four of them walked back through the dark passageway in silence, broken only by the clink of an occasional metal cup against the bars, and voices calling out from the deeper darkness of their cells. "Water?" "A bit of bread?" "Time for the yard, is it not, turnkey?"

The hollow tones of their voices suggested to Devon that they did not really expect a response, and they got none from the turnkey.

Then they were out in the bright white light of day again, the high layer of clouds glaring down as though reflecting some intensity of feeling from below. And Newgate was saying to the doctor, his voice a good deal less assured than it had been when he had first approached them, "Well, thank you, Doctor, for seeing the man, if only to confirm the misfortune of his condition."

"Oh, I'm sure he'll live long enough to pay your fee," the doctor replied matter-of-factly.

"At which time, I will surely bring your share to you as well," the barrister said quickly.

"No need," the doctor said; and Devon thought she saw the old man smile as they turned away, heading toward the woman's building, their original destination.

Devon could not hold her tongue longer. "I have never seen you pronounce death to a man so coolly," she said. "However terrible his crimes."

But the doctor only smiled. "Could be the pox as likely as the plague of the man-about-town, either one," he said. "Hard to tell at this stage. But either way, it's the sole punishment he'll ever get for the deaths of a mother and child."

"Why is that?" Devon asked in confusion.

"No man is likely to go to the gallows for killing his wife," the doctor said bitterly. "Another man's perhaps, but never his own. Unless she should have money, of course. So let him squirm a little in the meantime – small enough a price to pay for infecting others for his own pleasure."

Devon was contemplating those words as they passed through another gate and were admitted to the women's section by a great burly man the doctor called Simon.

"Are they 'restless' today again, your guests?" the doctor addressed him.

"Restless enough," was the man's grave reply. "They've got 'em on the wheel, work off some of their dark energies."

"How kind for them," the doctor said. "And maybe someday their betters will find some real use for all that labor, and pay f'r it, so when the poor lasses are free – if ever – they'll be able to live until they find work."

They progressed to the little bare anteroom where the doctor always made Devon wait when he visited the women's wing. But this time, he grumbled, "Ye might as well see where the wives end up when they kill the husbands about to kill them."

Devon hurried to keep up with the two men in the binding clothes she'd been given to wear, the layers of stiff petticoats beneath the skirt and the long laced-down bodice that fit over it.

The sight they came to, though, made her stop still in the doorway, while the men proceeded to a woman lying on the floor at the far end of the long, bare room.

Ahead of her, on several giant wheels, women were climbing steps, one after another, each tread only bringing the next step up. The women's expressions, what she could see of them, were blank, their backs hunched, arms bent to the bars, lifting their legs, then pushing on their knees to press the next step down as it came around again.

"Mother of God," Devon whispered, an expression she'd heard her mother use when she'd seen through the shop window some particularly brutal scene being enacted without. Another reason Devon's access to the street had been strictly limited. *Now I'm seeing it all, and more, Father,* she said in her mind, hoping he could hear wherever he was.

Then a voice behind her said, "What are you doing here?" so harshly that she whipped around to see a man in a guard's uniform, its buttons open at the throat, the sleeves rolled up, clutching what looked like a riding crop.

"She's with me," the doctor called from the end of the room. "Come here, girl, give me a hand. You too," he addressed the guard in a louder voice. "This woman must be taken to the infirmary at once."

Devon hurried over, the guard following, but was not yet to them when the woman's body began heaving, small trickles of saliva oozing from her lax lips.

Then another commotion, this time from the wheels, distracted Devon's attention. At the nearest wheel, one of the women had a young boy by the neck, and another had gripped the attacker's hair in both hands, shaking the head back and forth, apparently to loosen the woman's grip on the child.

"Leave him be!" the second woman screeched, followed by a string of epithets as strong as any Devon had heard in the alley below her attic window.

"The brat bit my leg!" the woman cried, one fist leaving the child's throat to grasp the hand in her hair.

"Then he'll be dead of the poison in you soon enough," the other woman rasped, giving the head another mighty shake.

The guard nearly knocked Devon over getting past her to seize the two women, one in each hand, prying them apart like the dogs that Devon had seen boys set on each other in the alley, taking wagers on which would kill the other first.

Then Devon had to stoop to aid the doctor, who was holding the woman's jaws open with both hands. "The handkerchief," he said to Devon. "In my pocket."

She knew in which pocket the doctor kept his handkerchief and plucked it out and, without further instruction, stuffed it into the woman's lower mouth to keep her from swallowing her tongue. The woman's breath, joined with all the other odors of unwashed bodies, urine and ordure, nearly made Devon gag, but she held it back.

Then the turnkey lifted the body easily, the woman's long gaunt limbs hanging like a doll's from his powerful arms as he carried her off through the door from which they'd come.

Devon turned, saw the two women immobilized now at either end of the guard's arms, the others stopped at their treading, shrieking profanities at the intervening guard. The children, mostly naked or in tattered rags, had appeared to wake from the listlessness Devon had first observed and were shrieking too, pounding on whatever came to hand – the guard, the women, each other…

Until Devon was pulled away, to accompany the men down another long hall, stinking also of urine, to a doorless room at its end, where a scattering of bodies lay in disarray about the floor, some on frayed rugs or straw or piles of dirty rags, some on the bare stone itself, a few moaning but most of them silent, their eyes closed or staring blankly into space..

The woman just brought lay on the bare floor between two others, their eyes closed, either unconscious or dead, Devon guessed.

The doctor bent over her, removed the cloth from her mouth, and peered beneath one eyelid, then the other. Devon stood in the doorway, unwilling to go farther, seeing in the angular array of bodies those others on the floor of their loft not so many weeks ago. But these women hadn't been taken by disease; they were doomed here by what? True crimes; or as the doctor had suggested, having defended themselves from husbands like the wretched creature she'd just seen in the men's section? What would be their future?

What would be her own?

Chapter 6
Shopping

Man is the only creature that consumes without producing.
George Orwell, *Animal Farm*

By the time the cooler seasons fell upon the city, the dark coming earlier and with winds of increasing chill, Devon and the doctor went less frequently about their rounds of patients. Doctor MacBride kept to his bed some days, sometimes several days at a time. Devon could hear coughing coming from his end of the bedroom floor; but her pleas to Mrs. Dofferman to be allowed to attend him fell on closed ears.

"That is my position," she would say, with some pride; and Devon knew from her manner that it was no use to argue.

Instead, she came to see a good deal more of the woman herself. On the days when the doctor did not venture from his bed, Mrs. Dofferman would eventually accede to Devon's requests for productive work and let her help in the kitchen, sweep the floors, empty the chamber pots, or dust and polish the surfaces of all that furniture.

That became Devon's favorite task; it gave her an opportunity to inspect all those curious pieces, and the even more curious objects that stood on them.

There seemed to be no order to the patterns of the plates and cups stacked on racks in the kitchen, having overflowed the pantry. More were laid behind glass in the curved corner cupboards of the dining room. It seemed that each had been selected on impulse for its individual attractiveness alone, with no intent for its future use.

The same appeared true of the legion of curios: crystal lanterns set near nothing that needed lighting; painted bed warmers separate from any bed; little spoons set in their own little slots on a rack far from the kitchen. Pewter and porcelain and china of every description – far more than a family of any size could use.

Such excesses Devon found quite shocking when she imagined what the price of each piece might buy in the way of food for families of her own class or poorer. Knowing little about sin – a word she'd heard often enough from preachers in the streets but had never heard fully defined – Devon concluded that such amassing of objects with no intent to ever put them to use must constitute some kind of sin. There had been earnest deliberation and periods of saving in her own family before the smallest purchases were made – a mirror for the shop to replace a broken one; a new tea kettle; another place setting for another child when its hands grew dexterous enough to wield a fork. And nothing, from soured milk to mendable hose, ever went to waste.

It seemed even more odd that such overspending should exist in the house of a man such as the doctor, who spoke so scornfully of the excesses of the privileged classes. It made her all the more curious about what sort of person this absent wife of his must be, and how he had come to be associated with her.

But the doctor never spoke of her; and the subject seemed to upset Mrs. Dofferman so much that Devon came to avoid it altogether. Still, she felt she must do her part in avoiding any unnecessary spending, and steadfastly refused the doctor's gruff orders to Mrs. Dofferman to "Get the girl some decent clothes of her own, for pity's sake." Instead, she cut down some of the wife's older, plainer pieces, to fit her more slender body – a skill she had learned well from her mother. And in the process, she eliminated a few layers, to make them easier to move around in.

But she did quite enjoy going out with Mrs. Dofferman when she did the shopping for the household. Whether food or linens, candles, soap or writing paper, every quest would take them into a different street, each with its own peculiarities of people and place.

Devon was especially admiring of the manner in which Mrs. Dofferman met the streets. Despite her long skirts, the woman strode along the streets and walks very like a man, forging through the tangles of carts and carriages, wagons and pedestrians as though they were so many scraps of debris in the way of her broom. And the rushing sedan chairs were no match for her when they tried to detour onto the footpaths. Their "Have a care" as they hurtled toward you brought only a "Have a care y'rself!" from the woman, who invariably held her ground, making the encroaching carriers give way. Devon stayed close beside the woman's bulk during these outings to avoid being overrun; but the immense variety of people and vehicles that seemed to fill the streets of downtown London from morning till night provided endless fascination.

Often, Mrs. Dofferman would keep up a steady muttering as she strode along, in a language Devon did not comprehend but thought might be a form of English spoken in Scotland, perhaps long ago. It was as though the woman wished to counter with the language in her head the din around her – the incessant rumble of carriage wheels and the sharp raps of their horses' hooves, the cries of apple vendors, street peddlers, milk women and town criers. Devon only wished for greater quiet when they came upon a ballad singer, so that she might memorize the song and take it with her for the long, over-silent hours in the doctor's house.

It was on one such errand – to Mobley's in the Strand, for a book the ailing doctor had been demanding – that Devon again encountered the barrister Pierce Newgate.

The Strand was perhaps the most intimidating of their regular destinations, its boulevard so wide and crammed with shoppers and their vehicles, it was generally impossible to see more than one person ahead. And the seemingly endless array and variety of goods displayed in the windows of the shops made Devon quite dizzy after a few fast-paced blocks. But it was still an adventure she was always ready for, whenever an excuse could be found.

When Mr. Newgate re-appeared, Devon and Mrs. Dofferman were just emerging from the bookseller's, Devon with great reluctance, since she could happily have stayed for days on end within the musty shelves, the piles of volumes seeming to contain within their covers all the secrets of the universe.

The two were lingering just outside the door, waiting for their eyes to re-accustom themselves to daylight, while Mrs. Dofferman struggled to open her umbrella against a steady smattering of rain.

"Why, it's Miss Quail, I do believe," came the familiar voice suddenly beside her.

He would not let himself be jostled aside by the steady stream of pedestrians as he went on, "And looking so lovely too. Is that a new frock perhaps?"

Devon was searching for a reply when Mrs. Dofferman spoke up. "And who might you be, pray?"

"Why, Pierce Newgate, Esquire," the man replied, giving her a proper bow from the waist and offering his hand. Which she did not take.

He was not deterred. "And whom might I have the pleasure of addressing?"

"This is Mrs. Dofferman," Devon spoke up finally. "She is housekeeper to the doctor. Doctor MacBride," she added, in case he had forgotten her protector.

"Ah yes, the good doctor. A fine man, fine." He continued to direct his words to the older woman, though his gaze took frequent side trips to Devon's face and form. "He was good enough to examine an unfortunate client of mine. Gravely ill he was, and needed help in settling his affairs. I will be in touch with the good doctor soon with his fee in the matter."

Then he turned his body slightly to include Devon in the area of his address. "I was just on my way to a merchant of miniatures, to buy my wife a little gift. She has collected the trifles since she was a child – which in some ways she is still. I wonder if the young lady might accompany me. I'm sure she would be charmed by the little works: an entire world that can fit in the palm of your hand. Most extraordinary." He smiled with such apparent enjoyment that Devon found herself wanting to see for herself such miniature marvels.

She looked to Mrs. Dofferman, who as usual in her about-town manner, was frowning. "Might we go?" Devon asked, assuming the invitation was for the both of them.

"Not this body," Mrs. Dofferman replied. "It has had enough of city streets for one day."

Her intense gaze remained on the barrister. "You know Doctor MacBride then?"

"We are colleagues, you might say," Newgate assured her. "He is well, I hope?"

"No, in fact he is not." Her tone continued to be unfriendly. "The man is down more than he is up these past weeks."

"No! I am most sorry to hear it. I hope you will extend to him my heartfelt wishes for a speedy recovery. I must visit him soon."

But Mrs. Dofferman was looking at Devon now. "I must be getting back and off these legs. If ye'd like to stay out a bit longer…" Her head swung back to Newgate. "Where did you say this shop was?"

"Not so far as Covent Garden," he said.

"Well then?" It was a question she addressed to Devon, who found herself uncertain as to what her response should be."

"It is agreed then," Newgate said promptly. "I promise not to keep the young lady out overlong."

And without further discussion, Newgate repeated his bow to the older woman and shifted his umbrella over to shield Devon's head, grasping her elbow firmly and steering her out into the flow of pedestrians that filled the walkway, even more densely now that the hour approached tea time.

"So tell me, how do you come to be with the doctor?" Newgate asked when they had found their pace among the throng. "Are you apprenticing perhaps, to learn the midwife trade?"

"He took me in when my family… died," Devon said, embarrassed to hear the tremble in her voice on the last word.

"Ah, I didn't know," Newgate said, his voice carrying such feeling that Devon was further moved. "I am aggrieved to hear it. They went suddenly then? All of them?" His hand on her elbow firmed its support and moved a little upward.

"From the influenza," she said, hoping that would conclude the subject.

"It's always the good folk who are struck the hardest," Newgate went on. "A good and honest man your father was. And your mother – such a beauty." He squeezed her arm again. "You are the very image of her, you know," he added.

The remark was more upsetting than she could have defined with reason. "Oh no," Devon said quickly. "I am unlike my mother."

She wanted to say more, but could not think how to put into words exactly what she meant. There was a quality to Mary Quail that Devon felt utterly lacking in herself – something to do with serenity, contentment. There had been an inner glow that had seemed to shine through her mother's very skin, making a dramatic contrast with the soft frame of her curly black hair. And while Devon possessed the same fair skin and black hair, she felt herself a pale reflection of her mother, seeing in her own image when she was faced with it in the shop's mirror too much restlessness, willfulness, to qualify for any such comparison.

"The very image," the gentleman was repeating now. "And I have an eye for beauty. Believe me, child, you will turn many heads, and be able to secure for yourself every advantage such attractiveness can acquire."

Devon was thankful no response seemed required of her, for she felt at a loss to know how to respond to such a remark, and just focused on keeping up with the man's long, confident strides.

Then they turned off into a dim little court and Newgate was saying, "You shall be of great assistance to me in selecting just the right piece with which to please my wife. While a woman in years, I fear my Sissy's tastes are still those of a child. A charming child, mind you, I'm sure you'd get along famously. Yes, in fact, that's a capital idea: you must come visit her at the house. I'm sure the two of you would become fast friends."

He was speaking and moving so quickly, Devon could hardly keep up with either.

"Yes, she would welcome your company, I'm sure," he went on. "A playmate. Painting, music: she prefers play to dealing with the harder facts of life. But then, that's why she has me, isn't it? It's a proper bargain."

But Devon's mind had snagged on the word *play*. She had scarcely thought of herself as a child for years, having taken on so many of the chores of the 'woman of the house' while her mother worked in the shop to support the family. She was trying to remember the last time she had done anything akin to 'play' and was having no success.

Then the man stopped beside a sign hung on the rail of an old brick building: *F. Finch, Fine Miniatures*, with an arrow pointing to the stairs that led down to a door beneath the level of the walkway.

"We may have to wait a few moments for our host," Newgate said after he'd given the clapper of the brass bell on the door several vigorous clangs. "Mister Finch is getting up in years and moves a bit slowly. But the wait is worth it."

Eventually, an old gentleman did appear, the door creaking slowly open after the bolt had been thrown. He peered at them with squinted eyes before he recognized his caller.

"Mr. Newgate, sir, come in, come in. I have just been thinking that it had been some time since Mister Newgate last paid us a call."

They were ushered into a room dimly lit, with a ceiling so low it seemed the old man's back must have become bent just from stooping to avoid hitting his head on the rafters.

But the man went about lighting oil lamps as he spoke, until the room was filled with a soft glow and the glass-topped cases that formed three rows in the low room emerged like magical creatures from the gloom. Devon soon became so absorbed in peering through the glass at the wealth of tiny scenes that she heard little of the conversation around her.

"…Well enough, though she doesn't come out much. She prefers the home."

"…such a lovely young woman…"

"…Yes. But it is hard, you know."

The long cases were lined with dark green velvet and seemed to contain a miniature of every kind of figure and object imaginable. There was a replica Devon recognized as the Tower of London, though she had seen it only from a distance; and a tiny organ grinder with his monkey. The figure of a young girl with long blonde braids was carrying a pole on her shoulders, from which balanced a metal pail at each end. Devon was trying to peer inside the pails when the old man approached.

"Let me take some out for you," he said, picking among the many keys he held on a large ring.

One after another they came out, as Devon spied some particular creation – a juggler in a bright patchwork costume, five yellow balls suspended with near-invisible wire about his head. A tiny chimney sweep perched on a rooftop with broom in hand and a bright smile on his grimy face. A whole cluster of ballad singers, their arms about each other's shoulders, their mouths wide open in song. Each was done in such fine detail that it seemed the thing itself must simply have been shrunk. Where there was metal in the living, there was metal; and where there was wood, wood. The bodies looked soft, like flesh, and the hair was surely real human hair. Devon reached just the tip of her finger to touch the golden braid of the young milking girl. It was silkier than her own.

"Exquisite, are they not?"

Newgate's voice, so close to her ear, startled her. She had quite forgotten his presence in her fascination with the tiny works of art.

"Did you really fashion all these yourself?" she asked the old man.

"No, these hands aren't limber enough for the work anymore. My wife and I did it all originally. Now our children do most of them. And their children are learning the craft as well."

"Cottage industry," Newgate spoke up loudly. "I wish more families in this city understood that need, get the poor rates down and the beggars off the street."

The man did not reply, but moved to the next case down from the one Devon had been studying. "There is a piece here," he said to Newgate, "I especially thought of for your wife. Done by my eldest granddaughter, who has become the best in the family at the work, I think."

He opened the cabinet and carefully lifted out a wide, elaborate scene.

Devon moved over beside Newgate to look, while the man moved an oil lamp closer.

It was quite beyond belief in its intricacy. The surface of the whole was carved out in tiers, in one of which were clustered a group of men playing all manner of musical instruments, the golden pipes of a grand kind of piano rising behind them. And in other tiers sat ladies and gentlemen arrayed in the richest dress, with velvet gowns and waistcoats, plumes woven into the ladies' hair or tucked into the bands of their wide hats. The men held canes tipped with gold, while many of the ladies' hands were buried in fat muffs. Devon couldn't resist moving forward to touch them – yes, they felt like real fur.

But the scene was not the interior of some castle or grand hall; there were a dozen little trees anchored in the base at the bottom of the scene, their leaves looking as frail as flower stems, their branches arching over the figures on the grounds below the tier of musicians. Some of those below were dressed as finely as those in the boxes, others more roughly; but all appeared engaged in lively talk or dancing, or eating perfect miniatures of little cakes.

"Vauxhall Gardens!" Newgate exclaimed. "Why, it is perfect. You have trained your ladies well, sir. The lass has captured all the delight of the place. She must have spent much time there. I would not be surprised if we had met on those grounds at one time or another."

He seemed to be waiting for a reply from the old man, which did not come.

Newgate cupped the piece in his two hands and lifted it closer to the light.

In his hands, the piece appeared smaller, the details of its execution even more miraculous.

"How much, sir?" Newgate said. "You have guessed rightly of my interest, but perhaps the price is too dear."

"Three pounds only," the old man replied.

"One," Newgate said immediately.

"Ah, sir, you know that wouldn't even pay for the materials."

"One-and-six," Newgate came back, setting the piece down on the glass case without ceremony.

"Two-and-six would be more fitting," the old man came back, his voice having taken on a mournful quality.

"Two. And that's my final offer." A note of irritation had crept into Newgate's congenial tone.

"Two then," the man said softly, not looking at Newgate anymore. "At least I know the dear Miss Cecily will enjoy it."

"Indeed she will," Newgate said briskly, and reached into the pocket of his waistcoat for his money clip.

Then he paused, seeming to become aware of Devon again. "And for the milkmaid? Suppose I give you two-and-six for them both."

"Ah." The man's face grew even more distressed. "It would have to be three, sir."

"Three it is then," Mr. Newgate said expansively. "It is just money after all, isn't it? The ladies are worth it." And he beamed down at Devon. "For you, my lovely," he said, and extracted three notes from his golden clip, where a great many more remained.

Devon was beginning to protest when Newgate, anticipating her refusal, laid his hand with the money clip on hers. "Please. Allow me to do this," he said. "It would make me so happy to please you."

Not knowing how to respond to such a statement, Devon could only watch as the old man folded the two pieces in muslin, wrapping the soft cloth gently about each like a winding sheet.

"In separate packages?" he inquired, as he turned to where containers of various types and sizes were ranged on the shelves behind him.

"Quite," Newgate replied. And before Devon had fully absorbed what was happening, she was again on the street outside, the girl bearing the pails lying wrapped and boxed in her hands.

"Thank you," she said. "Though really, you shouldn't—"

But his voice cut her off as the man opened his umbrella above her head. "Nonsense. A lovely young woman such as yourself should have a lovely little girl to play with and admire." And he peered down the street, as though getting his bearings. "Now. Shall we stop for tea?"

"Oh, I must be getting back," Devon said. "Really. Mrs. Dofferman will be expecting me. And I should try to be of assistance with the doctor's supper."

His hand made a brief gesture in the air, like the doctor's dismissing money from his patients. "A fine young woman should not have to bother her head with such things," he said. "Or her hands with such chores. I'm sure you have had enough of that sort of work in your father's house. Now it's time for some lucky man to spoil you a little. Come – perhaps we can find some amusing little pastry to eat along our way."

And with his hand higher on her arm now, just under her breast, Newgate moved her off down the street at a brisk pace, the air seeming to Devon to have grown darker in the short time they'd been inside the shop.

"Too bad we're so far from Gunther's: an ice would be most refreshing right now. But if you must be getting back, we'll see what we can find between here and Pilgrim Street. That is where the doctor resides, is it not?"

It occurred to Devon to wonder how he knew that; the doctor hadn't recognized him when he'd approached them at the prison.

But he was continuing to talk as they moved along. "You don't mind if we walk, do you? So good for the constitution. And you can tell me all about yourself along the way."

Devon was beginning to feel like one of those tops she'd seen boys spinning in the alley. She had always taken her parents' warnings about "young men" to mean such boys, while the only grown men she'd really known were her father and the doctor, or while under their protection. She was not sure that the same rules applied.

Newgate was not waiting for her thoughts to catch up, however, but was continuing his cheerful conversation as they crossed the court and into another broad street, heading east, where the spires of the churches were barely visible now, enveloped in a thick mist.

"My wife is not a bold young woman such as yourself, you understand," he was saying. "She is a more delicate creature, and has had to be protected all her life – first by her father, and now the task has fallen to me."

Devon was not at all sure the term "bold young woman" could be applied to her; but she couldn't help being pleased that she could be seen as such.

"You must come visit her," Newgate was continuing. "Sissy would enjoy your company, I'm sure. She gets out so little. And you'd be entranced as well by her full collection of the miniatures. There is hardly room for them all in her suite. There's a remarkable replica of the Tower, with one of Henry the Eighth's wives inside, awaiting her execution. Crown and all. Even a tiny gallows. You've been to the Tower, surely."

Devon admitted that she had not.

"We must go then, one day soon. Quite the most magnificent view of the Thames and the city. I do so relish this city, even its darker parts. The lower classes too can be so intriguing; I never tire of the spectacle. Like continuous theater, it is."

Then he had stopped before a shop bearing the name *James Bright, Confectioner*, with a legend below it: *All Sorts of Biskets, Cakes and Sugar Plums.*

"Shall we?" he said, making a sweeping gesture toward the door such as she'd seen footmen make to the boarders of a fine carriage. "His creations do not equal Gunther's, of course," he said, "but they should pleasure our mouths sufficiently for the rest of our journey."

Feeling she had very little choice in the matter, Devon entered the well-lit shop, its interior pleasantly warm and sweet-smelling after the chill rain outside.

"Now what shall we have?" Newgate said, propping his umbrella among others by the door and rubbing his hands together as they approached a case in which more sorts of cakes and pastries were displayed than Devon had known existed.

"Ah, apricot," Newgate was saying. "Or peach. Wouldn't that taste fine with a spot of tea. Come." And he turned to hustle her off to a chair at one of the little tables in a far corner of the shop. "We must do this properly," he said. "What will it be, peach or apricot? No, don't demur now, just tell me. Apricot? Is that what we want?"

Without waiting for an answer, the man strode off to pick their pastries, taking as many notes from his money clip as he had given the old man for the miniatures he had just purchased.

He was back in moments, bearing three enormous confections on a china plate. "An apricot for each, and a peach for good measure."

He laid a linen napkin on the table before her and placed one of the pastries upon it, cutting it in quarters with a knife he produced, with a magician's flourish, from his other hand.

Then he sat down and, with a contented sigh, bit into his own – uncut – pastry. "Ah, Mr. Bright has done it again. Now, let's hear about Miss Devon Quail. How are you enjoying what you've seen of our fair city, now that you're more out and about?"

Devon didn't know quite what he was asking, but began to speak of her experiences in the past weeks. He seemed to listen intently to her, the hand unoccupied with his pastry lightly touching hers now and then, as though punctuating his brief responses to her remarks. It occurred to her that listening might be as important to his profession as to the doctor's, who paid close attention always to his patients' accounts of their ills. And while Mr. Newgate's gaze was rather more intense than she was comfortable with, Devon appreciated the attention paid to what she had to say.

It was nearly dark when they arrived back on Pilgrim Street, and Devon was worried that Mrs. Dofferman would be concerned, or even angry. But that was all forgotten when she discovered that the doctor's condition had taken a turn for the worse, his fits of coughing now deeper in his chest and longer lasting. So both Devon and Mrs. Dofferman were distracted from all other topics while they worked to make him more comfortable. For the first time, the older woman let Devon attend him as well. Over his protests, she had called in another doctor, who had pronounced Doctor MacBride's condition "full-blown pneumonia" and prescribed tea with lemon and molasses, and a constant steaming of the room. When Devon entered, she found the bedroom filled with vapor and the doctor's face paler than the bleached pillow case. It was the worst vision she'd had since she woke that awful morning in the loft to find all of her family dead.

She tried to keep up her spirits for him, though. "You just need rest," she assured him, sounding to herself rather like her mother when one of them was ailing. So she tried to make her next words more in his own style, adding more gruffly, "What with the time you spend out in all sorts of weather, it's a wonder the cough isn't worse."

And she was rewarded with a faint smile from the patient as he said, "I see y've decided to usurp my position."

The doctor had been refusing food, but now let Devon feed him a few bites of the gruel Mrs. Dofferman had prepared. Still, she was surprised by his reply when she offered to read to him from the book they'd just bought, a treatise of some sort by a man named Hunt. "Yes," he said, "I think I could use a bit of that. Hunt always speaks his mind, pure and simple."

After he fell asleep, though, Devon watched over him with a great lump of sadness in the center of her breast, and fear at the threat of another loss. She had always been fond of Doctor MacBride when he had come to visit her family, summoned or not. The rough facade he put on much of the time, she had come to understand, was only a poor shield for the softness of his heart. But in these last months that she had been privileged to accompany him on his rounds, she had grown to love him deeply for his caring, especially his dispensing it more liberally to the poor than the better-off. Such a man, she thought, should not be allowed to die and leave so many who needed him.

Devon regarded him intensely in his troubled sleep, herself breathing deeply in and out as though she could breathe for him, until Mrs. Dofferman came to take over, insisting she "Get t'yr bed now. I can't handle more than one invalid at a time."

It wasn't until the next morning, together scrubbing and rinsing and drying the few breakfast dishes, that Mrs. Dofferman seemed to remember the circumstances under which they had parted on their shopping excursion.

"Did you get along, then, with that gentleman well enough?"

"Yes, I suppose so," Devon said, a bit surprised that her response wasn't more enthusiastic, considering all the treats the man had showered upon her. Though already that afternoon seemed a very long time ago.

"He bought me a gift."

"A gift?" Already the woman's tone was sharper.

"A sort of doll. He was getting another for his wife," she added quickly.

"Dolls? You're too old for dolls," she said with a huff. "As I'm sure his wife must be."

So Devon fetched the little figure to show her.

"Someone has put a lot of care into this," the woman said as she turned the figure carefully in her large hand. "What did he pay for it?"

"A pound or so only. Three for the both of them."

"It's worth more than three itself," Mrs. Dofferman said. She turned with a sharp look. "And did he want anything for it?"

"'Want anything'?" Devon repeated, unsure whether the woman was referring to the seller or the buyer of the figure.

"Did he propose anything indecent to you?"

"No!" Devon could feel herself flushing at the question. Did Mrs. Dofferman think her a girl who could be bought, like those she'd seen in the streets? "He only got pastry and walked me back."

Then instinct prompted her to add, "He wished me to meet his wife and keep her company," and found that her own mind eased just speaking the words.

"Uh huh," the woman said, sounding less eased.

"She keeps to the house apparently. And collects little figurines to keep her company."

"Sounds like a poor substitute for a family," Mrs. Dofferman responded.

"He did ask me to speak about my experiences attending the doctor," Devon felt compelled to add. "And he seemed to attend to everything I said."

"Hmph," Mrs. Dofferman said to that. "Take care when they seem to pay attention. What they may be attending to is the fastest route to your bed."

It was said with no more than the woman's usual sour tone; but Devon found herself going over the events of that afternoon in her mind more than once, trying to fully comprehend their intent, before the next time Mr. Newgate came to call.

Chapter 7
The High Life

Man is the only animal whose desires
increase as they are fed; the only animal
that is never satisfied.
Henry George

Devon was back in the mews of the carriage house at the time, talking with Mynors, the coachman, while she stroked the great head and glossy coat of Sam, the doctor's horse he was grooming. Having heard Mynors utter barely a word in all the months he had piloted the doctor and herself through the poorest streets of the city, Devon had been pleased to find that, encountered on his own, he might have quite a bit to say – especially on the subject of the various classes of London society.

This particular day, he was explaining in some detail the differences between one type of carriage and another – stanhopes from tilburies, broughams from britzkas, phaetons from tandems or tin-whiskies. And Devon listened, fascinated by the names alone, and which people Mynors said rode in which kinds – all the while admiring the dignified beauty of the horse, who stood quite still while he was being groomed and petted, only the occasional rippling of his side or flick of his tail giving evidence that he was more than a statue.

Then around the corner at her back she heard footsteps and a now-familiar voice say, "There you are, my girl. That housekeeper said you were gone, but I thought I'd look around for myself."

She turned to see Mr. Newgate approach, dressed quite elegantly in a long coat with a fur collar, striped trousers, polished boots, and a starched cravat.

"Good morning," she said politely, already wishing he had taken Mrs. Dofferman's word for it, though she could not have said exactly why she felt it.

"Aren't we looking lovely today?" Newgate said as he came closer. "But that frock, my dear! It was more suited to its former owner than to a young woman such as yourself."

"You knew the doctor's wife?" It was a coincidence she found surprising.

He laughed. "There are few in London did not know the fetching Polly MacBride. Or the Polly Duckett before her."

Devon would have liked to inquire further about this lady of whom the doctor never spoke and Mrs. Dofferman spoke of with such bitterness that Devon no longer brought up the subject.

But Mr. Newgate had other things on his mind. "I thought this would be a perfect morning for a ride through Regent's Park," he said, "and wondered whether you might join me. My britzka is right out front, ready and waiting."

Out of the corner of her eye, Devon saw Mynors's head nodding slightly, as though the information about the carriage this man drove had been a significant clue to his character. She made note to speak to him about that later.

Devon had heard of Regent's Park – a kind of wonderland of trees and meadows, pools and fountains, with fine houses set around. *A playground for the King*, the doctor had called it, in his most scornful tone.

Devon looked to Mynors, but his face had closed down to its usual impassive mask.

"I'll have to inquire of the doctor," Devon said.

"And how is the good doctor?" Newgate asked cheerfully.

"Not well, I'm afraid. But he does seem to be doing a little better these days, since Doctor Palmetter has been tending to him."

"I'm glad to hear it. If we barristers who represent ourselves in court are said to have a fool for a client, so must the man of medicine who tends himself when he is ailing. Do, by all means, go tell the man that Squire Newgate has come to take his charge out to that country within a city, to put some bloom back in those pale cheeks."

With some reluctance, but also with no small amount of curiosity, Devon went inside to obtain permission.

She found Mrs. Dofferman first, and in an ill humor, but willing enough to get her out from underfoot. "Don't bother the doctor, he's sleeping. Just be sure it's to the park the man takes ya."

Devon didn't find the remark encouraging, but went to change her dress as instructed, to what Mrs. Dofferman called "the Missus' out-for-the-day frock" – as opposed to her "out-for-the-night" gown – which Devon had been forbidden, though she'd never have entertained an interest.

The day frock was one Devon felt some better comfort in, its inner layers all muslin and soft to the skin. She tucked a handkerchief into the bodice to raise the neckline, though the tiny pearls woven into the puffed sleeves still felt far too grand to be wearing for only a carriage ride.

Mr. Newgate seemed pleased with it though, when she appeared in the entrance hall where Mrs. Dofferman had made him wait. "Ah, now that one suits you better," he said, coming closer. He reached a single finger to rearrange a curl at her left temple. "Shall we be off?"

Little she had heard of the opulent splendors of the Regent's Park and its environs had prepared Devon for the scale of what she saw that day. Traveling farther west and north than she'd ever been in the doctor's coach, the streets and houses both seemed to expand the farther along they went, plain fronts becoming studded with pillars, porticoes and bays. The narrow, busy streets swelled to grand avenues and squares, where people simply strolled about, dressed as though for some elegant occasion, though it was only the middle of the morning and the week. They made those parading down Fleet

Street that first day in the doctor's coach seem quite ordinary by comparison.

Devon had to crane her head so far out of the carriage and tilted back to see to the tops of the ornamented structures, that the bonnet Mrs. Dofferman had made her wear slipped off into the street – to Mr. Newgate's great amusement.

He waved his hand in dismissal when she asked him to stop the carriage to retrieve it. "We can find one of Sissy's that will be more suitable," he said, making Devon wonder again just how old his wife was. But Newgate had his driver stop to put the top of the carriage back; and despite the chill in the air, Devon was glad for the wider view.

Entering the park through a gate built with narrow twin houses on either side – though for decoration only, it appeared – the carriage rolled along drives so smooth its wheels seemed to purr. They passed meadows green as fine silk and a wide pond of water from which streams spread out in all directions, flocks of birds with iridescent heads and larger ones with long white necks floating on its surface.

Compared with any street or market in any other area of the city she'd seen, this vast space appeared to Devon practically deserted. Fine carriages and couples paraded along the tree-lined lanes; children dressed like miniature adults leaned over pools, restrained by their nannies' hands. And here and there stood a great stone structure, its lawns spread out about it, as though every mansion Devon had ever heard of residing in the countryside had gathered here together in the heart of the city. Devon was reminded of the tableaux she had seen in the books of tinted prints she had pored over as a child whenever Boyle had been lucky enough to trade for a tattered copy. For while the figures in this scene moved, it seemed to be in slow motion, a series of poses only, until now and then a rabbit, routed from a clump of trees, would dash across their path, heading for some other patch of shelter.

Devon was too busy looking around her to attend much to Mr. Newgate's running commentary on the scene, telling her which house belonged to whom and what man had designed it – names like Maberly and Nash, Taylor and Cumberland – all spoken in a familiar tone, as though he knew all of them personally.

His speech was interrupted regularly with greetings he made to someone passing in a carriage or strolling along a path – "Sir Edgerton, good day, you are looking well, Sir." Or to a stout, matronly woman, "Ah, Madame Franklin, you are as lovely as ever."

But it was the size of the structures in the park that struck Devon as most notable. They appeared in the midst of the meadows like great chunks of stone and marble out of place in such a setting, and surely not housing enough people to warrant their size.

"How many families live in these houses?" Devon had asked after the first few she beheld.

Newgate had laughed. "Just one generally."

"Just one," Devon repeated, amazed. "They must have many children then."

And Newgate had laughed louder, giving her shoulders a little squeeze with his arm across the back of the seat. "You are quite wonderful, Miss Quail," he had said.

Then they came to a rather somber structure still under construction, its high walls straight and bare, with the pillars that would adorn it lying by its side. Devon was struck by how much it resembled the face of the Newgate gaol, tall and gray in the morning mist.

"These houses have many more to hold than just a family," Newgate's had added. "A veritable army of maids and butlers, gardeners and cooks – it takes them all to run a household of this size. There are frequent dinner guests, and I hope my wife and I to be among them shortly, as we should be."

An oversized matron passed the carriage. Walking slowly with a cane. "Lady Dunstan," Newgate addressed her in a reverent tone, "how very good it is to see you getting around again. I hope the trouble Lord Dunstan was having with the allotment of his estate is not still pressing on him?"

The woman didn't answer, just shook her head in the negative and continued on her halting way. A woman in plainer dress walked by her side with an arm under her forearm. As their carriage passed, Newgate called back, "Please remember me to him, with my very best regards."

They left the park that day by the York gate, passing what seemed to be a church, but colonnaded very like the mansions they had passed. They were rolling down High Street before Mr. Newgate said, "I've told my wife she can expect us for tea. She is so eager to meet you."

Devon started to protest that she had promised Mrs. Dofferman they would not be gone long, but he only added, "Sissy doesn't get out much, as I've told you. And she's been so ill. I told her of the charming child I met who is a ward of the doctor. Having no children of her own, in her condition, she is most eager to meet you."

Devon couldn't imagine being unable to have children; she herself planned to have a big family like her own. It seemed heartless to refuse to see this poor woman.

They traveled down another wide avenue, though the noise and bustle of the traffic had resumed once they'd left the sanctuary of Regent's Park. Newgate's carriage seemed to be nearly as heavy as the doctor's coach, but was being pulled by two delicate mares, whose names he said when she inquired were Nell and Gwendolyn. "After Sissy's mother and her aunt," he said. "Sissy used to love to ride. But she's been unable to for years now. Because of her delicate condition, you understand."

The square they finally pulled into was a somber array of brick houses facing a tidy expanse of green lawn. The narrow house fronts looked older than those they'd passed just outside the Park, all white and graceful in their curving order. The dark faces of these houses were broken only by little balconies of black iron half-circling the upper windows, too tiny for a person to actually walk out on.

Newgate mistook her gaze for admiration and said, "This is the oldest and finest of squares in all of London, built for the King's favorites. My wife's father, Admiral Wingsbury, was among the first to build here, and now the house has come to me, as part of my wife's dowry. Her mother died when she was an infant, and he wanted her to be well taken care of. But I will tell you a secret: I have my eye on those new terraces at Sussex Place – the grandest you have ever seen: ten domes and fifty-six

Corinthian columns, all in one great sweep, just at the edge of the park. You probably noticed them.

She had.

"I will show you the one I have my eye on at the next opportunity," he said as the carriage drew to a stop. But now, we must attend to our Cecily. We must keep her happy if we are to go again." And Newgate swung down from the carriage and reached a hand to help Devon alight.

But the space between carriage and curb was wide, and Devon had the usual layers of skirts to worry about. So gathering the skirts with her left hand, Devon held to the carriage door with her right and reached the pavement in a single energetic hop.

"Wonderful!" Newgate cried. "Ah, Miss Quail, you are a delight."

They passed through a black grillwork gate with *Wingsbury Hall* scripted in iron on its arch, and mounted the tall steps to knock upon a heavy burnished door.

"Marianne," Newgate said to the young woman who opened the door, "we will be three to tea. Would you inform Miss Cecily that we have arrived?"

The girl stood her ground a moment, staring rather boldly, Devon thought, at her employer and herself, before she stepped aside to let them pass, and, with another dark look, disappeared up the long curving staircase to their right.

The parlor Devon could see beyond the high pillars of the hallway looked like a more cluttered version of the beautifully balanced miniatures they'd seen in the shop.

Bordered with dark wood at floor and ceiling, the walls were covered with a somber pattern of deep blue flowers encased in stripes of gold, their vertical rigidity warring with the busy multicolored floral prints that cloaked the armchairs, overlaid with doilies on their arms and backs. The rug, of yet another pattern in vivid red and gold, looked as though it had resided there, unwalked-upon, for decades. Again, Devon wondered about all the unused space there seemed to be for such a crowded city.

Then from above came a light, musical voice, and Devon turned to see a young woman skimming down the staircase, the train of her white lace dress rippling behind her. "Percy!" she cried as she came, beaming down at Devon. "You have brought the child!"

She did not pause at the bottom of the stairs, but came rushing up to them, the delicate tap of her slippers echoing on the marble floor of the hallway.

First, she kissed her husband on the cheek he offered, then turned to Devon, touching her wrists, then her shoulders. "And isn't she lovely," she said. "But so tall!"

Indeed, though not uncommonly tall, Devon stood half a hand above the top of the young woman's head, even with its crown of golden braids. And in the white dress, gathered just below her small breasts in the princess fashion, the woman appeared quite a child herself, though surely older than Devon by a decade.

"Can you stay?" she begged Devon. "I have so much to show you!"

"Only a little while, thank you," Devon replied. "I must be getting back. Doctor MacBride is sick and may need me."

"The doctor, yes, Percy told me. How kind of him to take you in when your family died. I don't know what I'd ever do without Percy, now that my father is gone." And without another word, she turned, pulling Devon along by the hand toward the staircase. "Come. If you have only a little time to stay, you must come up at once. Perhaps you will find something among my collection you would like to have for yourself. I have so many, I'd love to give you some."

In the next hour Devon spent there, she thought she must have seen hundreds of the tiny replicas such as those in Mr. Finch's shop. Whole villages were laid out in miniature, with bits of thatch on the country cottages and pebbles on the paths, delicate little carts and wagons, horses and cows, and tiny people done up in peasant dress with bright kerchiefs at the men's necks and on the women's heads, wooden hoes thin as matchsticks in their hands. Curiously, most of the miniatures she was shown were country scenes. Maybe the people who could afford to purchase them, Devon thought, had had their fill of city sights and wanted something more peaceful.

"Isn't it just lovely?" the young woman kept saying as she pulled Devon from one to another of her miniatures.

"Oh, this one you must see," Cecily piped as she rushed to a miniature set beneath the front window with the unusable balcony outside it.

She reached for a tiny figure in the middle of what Devon recognized from books was a circus scene. The figure was suspended between two sticks; and by squeezing them together with her small hands, Cecily caused the tiny figure to flip over its bar, which made Devon join her in a delighted cry.

Then Cecily skipped to another small scene, and sent one after another of many miniature ladies twirling in their ball gowns beneath a sparkling chandelier.

The young woman folded her hands beneath her chin then and said wistfully, "Every time Percy goes out for a full day or more, it seems he brings me one. Now there are so many, I hardly know where to put them. So if you'd like one, please, please just tell me which and it's yours. Or more."

Then she was off to the high bed that filled one end of the large room. "Do come see," she called, lifting a wide blue bowl from the bedside table. "Though this one I'll never, never give away."

When Devon drew closer, she saw that the surface of the bowl was painted to look like ripples, over which a wooden boat seemed to float. In it were the slender figures of a man and a woman. The man was rowing, his head bare, the sleeves of his full white shirt pushed up, while the lady reclined on a pink silk pillow, her parasol propped over her bonneted head.

"Isn't it romantic?" Sissy purred. "Percy took me rowing once, when he was courting. And it was the most enchanting day. He says he will take me again sometime, when I'm recovered. I lost the baby, you know. Three months before it was to come, it went away. But he says perhaps in a while, when I'm stronger, we can try for another. I do hope so. I just love babies, don't you?"

Chapter 8

Sissy and Her Percy

I paint self-portraits because I am so often alone,
because I am the person I know the best.
Frida Kahlo, painter

Tyrants and sensualists are in the right when they endeavor to
keep women in the dark, because the former want slaves, the
latter a play-thing.
Mary Wollstonecraft, 1759-1797

In the next weeks, Devon saw a good deal of Cecily Newgate – or Sissy as she insisted Devon call her.

Newgate would call often, "happening by", it seemed to her, just when Devon's restlessness had reached its limits. The doctor had rallied somewhat after his bout with the lung disease; but his health was far from good. And on those days he ventured out at all to make his rounds, he was often so worn by late morning that he did not protest when Mynors turned the coach back toward Pilgrim Street.

So when Mr. Newgate dropped by, on his way to visit a client in Lambeth or Hampstead or Kennington – places Devon had never been – she was glad for the chance to get out of the house and visit new areas of the city. And when his appointment was finished, which often took only a brief time while she waited in the carriage, they would stop by some charming little shop for tea, or to an art gallery or afternoon concert at the Vauxhall Gardens. Or once to a cricket match at Lord's.

On those occasions, Devon always inquired whether Sissy might not join them. But Mr. Newgate invariably responded that he had not brought his wife because she was not up to it. "Female troubles" he called the health problems that kept Sissy to the house.

It made Devon wonder all the more whether the pain and blood she'd been experiencing for the past few weeks was not an indication of malfunction of her female parts. "It's only to be expected," Mrs. Dofferman had told her. "Just one more of women's burdens." But Devon couldn't help but wonder whether such a burden might not have cost Sissy her baby, and whether she herself might be subject to the same fate. Her mother had had two miscarriages, after all, after Devon had been born. It seemed that maybe the blood itself was to be feared.

Often, Mrs. Dofferman would quiz her upon her return from an outing with Mr. Newgate. Had his wife come along this time? Had he behaved like a gentleman? And except for those periodic occasions when they had ended the outing with a visit to Sissy, Devon had to reply no to the first question, but always yes to the second. For while Mr. Newgate told her often how fond of her he was, so did Sissy. And Devon could find no logical reason to believe that his occasional hugs about her shoulders or squeezes of her hand were any different from the many hugs and squeezes Sissy lavished upon her.

"My little girl," they both called her, even though she was already taller than Sissy and often felt older as well.

But Sissy was fun. Their time together, whether spent singing or dancing or painting, or simply studying in wonder the fine details of the legion of her miniatures and imagining the variety of lives they illustrated, Devon found Sissy to be every bit as enjoyable and instructional as Devon's time out in the wider world with her husband.

Those hours with Sissy, in fact, on reflection, seemed to mark the only times in Devon's life, really, when she could remember ever just *playing*, like a lighthearted child. Though she must have, she would say to herself, before the twins and the other children had come along to fill her every hour. Hadn't she? Of her early childhood, Devon could remember only being in the shop with her parents while they worked; and it was necessary to do whatever she did quietly – playing with her only stuffed animal, a bear named Barney, or the various ornaments to adorn the garments her parents were fashioning – so as not to disturb the customers. And she could remember quite vividly the many customers who told her mother what an adorable child she had. "And so well-behaved!"

Sissy had more talents than that for merriment, however. When Devon first admired the many paintings she saw – not the somber oil portraits in the downstairs parlor, hung in heavy gilt frames, but the sunny, fanciful scenes that adorned the walls in Sissy's suite of rooms – the young woman blushed with pleasure. "Do you like them, truly? They're only play, of course; their lack of instruction is plain. But I do so enjoy it."

Devon had stared at her. "You painted these *yourself*? Truly?"

Sissy had grabbed her hand and led her to a tiny studio at the back of the house, where an easel was set before the single window, surrounded by jars holding brushes in every tint of water. Canvasses were propped everywhere, some blank, some half-finished, done in swirls of soft but vibrant colors. Some of the scenes Devon recognized as inspired by the miniatures in Sissy's collection, often enlivened with so much light and color, they fairly seemed to dance.

"But they're beautiful!" Devon breathed. "They're wonderful!"

There were tears in Sissy's eyes as she rushed to hug her tight. "Really?" she said. "Really? Oh, my precious friend!"

Then, in a far corner, Devon noticed another several canvasses propped with their faces to the wall. She went to them and crouched, turning each one to examine it. They were all clearly self-portraits. But while the clothing and backgrounds were as bright as the others, the faces did not look happy. Some looked shy, some sad, and one downright despairing. It made Devon's heart hurt just to look at them, and she didn't know quite what to say.

Then Sissy was behind her, pulling her up and away from the paintings, laughing with embarrassment. "Oh, don't mind those. They are just some self-indulgence on my part."

Devon came away from that visit with a confusion of feelings. Here was a young woman who'd been represented to her as a near invalid, yet she appeared to have boundless energy. And she seemed happy, but painted herself sad, despairing.

Later, in her memories of their times together, Devon would find that she had to hang on to the happy times. Especially the dancing. Sissy would wind the music box that stood on a stand in her bedroom and – refusing to accept that Devon did not know how to dance – twirled her about the room, while the resplendent couple atop the music box spun and spun to a tinkling waltz. Sometimes they twirled so hard that they eventually toppled against a wall and fell laughing to the carpet in a heap of petticoats.

Yet Sissy did sometimes come down with the spells of indisputable illness her husband had told Devon about. At those times, when Newgate told her he had promised Sissy to bring Devon to see her after some outing, the young woman greeted Devon from her bed, and seemed to be only a pale replica of herself. The delicate tissues of Sissy's eyelids seemed too heavy for her to keep raised as she reached for Devon's hand on the coverlet. Devon would force a smile past her fear as she held the slim wrist and felt its pulse so weak beneath her fingers.

Each time, Devon wished that she could bring Doctor MacBride to see Sissy, to divine the reason for such chronic illness. But when she'd said as much to Mr. Newgate once, he had seemed offended. "Doctor Thurston has attended the family for generations," he said as they rode in the carriage to take Devon back to the doctor's house. "It is apparently hereditary, and you can be sure that everything that can be done is being done."

Then he had covered her hand with his and his tone had softened. "I'm glad you have become such a good friend to my wife. She has needed such a friend. But you must understand that not all women, particularly those of her class, are as strong as those you may be accustomed to in the working classes. She has been delicate all her life, and her energy, while high at times, fades quickly. So we must bear with her. There is just nothing else, really, that can be done."

"On his death bed," Newgate went on, his voice almost dream-like now, staring straight ahead in the carriage, "her father said to me, 'Son,' – for he thought of me as a son surely – 'Take care of my little girl. You are all she has now.'" He turned back to Devon. "So you see, you must do some of her living for her, be her other half, so to speak, and come back to tell her of your adventures. She has come to depend on you for that."

And sometimes Sissy was able to come with them. Such as the time they went to the Sadlers' Wells to see a quite marvelous performance by Grimaldi the Clown. It was that outing, in fact, from which Devon returned to Pilgrim Street to find Dr. Palmetter at the house again, and the perpetual worry lines on Mrs. Dofferman's brow grown deeper yet.

"It's the fever again," the woman told her in the kitchen. "I cannot get it down." And with the great wooden mallet, she pounded the chunk of ice on the table as though it were the disease itself.

"I shouldn't have gone," Devon said, remembering her concern at the sound of the doctor's cough that morning. It was a Sunday, and the outing had been planned for weeks; but she had gone up to Doctor

MacBride's room and asked if he did not want her to stay and read to him. But he had barely opened his eyes, waved her away with a weak hand. "Get y'rself some air, girl," he said. "Ye don't need to be breathin' more of mine."

Now, she regretted having gone at all, and did not leave the doctor's side all that night, while his chest labored for each breath and the fits of coughing that seized him seemed interminable. Mrs. Dofferman had, at Dr. Palmetter's instruction, fashioned a gauze tent about the bed in which a steady stream of steam was maintained, to ease his breathing. But if it was so eased, Devon hated to think how it would have been without such measures.

Devon had a lot of time to think that night. And some of the thoughts she had been trying to keep from her mind settled upon it now. What if he dies? What would become of her? If Mrs. Dofferman were to remain in the house, Devon could probably stay too, serve as a maid or take in washing perhaps. But what if the doctor's wife returned and didn't want her about? Surely there was no reason she should. Then Devon would have to find some way to make a living for herself.

Whatever assistance she had been to Doctor MacBride or Mrs. Dofferman surely would not suffice to provide enough income to live on her own. Servants lived in the homes of their employers, but she shuddered at what her father would say to that. *No daughter of mine will ever be in service.* He had said it often enough. But what else was there for a girl? She could sew a decent hand, from her mother's instruction. Were there tailors or clothing factories that employed young girls and would pay enough to provide a living? Or could one actually apprentice for skills such as midwifery, as Mr. Newgate had once implied? She had helped Doctor MacBride deliver babies often enough, but doubted that would qualify her to do such a thing on her own. Did one train and then get some sort of certification to qualify as a midwife? And if so, how would one go about finding such a program?

She couldn't ask Mrs. Dofferman about such things, not in her present state of worry. The mere question would make more real the possibility of the doctor's dying. Devon could scarcely bring herself to think of it either. But during that long night, she wished her parents, or the doctor, or *someone*, had given her a little preparation for the possibility of being alone in the world this early in her life.

Devon regretted now the occasional impatience she had felt with Sissy when the young woman seemed to accept so easily the restrictions placed upon her. She seemed never to question the boundaries that had been set for her forays out of the house without her husband. They were limited to strolls around the circumference of their own little square, or brief shopping trips to Regent's Street. "But only as far north as Oxford," Sissy told her. "And not so far west as Bond Street. Percy says the macaronies on Bond Street, going to their clubs, will think me a wonton woman to be parading there unescorted.

"Did you know there are even houses of ill repute in Covent Garden?! Did you know that?" Sissy had said, her eyes wide. "Who would expect such a thing? And just the other side of Regent's Street are all those dreadful Soho people, drinking and fighting with their bare hands. Even in a carriage, I know I should not be safe there."

Having by then spent more days in Soho with the doctor than to the west of it with Mr. Newgate, Devon was far from convinced that Regent's Street marked the boundary of civilization. But she could sympathize with the caution the young woman felt in general. Hadn't she herself spent the first twelve and a half years of her life confined to her tiny home, seeing the world only through the closed pane of a loft window? And many of the scenes in the alley below that window had seemed to provide ample proof that her father's warnings of the dangers there for a young girl alone were well founded.

So Devon felt most fortunate that, through the doctor – and even Mr. Newgate – she had been given a chance to see some of that wider world in safety. Even accompanying Sissy occasionally on her shopping trips – to Court Hope's to pick new paper for the upstairs sitting room, or to the Messrs. Swan and Edgar for Sissy's dress fittings – gave Devon new perspectives on the world that others inhabited. And while she preferred riding through the countryside or attending some concert or performance, whether indoors or out, there was a certain fascination to be found in simply studying the parade of ladies and gentlemen – the latter turned out no less elegantly than the former – walking primly with their little dogs or maids, as though the purpose of their day was not to get where they were going, but simply to be part of the procession. Still, Devon had marveled that one could take so much time to shop and still have the time to earn the wherewithal to spend on shopping.

When she had posed that question once to Mr. Newgate, he had only laughed his boisterous laugh and given her another little squeeze and a most peculiar answer. "That's why those who work, work," he'd said. "To pay for those who do not." He had added to her frown, "That's why I must be out and about so much, to make the contacts to pay for Miss Sissy's pleasures, since she cannot."

Devon had made a silent vow then and there to pay, herself, for whatever pleasures she felt she could not live without in her life.

"I'm sure Sissy would be glad to help," she had said to Mr. Newgate that day, "if more income were needed."

But Newgate had only laughed the harder. "Ah, don't you see? That's what marriage is for."

Chapter 9

A Manly Sport

Sports do not build character.
They reveal it.
Heywood Hale Brown

Boxing's just show business with blood.
Frank Bruno, English boxer

After that day, Devon vowed not to leave the doctor's side, for any reason. Besides, in the past weeks, preoccupied with her concern for the doctor's health and her own future, Devon had become to Newgate "not so much fun to be with anymore."

Fine, she thought, she did not consider herself put in this world to provide "fun" for Pierce Newgate.

And she'd kept to that vow for two weeks, keeping vigil over Doctor MacBride or asking Mrs. Dofferman what she could do to lighten her burden. Until both had let her know with little gentleness that she should try to entertain herself elsewhere.

So the next day when Newgate's coachman stopped by to see if she would be available to accompany the Mister and Missus to Lambeth on the morrow, Devon had accepted.

But when Newgate arrived the next day, it was not in the britzka, with Sissy beside him, but by himself in a rakish new coach, without even a coachman in attendance.

"A phaeton," Newgate told her with pride. "It's the latest thing. Isn't she gorgeous?"

Devon didn't even ask about Sissy; it was obvious that there was only room for two on the red velvet upholstered seat. It seemed to finally confirm Devon's suspicions that at times, Newgate's tales of Sissy's indispositions were probably just his way of getting Devon's company to himself. For what reason, she tried not to ask herself.

The horse also was new, and a real beauty. Devon stroked him down his velvet nose as she tried to decide whether to go at all.

"Sissy is feeling poorly," Newgate said quickly, sensing her annoyance. "But she asks that you stop by for tea when we return. She will be most disappointed if you do not."

Devon supposed that she might as well go then. It had been so long since she'd been out of the house. And if Sissy was expecting her…

His appointment, Newgate had said, was in Lambeth. But when they reached the town proper, Newgate kept the horse moving at top speed. He had said little on the trip so far, and seemed more tense than his usual bonhomie manner.

When he finally pulled the horse to a stop, it was at a tavern beyond the last row of houses.

"Come," he said, reaching to lift her down from the seat. "This is not a place a young lady should remain alone in a coach."

He gave her no time to demur, just pulled her with him by the hand as he crossed the expanse occupied by many other horses and carriages. "This is something I want you to see," he told her as they approached the tavern.

Devon was wishing she hadn't come at all, even before he opened the heavy oaken door into a smoky darkness. Ahead was what seemed to be a solid wall of men. As her vision adjusted, the bodies appeared to fill every space in the huge room beyond, crowding between the tiny tables, some even standing atop them.

But Newgate didn't pause. He pulled Devon with him, winding his way through the tight-packed crowd toward the center of the room, where a gas lamp glowed yellow over a raised platform. They didn't stop until they reached it.

The platform was ringed by a rough rope, and those gathered there were extending fistfuls of pound notes and gleaming guineas toward the man seated on the platform itself.

Newgate dropped Devon's hand then and reached into his pants for his money clip. "On Belcher," he shouted to the man as he stretched the notes toward him. His voice was tight with tension, as though he might miss his chance if the notes didn't reach the man's palm in time.

All around there was noise and the press of bodies, some roughly dressed and stinking of smoke and grime, others as elegantly turned out as any businessman on Bond Street. Everywhere, the odors of beer and body odor lay like a pall, until Devon felt she would be sick right there and then, so little breathable air there was around her.

Then the noise became a roar, as two men strode through the crowd from the far end of the room, and were actually lifted by a myriad of arms to the stage when they reached it. Only then did the money collector drop to the floor, to be replaced by a stout yeoman who shouted, "Belcher and the Gas Man! Last chance to place your bets."

The two men were stripped to the waist, and bounced about the stage on the balls of their feet, their arms raised, fists pummeling the air.

"Last chance to place your wagers!" the money collector repeated from below, as Devon was pressed from behind even closer to the platform by those trying to get their money into the man's hands.

"Which will it be, boys?" the man on stage called out. "Belcher or the Gas Man? Both these bruisers mean to win the day. Which will it be? Let's see the shine of your coin and the slap of your pounds!"

Newgate's hand gripped her elbow, and Devon turned to see his face close to hers, hissing, "Watch this now. It will be thrilling!"

Devon felt a rush of panic as the crowd closed in even tighter, as though the whole of Eagle and Childe Alley, peddlers to pickpockets, had broken through their shop door and poured into the confines of her home, bringing with them all the lords of West London.

Then the two men were at each other, their huge fists smacking against the other's flesh as they landed blow after blow against the head and face, chest and stomach of the other, aiming for any unprotected spot. And the crowd of men around them roared encouragement.

"Pound the smile off his ugly face!" one well-dressed gentleman yelled.

"The Gas Man's stomach is his weak spot!" yelled another, so close beside her that Devon could smell the whisky on his breath, even over the general pall of sweat and liquor.

From all sides the crowd pressed in, howling their support or opposition to those on the stage. Devon's head rang with the din, her knees buckled, and she would have fallen had there been any space to fall.

She couldn't tell how long the ordeal went on, was only aware of an eventual thud she could feel as well as hear, as one went down upon the platform and the crowd surged forward, screaming for blood.

"You've got 'im!"

"Pulverize him!"

"Get up, you craven woman!"

Just as merciful darkness was overtaking her senses, the bodies all around her turned from solid flesh to a mass of writhing sinew as each seemed to turn upon his neighbor, fists flailing, mouths gasping as blows were thrown and taken.

Turning desperately to find some hope of exit, Devon's panic rose as none of the bodies milling around her looked familiar, and she was knocked against a table by a falling form.

Then Newgate, clutching a fistful of notes high above his head, surged toward her from the table on which the money collector was now standing. He gripped her arm with his free hand and pulled her behind him as he plowed his way back in the direction of the door, pounding on every available piece of flesh until the bodies, falling back, made an opening wide enough for them to squeeze through.

Outside, the sudden smack of air hit Devon's face with a force equal to the suffocating lack of it she'd just left. The clutter of empty carts and carriages that filled the courtyard reeled in her vision. Then she was being pulled again, then hoisted onto the seat of the little phaeton, which she clutched as Newgate sprang up on the other side. He seized the reins, shouting, "Go, Beast! We've won, we've won!

The vehicle jolted forward, a patchwork of dirt and trees and sky spinning in Devon's vision as they careened out of the courtyard and down the road.

Devon sank back against the velvet cushion, her eyes shut tight to stop the whirling; when out of the darkness a mouth closed down on hers, its sharp teeth biting into her lower lip with a taste of whiskey.

"Wasn't that a thrilling match!" the mouth said, withdrawing. "I'll bet you've never been so close to such a spectacle before!"

He snapped a switch over the horse's rump, though the animal was traveling at top speed.

"Did you see? The Duke of Tunningford was there! And didn't the Belcher distinguish himself as mightily as Gentleman Jack ever did! Newgate flung his head back, breathing as heavily as if he himself had been in the ring.

Devon couldn't seem to catch her breath. Her whole body was shaking as though in the grip of some cold fist, and she was helpless to stop it. She shrank back against the side of the coach, as far from Newgate as she could get on the narrow seat.

Newgate frowned at her, tried to put his arm around her shoulders, his other hand gripping the reins. "What's this?" he rasped. "No need to be afraid, you're safe with me. Did the scene frighten you a bit? Come now, would I let any of that rabble get to you?"

She shrank from him, and his scowl deepened, then was erased completely by an even smile. "Come on, what's a little kiss between friends? I'll tell you what we'll do. How about dropping by the Royal Amphitheatre? It's just down the way here and you loved the horses that one time we went. Remember? Astley and that fine young woman doing those fabulous acrobatics? That's more your sort of sport, isn't it? Let's go there straightaway." And his teeth gleamed in the fading light.

Devon managed to persuade Newgate that she really didn't want to go to the amphitheater or anywhere else, only home. She felt ill, she said; she needed to lie down.

"Then perhaps we shouldn't make the full journey tonight," he said. "There are several inns not far from here. We could take a room, let you get a little rest before we make the trip back. Look, it's nearly dark. Let's do that, let you get a little rest."

Devon sat up straight then, assured him that she could make the trip back just fine, that Mrs. Dofferman and Doctor MacBride were waiting for her, would be worried if she did not return as expected. It was only the smoke and the crowd that had made her a little, faint, she said, and the brisk air was reviving her now. She just wanted to go home.

Newgate's face turned darker. "Your doctor will not live forever," he said through a tight jaw. Then he said no more, only cracked the whip many times against the backside of the horse, its sides already heaving and glistening with sweat.

It was not until the wheels had rattled across the Westminster Bridge that he reined the horse in slightly, turning him south instead of north.

Devon's panic returned. "Where are we going?" she said, trying to keep her voice steady against the fear.

"There's something I want you to see," Newgate replied, his tone as sharp as his features, in profile against the city lights.

They traveled on in silence until, after a turn, then another, they pulled up before a long gray building looming behind an iron fence, its walls jutting forward at either end as though to enclose anyone who came within their reach.

"The Asylum For Female Orphans," Newgate said, repeating the words she saw etched in the stone above the pillared entrance. His voice was low, but tight. "For young girls whose parents have died and who have no other living protector. I understand some quite dreadful things happen here to these unfortunate young women. But then, it's either that or the streets, isn't it, without anyone to take you in and care for you like a daughter."

Devon didn't look at him, only stared at the forbidding gray building looming over the night street; until finally Newgate slapped the reins on the horse's rump and sent the phaeton lurching forward again.

"To Pilgrim Street," he said, as though addressing the horse. "We will take Miss Quail home to her doctor. For now."

Chapter 10

Alone Again

Death is not the greatest loss in life.
The greatest loss is what dies inside us while we live.
Norman Cousins

The doctor died that Sunday. Devon was grateful that she was with him when he went, holding his hand, though he had shown no signs of consciousness for hours.

While she'd attended him these last days, in the stiff chair by his bed, she had begun to sing the songs her mother had sung when she'd tucked in the little ones for the night – faintly plaintive, peaceful songs, some in the native Gaelic that her own mother had sung them to her as a child. Devon didn't understand all the words herself, but she knew how they felt. And when the doctor didn't object, she had concluded that they soothed him, too. Though it may only have signaled his weakness as the end drew near.

Newgate had come by twice that week, but, at Devon's behest, Mrs. Dofferman had told him that she was attending the doctor and could not be disturbed.

He must have heard that the doctor had died, though, for he was back after only two days, and Devon could hear him all the way from her room upstairs, demanding to see her.

"I will not be put off, Madame," he said, his voice near to shouting. "Yes, the child is grieving. Of course. But my wife and I are as near family as she has, and we must be allowed to comfort her."

But Mrs. Dofferman's voice was just as strong in refusal; and eventually Devon could hear the sound of Newgate's boots rap down the steps, and his fierce "Move, Beast!" reaching clear to her window from the street below. She turned her face into the pillow, feeling a spreading fear join the heaviness of grief in her chest.

All that week, Devon stayed within the confines of the house, the steady sheets of sleet outside making the city seem all the more alien and unconsoling. Even when the sleet turned to snow, covering Pilgrim Street with a veneer of white, it only looked to her deceptively clean.

She spent most of her time in the doctor's study, sitting in his worn brown leather chair beneath the legend on the bookshelf behind it:

A doctor is a man who writes prescriptions til the patient either dies or is cured by nature. — John Taylor.

Clearly, Devon knew that that was not the kind of healer Doctor MacBride had been. She had never seen him write a prescription. His philosophy was more clearly reflected in the volumes on the rest of his untidy shelves: *Nature's Remedies*; *Account of the Fox-Glove*; and *Commentaries on Anatomy*.

Devon had thought a study of his books might take her closer to him, or at least give her some idea of how to follow in his path somehow. And that proved almost literally true; for soon the words in the texts, so dense with medical terminology, were replaced by scenes from the many homes they had visited, and the people they had cared for there. Sometimes the scene was not a house at all, but a street where a beggar had dropped from hunger or from too much cheap wine.

She became compelled to relive them all, down the narrow halls of the hospitals or the cold floors of the prisons. Even that most nightmarish afternoon on the Deptford Docks, where men and women alike were being led in irons onto a barge-like ship, to be transported to Botany Bay, somewhere on the other side of the world called New South Wales. Several of the women had clutched babies to their chests, the both of them encircled by the iron hoops that ringed their arms, as they stumbled against the chains that bound all of the prisoners together.

The doctor had been looking for one of his patients that day, one he had heard had been tried and sentenced to deportation the same day, for stealing a leg of mutton to feed her family. He hadn't found her, hadn't even gained permission to treat the prisoners who passed them, barefoot and with running sores on their arms and legs.

"The men will work the land for the freedmen already there," the doctor had answered her question. "Free labor makes cheap goods for the motherland. White slavery is what it is. And the women unable to do the work? If they were not prostituting themselves to make a living before, they will be now."

It was more than a week before Devon's perpetual restlessness caused her to venture out as far as Fleet Street, walking aimlessly among the throng or searching a bookseller's cart for a treasure she might one day have access to. Until someone's stare, or the seller himself, drove her away when her modest clothing and manner apparently persuaded him that this girl, out on the streets alone, would not have the wherewithal to make a purchase.

She began going out in the coach then with Mynors, on errands for Mrs. Dofferman, whose lethargy seemed even greater than her own since the doctor's death. The woman's ruddy complexion had faded to a dull gray, and even her voice had lost its force, unless anger momentarily brought it back. She moved like an old woman now; and once Devon had found her in the doctor's room, kneeling before an open drawer of his chest, one of the doctor's threadbare sweaters pressed to her face. Devon had stolen silently away so as not to embarrass her.

The next time Devon was alerted to a knock at the door, though, the voice she heard surprised her. It was not the one she dreaded, and she went to the top of the stairs to listen.

"Oh, I would so love to see her," Sissy was saying. "The poor dear. How lonely she must be. Percy has offered to take us to a musical concert at the Hanover House, right in our own square. He says we may go if he is with us. Then we could have a little supper and bring her right back. Unless she could stay the night? There is plenty of room in my big bed for us both."

Mrs. Dofferman must have heard Devon on the stair, for she turned to look up at her, and Sissy took another step into the entry hall.

"There she is, our precious girl!" she said, pressing her hands together as though in prayer. "But how pale you look. You must come with us, my sweet, right this minute. We will have such a lovely time. Say you will."

So Devon went. And indeed, Newgate did act the perfect gentleman all that evening. At the concert, Devon quite lost herself in the sweet songs of the strings and the piping of the woodwinds. Everyone sat about on delicate chairs in perfect silence while the musicians played – so different from the shifting bodies and whispered comments that had accompanied the one opera she had attended with the doctor at Covent Garden. Much less the rowdy confusion that had reigned at the melodrama she'd gone to with Newgate in Drury Lane. There, the men seemed more interested in the deep cleavage of the women selling oranges than in anything transpiring on the stage. In Hanover House, everyone seemed to be actually listening, and no one spoke until the last note had died and the flutter of applause began from gloved hands.

The music stayed with Devon all that evening, and soothed her like nothing had since the doctor's death. So when Newgate vowed he would take her straight home following supper, after she'd firmly declined Sissy's invitation for a "just us girls" overnight, Devon felt less fear than she had earlier, after the trip to Lambeth.

Still, Devon urged Sissy to come with them when it came time to take her back after supper.

But Newgate quickly interrupted. "Miss Cecily must get her rest," he said. "One adventure of an evening is quite enough. I will see you safely home, my dear."

"But couldn't she stay?" Sissy pleaded, as though she hadn't heard Devon's decline of the invitation.

But apparently she had, and didn't wait for an answer, only kissed Devon's cheek, as she had repeatedly throughout the evening. "I have so missed your company," she whispered to her.

"If we get Miss Quail home in time tonight," Newgate said in a most reasonable tone, "perhaps she can be persuaded to come to us again. The ball at the Pantheon is coming up, you know. I'm sure that the masque would be a great delight to the child."

"Oh, yes!" Sissy clapped her hands. "The masque!" She seized both of Devon's hands. "Oh, you must come. It is quite the most exciting event of the season. Say you will!" She turned to Newgate. "Next week? Is it this next week already?"

"The twentieth," Newgate said. "The twentieth of April."

"My birthday," Devon said without thinking. "I had forgotten."

"Well then," Newgate said, "it is settled. We shall take Miss Quail to the masque for her thirteenth birthday."

Devon wondered how he could know that. Had she ever mentioned her age to him at all? She must have. But she was puzzled by his comment in the coach on their way back to the doctor's house.

"Finally grown and legal you'll be," he said. "How rewarding for you."

Newgate had not tried to touch her, except to help her into the coach; and his hand rested only briefly on hers as he said goodnight. "We shall see you on the twentieth then. Why don't you plan to join us for supper before? Then the two of you can dress up together. There's such high spirits on Masque Night, everyone trying to guess who everyone is behind the mask. Will you need something to wear? I'm sure Sissy would be thrilled to take you shopping for a perfect dress. She does love that sort of thing, it's like playing dress-up for her. And the cost would be immaterial, as well endowed as she is."

Devon assured him that whatever she needed she could surely find in Mrs. MacBride's closet and could alter it to fit. Mrs. Dofferman was always urging her to make use of those clothes. "Even if the woman returns at some time, she will have no use for anything that is not the very latest style. And that she will surely bring with her," the older woman said.

Devon was relieved that Mr. Newgate had apparently realized the impropriety of his behavior that last dreadful trip to Lambeth. He had seemed, after all, to have been under the heavy influence of drink. So Devon found herself looking forward to the upcoming ball. It would be a diversion for her mind from the melancholy that had possessed it ever since the doctor's death. Sissy had taught her enough dances that Devon should not disgrace herself at least.

And Sissy would be there too, after all.

Chapter 11
The Masque

Are all men in disguise except those crying?
Danny Abse, Welsh poet

Devon enjoyed fashioning her disguise for the evening.

"Everyone comes in costume," Sissy had said. "And there is such mystery about who is who. Last year four ladies – *four* – came as Marie Antoinette. One even had a head that would come off, she would hold it in her hands and still be talking to you! It was quite the rage. I was Little Miss Muffett, and Percy was the spider-that-sat-down-beside-her. All dressed in black – he was so handsome! And all those hands! The ladies made such a fuss over him, I think it quite turned his head."

That made Devon comb her memory of nursery rhymes, for some costume that would excite the least notice and would be possible to put together from what was at hand, so she wouldn't have to bother Mrs. Dofferman with the matter. The woman had seemed to grow more distant by the day, and Devon felt helpless to ease the burden of her grief, except to stay out of her way as much as possible. Devon had already taken over most of the house cleaning. Mrs. Dofferman continued to do the cooking; but neither had much appetite, so it was simple fare only.

The costume Devon finally came up with, though, was inspired by neither history nor nursery rhyme, but by the little milkmaid figurine Mr. Newgate had bought her in Mr. Finch's shop. The modesty of it appealed to her, as well as its reminder of her true station. And it was easy to duplicate: the blouse she simulated by altering a torn one of the doctor's wife's, adding more cotton cloth to the neckline to make it less revealing. There was a skirt full enough to do, with an added petticoat beneath and a white apron on top. And while her dark curly hair bore little resemblance to the long blonde braids of the milkmaid, Devon gathered it with a ribbon on each side and felt that it at least suited the youth of both the figurine and herself. For once, in fact, she thought, gazing in the mirror in the bath, she actually looked her age. She smiled at her reflection, and realized it was her first smile in quite some time.

But from the outset, the night of the masque took an ominous turn. Newgate's coach arrived for her at six, as arranged; but neither Mr. nor Mrs. Newgate was in it. They had planned to dine out; but Stiles, their coachman, was the one who came to the door, hat in hand, to "fetch the little miss" that evening. And when they descended the concrete steps, it was the phaeton, not the larger britzka, that awaited them.

Stiles had barely acknowledged Devon's existence when she'd ridden in the carriage in the past; and his rigid profile did not invite conversation now. So Devon settled into the red velvet cushions for the duration of the long ride west through a heavy rain, the few pedestrians they passed hunched under caps or umbrellas, picking their way through the mud. Both the city and its people seemed weighed down by the wet chill of the evening air. Even shielded by the drawn canopy above, Devon ducked her head instinctively as they rode through the Temple Gate, its stately arch seeming somehow threatening now, rather than the passage to safety it had seemed the last time she'd come through it in this very coach, traveling from the orphanage to the doctor's house.

Marianne, the maid, answered the door, with an even greater sullenness than usual to her stare. "The Missus is in bed," she said, before she'd even closed the door.

"In bed? Oh, surely she's not ill," Devon said, feeling a great dread settle on her spirits.

"She is," the girl snapped. "So I guess it be just the two of you. Again."

Devon wondered at the girl's open hostility, then realized they'd never been alone without either Newgate or his wife present. Devon got a clear message of jealousy from her now. *Jealousy?*

As Marianne took Devon's cape and hung it dripping from the clothes tree in the corner of the hall, she smirked at Devon's dress. "Who're you s'posed to be then? Some peasant girl looks like."

Devon didn't answer, only said, "I guess I'd better go up and see if there is something I can do for her." She was glad to be out of the girl's presence as she hurried up the curving staircase.

Sissy lay in her bed in her suite of rooms, and the look of her frightened Devon further. Her coloring was as pale as the ivory comforter under which she lay, her fine light hair limp against the pillows.

"You've come!" Sissy said, her tone a weak attempt to match the enthusiasm of her usual greeting.

"What has happened?" Devon asked, reaching for Sissy's hand as she lowered herself carefully to the edge of the bed.

"It's just this bothersome old sickness of the stomach," the young woman said. "Aren't I silly, getting ill like this all the time? My blood must be weak, like my mother's. That's what took her, you know, when I was just a babe: weak blood. All the women in my family had it, I suppose."

"You don't think perhaps it's something you ate?" Devon asked, rubbing the small cold hand between her own.

"I've hardly eaten anything. Just broth with a little egg and vegetable. Percy prepares it himself, he's so sweet. I'm glad you will be going with him, he does so love these masques."

"Oh, no," Devon said quickly. "I wouldn't think of leaving you."

Sissy boosted herself a little higher on her pillows. "But you must. For me. Oh, he'll be so disappointed if you don't. And look at you, how lovely you look, like a little girl."

Then Sissy's gaze shifted to the far end of the room, where in the curve of a bay window stood a gown on a dressmaker's dummy. "But my lovely dress will all go to waste. And I worked so hard on it, the whole week, until I had to take to my bed. Isn't it quite the most wonderful thing?"

Fashioned of glowing white satin, the gown's wide skirts were gathered in graceful little arcs at the hem by sparkly gold ribbons, which embraced the low-cut neckline as well. And on the faceless head of the dummy, set upon a wig of bright blonde curls, gleamed a golden tiara, with little points that sparkled like diamonds.

"Yes, it's beautiful. You are so gifted in all the arts," Devon said, turning back to her.

"Cinderella," Sissy said wistfully, still looking at the dress. "I was to be Cinderella. And Percy was to be my Prince Charming of course, taking me to the ball."

As though on cue, Pierce Newgate came through the door, the dazzle of his white coat and breeches almost hurtful to the eyes, festoons of fat gold braid hanging from his wrists and shoulders, a gilded sword fastened to his hip.

"Our beloved girl is ill again," he said, his mouth drooping briefly from the curve of his smile.

"I will stay with her," Devon said, turning back to Sissy.

"Not a bit of it," Newgate said briskly. "You, too, need your fun. Especially now with the death of your protector. And it's your birthday, my girl!"

Sissy squeezed Devon's hand. "Of course! I quite forgot! You absolutely must go. I should feel perfectly awful if you didn't. And Percy will need a partner for the dances."

"I know!" Newgate said, as though with a sudden inspiration. "She can wear your costume. Then you will be as good as going yourself." His bright smile turned to Devon. "You can be Cinderella on your thirteenth birthday. Like a coming-out ball."

"Oh Percy, how perfect!" Sissy clapped her hands. "You do think of everything, my dear."

A certain panic seized Devon. "No, I couldn't, really. It's not my dress, not my place. And I want to stay with you," she said to Sissy, hearing in her tone a note of pleading.

But by that time, neither husband nor wife would hear of her refusing, and Sissy became almost her animated self again as Newgate was relegated to the downstairs, while Marianne was enlisted to help Devon change out of one costume and into the other.

"Oh, it will be such fun!" Sissy kept saying from her bed, as the sullen Marianne unceremoniously pulled the Cinderella gown over Devon's head and down over her breasts and hips, billowing to the floor.

"You see? It fits you perfectly," Sissy said happily. "We're like sisters. And with your little slippers instead of my heels, it's just the right length. It needs only the wig and crown."

Devon stopped protesting as the wig and crown were fastened to her head with slender pins. At least they felt like a disguise, hiding her from all eyes.

"Perfect!" Sissy pronounced it. "Don't you see? Now everyone will think it is me." She plucked a gilded mask off her bedside table and held it out toward Devon by its little stick. "It will be almost like being there myself. And you will come back and tell me all about it, every detail – who wore what and who danced with whom. You must make Percy tell you everything that transpires. He will know who everyone is; he is very good with disguises."

Devon had to hold tight to the bannister as she descended the staircase again, toward Newgate's outstretched hand. "My dear, you are the perfect Cinderella." And he bowed from the waist and gave her hand a lingering kiss.

After that, the evening was a continuous, accelerating whirl.

Back out in the chill night air, Devon compressed the billows of the skirt with both arms as Newgate squeezed in beside her on the narrow phaeton's seat. She could feel the sharp edge of his sword against her hip as he cracked the whip against the horse's rump; and the gleam of his smile was as bright as the gas lamps that burned through the sheeting rain.

"No one is to know who anybody is," Newgate reminded her as they approached the doorman at the top of the steps to the great hall. "Keep your mask to your face," he said impatiently, giving an upward push to the arm that held it. Then he lifted his sweeping hat and fastened his own gilt-edged white mask by the elastic band that held it to his head, settling the wide-brimmed hat back on top.

Devon was only too anxious that no one recognize her, and held fast to the stick with one hand and her wide skirts with the other, wondering how women managed this sort of clothing on a daily basis. Just getting past the women in the entrance hall, skirt to skirt, was as clumsy a maneuver as she'd ever had to make.

But Newgate's desire for his own anonymity was apparently selective. As they made their way through the crowd, he stopped every little bit to raise his mask. "Sir Humphrey. Good evening, sir. Barrister Newgate." And, "Duchess, you are a vision of loveliness."

Only to the younger, truly good-looking women did he leave his mask in place as he kissed a hand or lavished a compliment.

After the crush of the entry, Devon was unprepared for the immensity of the dance hall they came to – a vast round room ringed with pillars in a double tier beneath a giant dome. Bathed in misty candlelight, coming not clear from the wick but tinged with green and purple, the whole dance hall seemed to wear a mask, its cloaked light caught up in the women's jewelry and their sparkling painted masks or faces. Even while dancing, both the men and ladies often craned their necks and tilted their masks to see who else might be present, playing a sort of hide and seek beneath their costumes.

Devon hung back and had to be pulled onto the dance floor, Newgate's grip firm about her arm. Then, with a little bow, he raised the arm he held, clasping his other about her waist, and moved her off briskly to the strains of a waltz

Devon's knowledge of dancing had been limited to Sissy's laughing lessons. From the waltz practiced in her rooms, they'd moved outdoors and danced to the tune of *Cherry Ripe*, played over and over by Ned, the gardener's boy, on his harmonica. They had "played ladies," as Sissy called it, doing an exaggerated box step out on the marble floor of the white pagoda in the garden, Ned only too glad to stop his work to accompany them.

But this was altogether different. Perhaps it was the cup of brandy punch Newgate had urged her to drink when they arrived; but now, gripped tight in his embrace, Devon felt out of control of her feet, or even her balance, as the costumed bodies swirled about her on the slick floor. So close to her eyes, the bright golden braid on Newgate's shoulder seemed to merge with the mass of twinkling ornaments hanging just above her head to form a gilded cage of light. Devon closed her eyes behind the raised mask, the distant weak flutings of the orchestra overwhelmed by the buzz of talk around her like a lone songbird in a tree full of magpies, her head swirling with her body as she was turned and turned and turned... If it hadn't been for the strength of Newgate's grip, she would surely have fallen to the floor.

Her confusion only increased throughout the evening. Whether they were dancing or were standing being greeted by strangers, Devon holding one of the cups of punch Newgate kept giving her with one hand and the upheld stick of her mask with the other, Devon felt awash in a sea of chaos.

"Why, Mrs. Newgate," one rotund woman exclaimed, coming up to touch Devon's cheek with a latticed fan. "It's been so long since we've seen you! And what a lovely gown; who are we, Sleeping Beauty? Most charming, my dear." She turned to Newgate. "And you!"

she said coyly, swatting his chest with the fan. "I expect we'll be seeing you soon enough." Then she was gone again, before Devon could collect her thoughts enough to speak.

She looked up to find Newgate's blue eyes gleaming behind his mask. He lifted a finger to his lips as he squeezed her hand, leading her back to the dance floor.

As the evening progressed, so did the temperature. All the heat from the mass of over-clad bodies seemed to rise to fill the great dome overhead and settle back over the crowd like a pall. Between the sweaty heat and the punch she drank to dispel it, Devon felt always on the verge of fainting and had to hold tight to Newgate's arm.

Then at last she was outside again, glad for the fresh breeze against her cheeks as the little phaeton moved off through the chill night air. The rain had stopped and the stars were out, shining brighter than the ornaments in that awful hall.

But Devon soon realized that the road back looked quite different from the way they'd come, and a deeper chill began to grow inside her.

"I hope Sissy is feeling better," she said finally, loud enough to reach him in the whistling wind. "I'm eager to get back to her."

His smile was the same glittery grin he had worn all evening. But there was irritation in his voice as he said, "Sissy will be fine. She has everything she needs and more. Tonight is *your* night, Cinderella," and he loosed one hand from the reins to reach beneath her cape and brush her breast. "It's not every night a beautiful young girl turns thirteen and becomes a woman."

She could smell the brandy on his breath, and his cheeks were flushed as he bent his face toward hers.

He laughed as she pulled back. "You will become a woman tonight, by god," he said harshly. "So enough of your coquetry, my girl."

He cracked the whip over the horse's back and yelled, "Lad's Lane, Beast! You know the way."

Devon's heart froze in her chest, constricting her throat so it was impossible to breathe, much less speak. Her mind raced, searching for ways she might jump from the coach and run away before he could stop it and pursue her. But the strange streets, mostly empty now, seemed to afford no shelter; and the coach careened along at such a speed, she thought both her legs might be broken by the fall.

Desperately, she looked about for signs of civilization, someone who might hear her if she screamed. But the streets turned to country roads, and the windows of the few farmhouses they sped by were dark. She could see no one.

The ride seemed interminable, but was over too soon. An arch loomed out of the dark, its painted sign reading *The Swan With Two Necks*; and the phaeton lurched beneath it into a wide courtyard, where Newgate jerked the horse's head back by the reins, pulling them to a rocking stop before a door with little multi-paned windows on either side that glowed like cats' eyes in the darkness.

"Don't move," he hissed, and dismounted, nearly losing his balance as his boots touched the ground. He peered up at her with narrowed eyes. "On second thought," he said, "you'd best come with me. We don't want you running off, do we?" And he reached in and pulled her from the coach by the wrist.

Inside the door, a little man looked up as though startled from sleep.

"A gallery room," Newgate said, laying two pound notes on the counter that separated them from the dim space beyond.

"Yes sir, Mr. Newgate," the man said, and put a large key on the counter without a change in his expression. "And will you be needing a call when the coach arrives?"

"No," Newgate replied gruffly. "We will be enjoying ourselves right here." And he pulled Devon back outside and boosted her up into the phaeton again.

She tried to jump out the other side, but he grabbed her cape and jerked her back. "We'll have none of that," he said irritably, and hung on to her skirt while he steered the horse to the far end of the yard and wrapped the reins around a post.

She was jerked down again, and pulled to a staircase that led to a second story, then roughly up the stairs.

"No, wait," Devon kept saying.

"I've waited long enough, my girl," Newgate growled as they reached the landing.

His grip was unbreakable as he dragged Devon past several doors and around the corner to another door, where he fumbled the key into the lock.

In a last attempt to free herself, Devon bent to bite the hand that held her. But his elbow swung up, knocking her back to the wet wooden flooring.

"Now look what you've done," Newgate said, glaring down at her from the open doorway. "You've soiled poor Sissy's gown." And he hauled her to her feet again and pushed her ahead of him into the room beyond.

Small and lit only by a dim lantern, the room held one chair and a rough wooden bedstead, the mattress lying slightly askew upon it, straw sticking out from one corner. A small mound of the straw had accumulated on the muddy floor beneath the rip.

Devon looked to the door again, her words coming from her with a strangled sound she didn't recognize. "No! You must take me home!" she cried, as loudly as she could.

"*Must*, you say? *Must?!*" Newgate pulled off her cape and threw it to the floor. "You still don't know who's master here, do you, my little quail? Well, it's time that I taught you!"

Newgate bent Devon backwards, his grip on her neck the only thing holding her up. "And you'd best learn this lesson well, my girl. Because you're all alone in the world now, and you have only one thing to bargain with for your safety." His free hand thrust the bodice of the dress down over her breasts. "I have been patient. But now the Maid will have her Prince."

Devon wrenched free of his hand, but with such force that she reeled against the bedstead and fell back upon the straw mattress.

His twisted smile was a mix of anger and pleasure. "So that's how it will be, is it? All right, my girl, Percy loves to play rough."

Devon scrambled backwards on the bed; but his boot came down on the skirt of the gown, halting her. And he kept it there while his undid his breeches. "You will learn to love this, my pet," he said. "Believe me, they all do. Pierce Newgate is known as the best of lovers all over London. And tonight, he will teach you everything you need to know to please a man."

Then he fell upon her, one hand clutching her hair, the wig long gone, the other reaching under the satin skirt to grip her between her legs. "This," he said, "is your most valuable asset. Without a dowry, this is the only thing you have to bargain with. And I am going to show you how to use it. From here on, we will keep the lessons up until you learn."

After that, there was only pain. Devon shut her eyes as Newgate tore at the cloth that stood in his way. There was a stab of agony, and Devon cried out against it.

"That's right, my little fledgling," he growled. "Beg for it. Beg your lord and master."

And the waves of pain kept coming, penetrating to her very soul, accompanied by his sharp cries, like those of an eagle as it swoops down on its prey.

Until at last it was over and his body fell limp upon her, his breath coming in rasps against her neck, the whiskey-sour smell of it enveloping her like drainage from a sewer.

Chapter 12

Progress of the Soul

She knew treachery, rapine, deceit, and lust, and ills enow
To be a woman.
John Donne, *Progress of the Soul*

Devon didn't know how long she waited there on the rough mattress, fearing to move a muscle lest it wake him and begin the torture all over again.

Until outside the tiny window, she saw the last of the covering dark begin to drain from the sky. If she could have crawled into the darkest hole to hide her shame, she would have. But even stronger now was her need to get away from this monster – as fast and as far away as she possibly could.

He'd been breathing evenly for some time, his body a dead weight. So with tiny, stealthy movements, she began to edge out from beneath him.

Inch by inch, pausing between to be sure he still slept, Devon wormed her way out from under his heavy weight, the torn tissues between her thighs burning with every movement. The time it took seemed interminable.

But at last both legs were free.

He muttered something unintelligible as her torso at last slid free as well and his body resettled itself on the stained mattress.

Moving slowly, out of caution and pain, Devon stooped and lifted off the muddy floor what was left of the gown Sissy's talented hands had fashioned.

But she dropped it again; she could not afford to be spotted as a woman alone, especially in a party gown so early in the morning.

Instead, she crossed to the chair and took from its back the jacket Newgate had taken care to hang there, and pushed her arms through its sleeves, turning the cuffs back until her hands cleared. The jacket was too wide on her; but with their padding, the shoulders seemed to stand by themselves, sporting their golden braid.

His breeches were still on him, though undone. She couldn't risk trying to remove them, even if she could have brought herself to touch him. But the jacket was long enough to cover her shift; and her white hose, though ripped at the crotch, were still on her legs; they would have to pass for breeches.

She sat and pulled on his boots. Too big, but at least they didn't come off when she stood and shook one leg, then the other.

Devon left the blonde wig on the floor and gathered her hair up beneath his broad hat. She was thankful the style of it dipped in the front, nearly covering her eyes.

Her cloak could be taken for part of the costume. It would have to do.

Her head was clear now – icy clear.

Devon made herself take a last look at Newgate. He was sprawled face down on the bed, still unmoving. His body gave off a stench of sweat and liquor, and something else that had been released by what he did to her; the smells made her shudder with revulsion.

She seized the doorknob and turned it.

The door gave out only a faint creak as Devon eased it open wide enough to slip through, then closed it carefully behind her. And she was out in the cold air again.

Its dull glare hit her eyes like a slap. But she had to keep moving. She rounded the corner and moved down the gallery, under which the horse he called Beast stood waiting, still hitched to the phaeton.

But before she reached the stairs, she spotted the small man from the night before coming up them.

She froze.

But when he reached the top of the staircase and spotted her in the Prince outfit, his mouth only curled in a knowing smile, and he moved down the gallery in the opposite direction without making any move to stop her.

The man knocked on the first door and called out, "Everybody up for the six o'clock coach."

Without waiting for a reply, he moved down to the next door, the smile still on his face.

Devon wasted no time, and clumped down the steps in the oversized boots, just trying not to trip.

When she reached the phaeton, Devon unwound the reins from the post and lifted them over the horse's head.

But as she looked into his face, with its fine brown, soulful eyes, Devon could not resist gently stroking his velvet nose and putting her lips to it. "Beauty," she said to him. "I will not call you Beast, for you are not a beast. *He* is the beast. I will call you Beauty, for that's what you are." And she moved to the high step and grasped the side of the coach, pulling herself up and into it.

Each move of her legs made her whole body burn, as though she now carried inside her the sword that had decorated his hip all last evening. And for the first time in her life, Devon felt hate. Hot, searing hate coursed through her chest, and it was a terrible feeling.

Throwing the sheathed whip to the ground, Devon gathered the reins and called, "Go now, Beauty! Take me away from here!"

The horse spun and moved swiftly across the worn bricks of the courtyard.

"Hey!"

Devon looked back to see Newgate braced against the rail of the gallery above, his shirt tail dangling over his twisted breeches.

"You bitch!" he shouted. "Get back here with that coach!"

But already the wheels of the little phaeton were gaining speed as they closed on the entry arch.

Then suddenly another coach, big and black, pulled by four horses, came charging through the arch. Beauty swerved sharply to the left, and they just missed colliding with the huge coach as it clattered past.

"Watch where you're going, sir!" shouted the coachman, while a dozen passengers peered out at them through its window.

"Yes, Beauty, thank you!" Devon cried, and the little phaeton went clattering down the lane, leaving them all behind.

But if Devon imagined that she was going 'home', she found another rude shock awaiting her at Pilgrim Street.

The ride had been swift and sure. Though Devon recognized almost nothing in the countryside they rode through, Beauty seemed to know his way back; and eventually the golden dome of St. Paul's appeared on the horizon. From there, Devon knew her way to Pilgrim Street; and the tall stairs to the doctor's house, when they reached them, appeared to her a safe shore in a storm.

But when Mrs. Dofferman opened the door – only a crack – Devon knew immediately that something was wrong. Her friend's shocked reaction to her costume was quickly replaced by a more grave expression, like fear, a warning. For someone Devon thought of as practically invincible, the woman's aspect shook her to her bones.

Then behind her there appeared another, younger, woman, whose expression was anything but hospitable. "Well now, open the door, Dofferman," she said, a mocking smile taking over her features. "Let's see what this…gentleman? is up to."

Mrs. Dofferman stepped aside.

Devon remained on the stoop, too cautious to go farther.

The woman's slender but curvaceous figure filled the doorway as she looked Devon over, the mocking smile fixed to her face.

"Ma'am?" Devon's voice was barely a croak.

"Polly MacBride," the woman said smoothly. "And who – or what – are you?"

"It's the young miss I was telling you about," Mrs. Dofferman offered behind her.

"Really? But I thought you said a child, and female." Her smile broadened.

"I have come from a masque," was all Devon could think of to say, her mind racing with the implications of this woman's presence for her present and future safety.

"And I thought *I* was modern," the woman said with the same ironic amusement.

"I am pleased to meet you," Devon said, finally finding her manners. "Your husband was very kind to me, very dear. His death has been a great blow."

"Mmm," the woman said, not changing her expression. "I expect it has. But it may be an inconvenience as well, since I have brought my own servants with me and have no need of whatever services Dofferman or yourself might have been expecting to continue to provide here."

Devon looked behind her to Mrs. Dofferman, but the woman's face was dark and closed.

"I see," Devon said slowly, and was relieved to hear that her voice didn't tremble along with her insides.

Then more trouble arrived behind her. A dilapidated coach, pulled by an even more dilapidated-looking horse and coachman, pulled up to the curb, and the fuming figure of Pierce Newgate dropped from it.

He stopped short at the sight of Polly MacBride.

"Why Percy," the woman said. "My, my. Has everyone in London quite lost all sense of style?"

Newgate's face flushed. To say that his put-together garb and state of dishevelment resembled a workman would have been an insult to all workmen.

He recovered quickly though. Taking in the sight of the new lady of the house, Newgate's expression changed to one of wry humor. He looked her over, from her over-red hair to her fashionable shoes. "Ah, our Polly MacBride has returned." He mounted the steps, pushing past Devon to bend over her hand with a lingering kiss. "And not a moment too soon to rescue us all from a most dreary season."

Her smile mirrored his. "At least," she said, "Pierce Newgate has not lost his charm along with his fashion."

"A small masquerade only," Newgate said, his tone giving no hint of the anger with which he'd first appeared. "My wife and I were taking this young lady to the ball at the Pantheon when Cecily took sick. I was just coming to see that she got safely home in the carriage I lent her."

His tone could not have been more casual, self-assured. It gave Devon more dread than his anger had.

"Ah," the woman replied. "She has arrived, all right, but I fear she cannot stay. There will be no room for others, since my full entourage is with me."

"What a shame." Newgate turned to Devon with a cold, steely gaze. "Well then, perhaps we shall just have to add her to our own staff. My wife has become quite fond of her. I'm sure Cecily will be pleased to have her as a live-in companion, with perhaps a few chores to take on as well."

"I can see *you've* become fond of her," the woman said, her meaning clear. "I doubt that she went to the masque in that outfit. Now if you will all excuse me, it has been a long journey and I am in need of a little rest. *In my own bed,*" she added pointedly. And without further pleasantries, she turned and disappeared into the dark house.

Newgate's voice did not even attempt warmth as he took Devon's elbow and pulled her down the steps, waving away the coach he'd arrived in and boosting her ungently into the phaeton. "Home!" he shouted to Beauty. "And you'd best mind only me in the future if you don't want to end your days in a glue factory!"

Mrs. Dofferman was back at the top of the steps and shouted down to Devon, "Crown and Cushion Court! Number twenty-four! My sister's!"

Her words were nearly lost in the clatter of the coach pulling away; but Devon heard them and committed them firmly to memory.

Chapter 13

Within Wingsbury's Walls

The world is still deceived with ornament.
William Shakespeare, *The Merchant of Venice*

Riding back to Wingsbury that morning, Devon was surprised to realize that she no longer felt fear for this man who sat beside her now, stiff as the toy sword that lay beside his haunch. He looked quite comical, actually, and hurled epithets at his noble horse every few moments, punctuated by the whip he'd apparently retrieved from the ground at the Swan With Two Necks. The triumphant smirk he had aimed at her as they charged away from the doctor's house had sagged to a sluggish scowl.

Was the vanishing of her fear, Devon wondered, because the worse that he could do to her had been done? Or perhaps had her seizing control, literally taking the reins, back at the inn changed her view of him – or perhaps of herself – in some fundamental way? After all – and she smiled at the thought – it was difficult to fear someone whose clothes you've taken and worn. As silly and pretentious as the Prince's costume was, its very claim to power lent it a certain air of authority. Perhaps

Mr. Downy, Newgate's tailor in Bond Street, had been right when he'd said of the new grey-striped waistcoat she and Sissy had gone to fetch one day, "Clothes do make the man, no mistake, ladies." Maybe these people had good reason for their obsession with attire. Perhaps it concealed what little substance they had beneath.

Apparently Newgate believed it to be so: wearing the outfit of a lower class, he turned his head away from every fancy carriage they passed; and as soon as he could, he left Fleet Street and kept to the most obscure lanes and alleys as he steered the phaeton back to Bedford Square. And while he fell into a shrill litany of the chores Devon would have to perform in "my house" now; and the access she'd have to give him to her bed to pay for her keep; Devon felt little more than scorn for his blustering. She knew what to expect now, and she'd be ready.

Instead, she turned her mind to where she might go and what she might do once she could be free of him. She'd already given it serious thought, after all, anticipating the possible return of the doctor's wife. There were a few of his patients well-off enough to have servants. And though he had made them come to him, she could surely find out where they lived, see whether any might have use for a young woman who would work hard for bed and board.

Although, she thought, her best chance of being steered aright might lie at the Crown and Cushion Court address Mrs. Dofferman had called out to her. The street's name was not familiar, but she would find it. She had escaped Newgate once; she could do it again.

The member of the household she had left out of her reckonings, however, was *Cecily* Newgate. As soon as they entered the house – by the back door, through the kitchen – it became apparent that whatever Sissy's illnesses were, they were not the passing "spells" they all had called them.

Marianne appeared before they'd fully crossed the cold kitchen, toward the "closet" Newgate said would serve as her quarters while she performed the function of cook. It was a position that had gone unfilled in the house, he said, except for the protesting Marianne, since he had had to let go a Mrs. Bench because "she could not keep to her own business."

At first seeing only Newgate, Marianne had run toward him, saying in a desperate voice, "She's worse. You'd best go see. She seemed stronger, wanted more of the broth, so—"

Then she stopped and her face hardened as she saw Devon behind him. "What's *she* doing here? She wasn't to come no more."

"She'll take Bench's place as cook," Newgate growled. "And you'll mind your tongue. What's this about more broth?"

"I thought it wouldn't hurt none," the girl mumbled, backing off a little.

"When did she take worse?" Devon demanded.

Marianne only glared at her, then turned to Newgate, the whine intensifying in her voice. "She can't be nothin' over me," she said. "I been here first."

Since there was clearly no useful information to be gained from the girl, Devon pushed her way past them and headed for the front stairs.

But Newgate's mocking voice stopped her. "You expect to go up like that?"

She turned, and he pointed at the Prince Charming jacket and boots she still wore.

"It might just be fitting," Devon responded hotly. "Perhaps she should know just how 'charming' her Prince is."

But the vision of Sissy's delicate, trusting face if she should guess the truth was enough to send Devon back into what was apparently the cook's room, to change into what turned out to be a very oversized uniform. Then she passed a frowning Marianne heading for the staircase again.

Newgate was at his wife's bedside when Devon arrived, holding her hand, a look of concern on his face that Devon would have mistaken for genuine had she thought him capable of any true feeling.

Sissy smiled up at her as she came near the bed. "Oh good," she said, "you've come back."

The voice sounded as weak and pale as the young woman looked, her eyes seeming to focus only with difficulty upon either of their faces. Devon's heart filled with pity and alarm. "Where is the pain?" she asked.

But Sissy only smiled, as though the question were either unanswerable or irrelevant.

"The girl has been kind enough to agree to help us out here with the cooking," Newgate said quickly. "And she can keep you company in your invalid condition."

How convenient, Devon thought, but did not even glance at him, moving closer to the bed until he was forced to stand and give over his place.

"I'm so pleased," Sissy said faintly. "Will you really stay with me? Truly?"

Devon sank to the bed, feeling suddenly weak herself. "Of course," she said. "As long as you need me to. We must make you strong again."

Devon could not avoid Newgate's self-satisfied smile as he withdrew from the room, saying, "I knew we could count on you."

It wasn't until that evening that Sissy apparently felt strong enough to question Devon about the ball, which now seemed lifetimes ago in her own mind, though the abrasions, both inside and out, burned ever more fiercely as the day progressed.

"Was it great fun?" Sissy asked, smiling up at Devon, her green eyes having regained a little of their vibrant color. "Did my Percy enjoy himself?"

Devon stared at the smiling face over the tray she'd just brought. Could she know? Beneath all that apparent innocence, was it possible that she knew of Newgate's, most likely chronic, betrayals?

As though in answer, Sissy said gently, "Percy does like his fun. He means no harm."

At a loss for a response to that, Devon made herself busy setting down the tray and arranging the tea on the bedside table within Sissy's reach.

The young woman's cold hand lifted to touch hers, then picked up the miniature of the young man and woman in the rowboat that always sat there in her sight. She held it to her breast and traced with a fingertip the two perfectly formed torsos, then the painted water at its base, as though the tiny figure of the woman herself were making the gesture. "He is a good husband," she said dreamily. "He has always been good to me. Daddy was wrong."

"'Wrong'?" Devon repeated.

"In not liking him, not trusting him. He said Percy would only hurt me, that he wanted only the money." She stroked the little figure of the man, who gazed raptly at the young woman in the boat. "But he takes care of his 'precious flower,' he does. And he brings me the world."

Devon didn't trust herself to speak then, unsure which would hurt the ailing Sissy more, the truth or the continuation of her illusions. There would be time, Devon decided as she descended the stairs, to speak up later, when the moment might be right and Sissy seemed strong enough to hear it. For now, the true owner of this house needed the genuine caring of at least one person in it; and for now, that seemed to be her.

As she reached the bottom of the stairs, Devon heard voices that made her pause. In Marianne's room under the staircase, off the dark back hall, Newgate's voice was saying, "Don't threaten me, girl." Then in a more appeasing tone, "Don't you see? They'll keep each other occupied. And with her to tend the kitchen, you'll have more time. *And* more of mine."

"Really, Percy? Will you come to me more?" The girl's tone wavered between doubtful and coquettish.

153

"Of course," Newgate said. "Haven't I told you so all along?"

Devon hurried on her way then, as silently as possible. But as she was searching the disordered spice shelves in the pantry for what she would need to build Sissy's strength back up again, Newgate appeared and lounged in its narrow doorway. He had changed his outfit and was once again the dapper gentleman, his confidence seeming to have returned with his clothing.

He gave her a mocking smile as he said, "Well. We're just one big happy family now, aren't we?"

Devon had found no yerba or St. John's Wort, but settled for a handful of flax seeds from a near-empty tin and turned to leave.

"You can't avoid me forever, you know," he said.

"You'd best avoid *me*," Devon snapped, pushing by him. "If you want your wife to keep to her fantasy."

His laugh was ready and mocking. "Do you really imagine you could go up against me? A girl of your class? Who knows what stories I might have to tell."

Still Devon did not look at him, but busied herself crushing the flax seeds with a wooden mallet. "She is very ill," Devon said between blows. "And I will stay with her. But you had better keep your distance. Have your fun with Marianne."

He moved quickly, grabbing her wrist, stopping the mallet's fall. "I have plenty of women for my amusement," he hissed. "I don't need such a bitter little tart. But make no mistake: if you try to come between me and my wife, you will wish you had never set eyes on this house."

"That," Devon retorted, "is something I already wish."

Newgate exited the kitchen chuckling. But not before he had plucked a small bunch of what looked like wild onions off the counter next to the soup pot, slapping them playfully against his cheek as he sauntered out.

The rest of that day Devon spent straightening the kitchen and the pantry. She prepared a soup rich in bone marrow and lentils and potatoes, although those she found in the root cellar had seen better days. She would have to go to market the next morning, she thought to herself, for fresh vegetables. And fruits. No wonder Sissy was feeling so poorly, kept inside with none of the right foods. The only times Devon had seen such weakness, such pallor, in a patient were in those households that could afford only bread and beer. In fact, now that she thought of it, Devon couldn't remember seeing Sissy put anything into her mouth but sweet biscuits and tea. Such a diet would sap anybody's strength – maybe even take a baby before its time. Always, in her own home, the first earnings went for sausage and beans and potatoes, a bunch of carrots and oranges, maybe a melon if there were a few pence extra. No liquor was allowed, beyond her father's occasional mug of ale on a Sunday.

"Empty stomachs make empty minds," her mother had said once, watching a man stagger past the shop's door from the Two Roosters Tavern. "If they ate their potatoes *before* they fermented, they might be able to provide for their families."

Devon remembered the moment because it was rare that her mother had passed judgment on her fellow creatures. But it had been a slow month in a cold winter, and they had had to buy food with the coal money and were all huddled together in the shop around the smaller stove that evening.

Devon had surely not felt fortunate in that moment; but now she saw that her family had always had everything they really needed. While here, with all the wealth anybody could want, the lady of the house was starving – and for more than food.

Devon slept that night on the carpet beside Sissy's bed, to be near if Sissy should need her. And for her own protection. Sissy had slipped easily into sleep after a supper of the soup and bread Devon had made. So she lay down now on the plush carpet – softer, in fact, than the blanket that had served as a mattress on her attic floor – and pulled a coverlet from the linen closet over her, the little pink pillow from Sissy's window seat under her head.

But it was not until she allowed her muscles to go slack, to prepare them for sleep, that Devon felt the full measure of her body's pain. The bleeding between her legs had finally stopped; she'd thrown the rag into the fire. But the flesh still burned and her muscles ached. The skin on her neck and wrists and upper arms had turned darker as the day wore on; she had been glad of the oversized uniform to conceal them from Sissy's eyes. But now she felt a weariness unlike any other she had known – of the spirit as well as the flesh. And she wondered if she would ever feel clean again. Like herself again. Like a person who belonged to herself.

She had seen Newgate only once since their exchange in the kitchen. She had been coming down the stairs with

Sissy's bowl and plate as he came up, returning from supper, apparently, with liquor on his breath again. He had taken hold of Devon's hair as she passed him, face averted, and sought to press his lips to her neck.

She had been surprised at the rawness of her tone as she'd faced him and said, holding quite still, "If you ever touch me again, I will loose a scream that will wake not only your wife but her father in his grave as well."

Newgate's face had registered a moment of surprise before he expelled another liquor-laden breath with his laugh. "Ah, I do like them scrappy. Where's the hunt without the fox?"

Now, as she lay on the floor beside Sissy's bed, Devon could hear from below a faint echo of the sounds Newgate had uttered the night before as he heaved and groaned over her interminably until his lust was spent. And now and then the guttural sounds were shot through with high-pitched squeals.

Sissy's slow, even breathing did not change; and Devon pressed the pink pillow over her ears until, at last, sleep overcame all sound.

Chapter 14

In the Country

Those comfortably padded lunatic asylums which are known,
euphemistically, as the stately homes of England.
Virginia Woolf, *The Common Reader*

From the respect paid to property, flow as from a poisoned
fountain, most of the evils and vices which render this world
such a dreary scene to the contemplative mind.
Mary Wollstonecraft (1759-1797)

Sissy grew steadily stronger in the days that followed, nourished by Devon's good food and constant care. And while Newgate's hands insinuated themselves upon Devon's person whenever he had a momentary opportunity – in the kitchen or the hall or at the door on her way back from market – he took her repulsions with a measure of amusement and said only, with his curling smile, "Our day will come again, my girl."

Meanwhile, the night sounds from Marianne's room continued – so loud sometimes that Devon was sure Sissy must hear them, too, though she saw no signs of wakefulness from the snowy bed beside which Devon spent her nights. And only once did Sissy seem to make reference again to her husband's "enjoyments."

It was the first day she had left her bed, and Devon was helping her back into it after a brief walk around the garden. Sissy sighed as she said, "I tire so easily. I am fortunate to have a husband with such patience."

As Devon plumped the pillows and pulled back the lace-trimmed sheet over Sissy's lap, the young woman said wistfully, "Men do like their rough-and-tumble. But my father always came back."

Now Sissy's days were mostly spent with her toys, that legion of miniatures to which Newgate kept adding after every extended outing.

But she was even more engaged with giving Devon "instruction as a lady". Sissy would hear no protest in her campaign to prepare her protégé for a life of leisure. One day it was makeup, the next "coiffeur" or French conversation – all while Devon put the beef to boil or rolled out the biscuits. Devon had no aspirations to lady-hood; but it got the young woman enlivened, so she put up with it.

Central to Sissy's campaign was dressing Devon like an oversized doll. Which at least got the mistress out of the house. The silent Stiles was put at their service, while Newgate was off in the phaeton to his "appointments". They rode out in the britzka several times a week – to Wigmore Street for the never-ending yards of silks and satins, bombazines and pelisses that filled Cavendish House to overflowing; then to Botibol's in Oxford Street to grace an already well-endowed bonnet with yet another ostrich plume or artificial flower.

Looking at her image in the mirror of an evening, as Sissy fussed with a hem or neckline that the Messrs. Swan and Edgar had not done entirely to her satisfaction, Devon thought the sight of herself, done up like some fancy lady, quite ridiculous. Those feathers she had marveled at on all the *belles dames* parading Fleet Street now seemed like just too much sugar on a cake. But to her protests that such finery was really not appropriate to her station, and that she'd never have occasion to wear such gowns, Sissy only replied serenely, "You mustn't say that. A lovely girl like yourself – you will be moving into high circles soon, and some fine young gentleman will take notice and claim you for his own."

From what Devon had seen so far of "fine young gentlemen", she had no interest, let alone in being "owned". But the prophesy of "high circles" became real all too soon.

Sissy came rushing into the kitchen to show Devon the invitation:

Colonel and Madame Otis Aliquott request the pleasure of your company at a gala weekend at Temple Aliquott, to include a ride to the hounds, on the 28th and 29th July in the year eighteen hundred and twenty-four. Respondez-vous s'il vous plait.

"It's perfect, don't you see?" Sissy exclaimed. "It can be your debut into society. We will dress you in that green velvet – well, for the evening. Perhaps the white frock with the little daisies for our arrival. That deep green is so perfect for your coloring!" She lifted one of Devon's dark curls. "You will be the 'raven-haired beauty' like in the novels."

Then she touched one of her own soft blonde loops. "I do wish I didn't have such silly hair."

Devon's protest, that the invitation surely did not include their cook, were to no avail.

"You are *not* our cook," Sissy scolded. "You are our dear companion, who is so gracious as to put wonderful food on our table." And she was off to begin immediate preparations for the trip.

For the next week, all Sissy's thoughts seemed to be taken up with how to outfit them both to perfection for the 'gala weekend'. She conjured up every detail, from the menus to the possible guest list, until Devon began to suspect that, for Sissy, the rehearsals for the visit might be more fun than the event itself.

Sissy even did a painting of the Aliquott mansion and grounds – neither of which, she admitted, had she ever seen, but heard they were "magnificent." On her canvas, the rolling hills were a fairy-book emerald green, and the house looked more like a castle, with its white peaks and spiraling towers. In the distance, figures clad in red sat perched astride horses so delicate they seemed more suited to the tiny carousel that sat on Sissy's writing desk than to mounts people rode on a hunt. And there wasn't a fox in sight.

Eventually, Devon gave up protesting.

"Of course she'll come," Newgate had said when his help was enlisted in persuading her. "It will give the party something new to pique their interest. That lot must be tired of the same old gossip."

161

"And do you think there might be some nice young men there who'd fall instantly in love with our Devon?" Sissy asked, clinging to his arm.

Newgate's smile curved a little wider. "Oh, I shouldn't be at all surprised. Who could resist her?"

It only added to the dread Devon felt at the very prospect of a whole weekend with strangers. Sissy's instructions aside, what did she know of proper manners and conversation for such society? Did they actually speak French – "a must" Sissy had said for "the right circles."

Still, it was good to see Sissy so animated again. Between the rounds to dressmakers and the preparations at home, the young woman seemed to be in constant motion, and Devon began to fear she would wear herself out before the Big Event.

Which apparently was just what she did. The day before they were to leave, Sissy was in such a whirlwind of activity that Newgate insisted she lie down, and brought her a hot cup of tea, prescribing a nap. "You know how you get if you overdo," he cautioned her.

Devon took the opportunity to go to the market for what she'd need to pack a lunch for the trip; and when she returned and there was still no sound from Sissy's room after an hour, Devon looked in to find her awake but still lying on her bed, beneath the feather comforter, her face pale and drawn.

"I'm just a little chilly," Sissy said when Devon asked if she felt ill. "And those silly old stomach aches again." Her smile was apologetic, as though she had committed a *faux pas.*

Devon was alarmed. Even with all the shades drawn to shut out the summer sun, the room was far from chilly.

Something that had been niggling at Devon's mind surged to the fore. These sudden illnesses, and at such times. "I'm going to summon Doctor Palmetter," she said, and turned to seek out Stiles to send a message.

But Newgate was there in the doorway. "Don't worry, I'm certain there's no need for a doctor," he said smoothly. "It's only her nerves again. I'm sure she'll be fine after a good night's sleep. Why don't we just retire and leave her to it?"

He crossed to the bed and took one of Sissy's hands and put it to his lips. "You must rest, my sweet," he said. "None of this rushing about. I'm sure by morning you will be quite recovered and we can go and have a lovely time together."

"I'll try, Percy," Sissy said weakly. "I don't want to disappoint." Then she added, "I do wish Doctor Harmon were still with us. He was so good to me as a child."

Devon stayed with her the whole night, while Sissy tossed and turned beneath the comforter, seeming to swing between chills and fever. Devon blotted her skin with a cloth by turns cool and warm, and Sissy thanked her every time.

Toward morning, though, she seemed to be resting easier, and Devon was persuaded to get a few hours of sleep herself, down in the cook's room she now occupied regularly, undisturbed.

"You won't be of any use to her if you are all groggy from lack of sleep yourself," Newgate said, the seriousness of his tone and visage seeming to signify a real concern. In spite of her suspicions of the man, all his self-indulgences, Devon perceived in him a genuine caring for his wife; she did not believe he would do her any real harm. After all, Sissy was his link to the social standing that was clearly important to him. Without her, he would be only one more ambitious barrister.

And by the time Devon woke, Sissy's stomach pains did appear to have stopped, leaving only the dreamy weariness she usually slipped into after one of her spells.

"I want you to go yourself," Sissy said, holding Devon's hand in her two damp ones. "I'm just too tired. But you must go and take note of every detail. Every one. And then come tell me them all. I shall be there through you, and it will be my great joy if you should find a true love of your own at this affair."

If Newgate were Sissy's 'true love', Devon thought, she fervently hoped she'd never find one.

But Sissy was adamant. As was Newgate. "All that can be done for her has been done," he said in the kitchen while Devon made soup. "Doctor Crown, one of London's best, was here while you slept and found nothing seriously wrong. He prescribed a tonic, which she has been given. And he will remain on call. Marianne will stay by her side at all times; I have ordered it."

Marianne would not be Devon's choice for a nurse; but surely, she wouldn't dare to do Sissy harm. And didn't she already have what she wanted, Newgate in her bed?

"She will be so disappointed if you don't go," Newgate said. "All her preparations will have been for nothing." Reluctantly, Devon had to acknowledge that that was probably true.

So Devon allowed herself to be shepherded out the door with the bag Sissy had had packed for days. At least, she thought, Newgate would have to behave himself. With so many of his kind – or those he wished to be his kind – in attendance, he would not risk their catching him in any crude behavior.

But she was proved wrong on all counts.

From the time the britzka had passed under the Highgate Archway and was rolling west, the morning sun behind them, Newgate's hand had settled on her knee.

When she pushed it away, his laugh was as merry as ever. "Just because my good wife is ill," he said, "is no reason for us not to enjoy ourselves."

"When will you understand," Devon said, pronouncing each word carefully, "that I do not enjoy your attentions? Keep them for Marianne, she apparently feels differently."

"Ah, Marianne is good for a romp, but she is not in your class."

"A maid and a cook? I should say they are identical in class."

"I'm speaking of something more intangible," he said.

"Then keep your attentions intangible," Devon snapped.

Newgate's voice took on a sharper edge. "You are becoming far too bold, my girl. I may have to take you down a peg or two."

Devon turned her back on him and stared out the window of the carriage as the density of the city's housing thinned to an occasional cottage on the blue-green heath. The sight woke in her a yearning like that she'd known gazing from her lonely window overlooking Eagle and Childe Alley – to be free of the wretched city and its wretched inhabitants.

It was always her mother's Ireland Devon pictured at such times, a freedom she'd never experienced but could feel in every one of her senses. A great green openness, with pure air and hills and streams and woods to explore. A small cottage in which to raise her own healthy brood of children. Although from what she'd experienced and heard so far, she was not keen to go through what it apparently took to conceive them. Surely though, she thought wistfully, that was not the way she herself had been conceived, her parents so much in love, so gentle with each other.

Thus carried by her thoughts, with Newgate slumped against the other side of the carriage, asleep and snoring, Devon passed the rest of the ride through the lush pattern of hills and hedges, cottages and fields, picturing herself as one of those peasants tilling the earth or carrying great baskets of its bounty to waiting carts. This is how people are meant to live, she thought, planting the seeds and harvesting the crops to feed your family. Seeing the seasons turn and turning with them – all a part of the natural order of things.

She hardly noticed that, as the coach progressed farther into the countryside, the land about her was becoming increasingly crossed with high hedges, the plots grown larger and larger, the houses in their centers smaller. Only an occasional figure could be seen, yoked to an ox, furrowing the fields in perfect order, no family around him.

Then her own lids grew heavy, and in the growing heat finally closed, her body and mind exhausted from the hours of worry and vigilance. Why, she said to herself, did Sissy always fall ill just when Devon needed her most, to keep Newgate's attentions in their rightful place?

She was aware of nothing further until Stiles' voice came from the seat above, calling "Temple Aliquott!" And Devon opened her eyes to see a sprawling estate, a patchwork of hedges that encompassed fields and skirted woods as far as the eye could see. And atop the highest hill, without a single tree or bush to soften the effect, stood a huge structure of odd design, with high-pitched roofs and domed turrets. Devon could think only of the castles she'd seen in children's books, where the royalty within were never favorably inclined toward visitors.

As they drew nearer, the great house appeared odder and odder. Huge domes bulged, not only at the top but along the sides as well, like great warts on an expanse of diseased skin. And the whole was cloaked with an elaborate filigree of ornamentation, the original frame peeking out in spots as though with timid eyes. Similar structures in miniature were set about the lawn, marking formal gardens whose trees and bushes were sculpted in echoing bulbous shapes.

Then the carriage stopped at the bottom of the terraced steps leading to the entrance porch; and Newgate, who had been freshening his toilet since Stiles' announcement, leaped out of his side of the carriage and came about to open her door, making a great show of helping her alight.

"You had best behave yourself here," he muttered through a tight smile as he led her up the stairs, his hand tight on her elbow. "Speak only when you're spoken to – and then briefly. Lovely young ladies here are seen and not heard."

Devon wondered whether plain ones were allowed to speak, but decided to keep the question to herself. She was studying the door, to see if she could detect a break in its gold leaf that would actually allow it to open, when it did open, and a tall man in an elegant red uniform ushered them in.

The hallway they entered was remarkable: white marble from floor to ceiling, with two statues in bays flanking the arch to the great room beyond. Also of white marble, the two figures, one man, one woman, were not young and slender like statues she'd seen fronting many London buildings. These were stockier, middle-aged, and draped in real cloth from hip to shoulder, with green vine-like wreaths atop their marble heads.

Then a portly gentleman strode up to them, wearing a uniform only slightly more ornate than that of the doorman, and clasped Newgate on both shoulders. Devon was startled to see that the man wore the same face as the statue – rougher, saggier, but the same features surely.

"Newgate, my boy, good to see you," he was saying. "It has been – what? Two years since that unpleasant tax business. But no harm done, thanks to you." Already he was moving on to reach for Devon, a gesture she instinctively drew back from.

"But this isn't our Cecily," the man said, the smile broadening on his ruddy face. "Oh, Newgate, you fox, what have we here?"

Newgate stepped forward. "Miss Devon Quail," he said proudly, touching her cheek with his introduction as though she were a marble statue herself.

Devon extended her hand as taught, only to have the man grasp both her shoulders instead. "Colonel Aliquott," he said, "at your service, my dear." Then he took the offered hand and kissed it.

"Oh, she's a looker," Aliquott said, addressing Newgate as though she weren't present. "A little young perhaps...But what have you done with your wife, you rogue?"

"Our Cecily is ailing again, I'm afraid," Newgate said. "Miss Quail has been helping to take care of her. A sort of companion. And Cecily insisted that she come in her place."

"Such a selfless young woman," the Colonel murmured, his eyes still on Devon. "A saint. But come, my dear, I will introduce you to my good wife."

By then, Devon was less surprised that the Colonel's wife looked very like the other statue in their hall; and the woman was equally effusive on the fine qualities of both Newgate's wife and his present companion. At least, Devon thought, she apparently was not to be snubbed at this gathering. Though the basis of her acceptance eluded her. One's appearance? Really?

But the most surprising meeting was yet to come. As they passed through the visitors already gathered in the large square sitting room with its clutter of ornate furniture, Devon spotted a face she could not immediately place, but which looked directly at her with a sly smile that suggested some complicity between the two of them. Then she remembered: Doctor MacBride's wife.

It was not until several rounds of introductions and refreshments later, however, that Polly MacBride approached her. The Colonel had invited Newgate to the terrace that opened off the sitting room, to survey his estate. Devon followed them, eager to see the grounds of this bizarre property.

It appeared as expansive as the whole of Regent Park, extending as far as the eye could see, beyond manicured lawns and hedges to a vast expanse of barren fields.

"It's just not worth cultivating anymore," the Colonel was saying to Newgate. "What with the poor tax and the rest of the rubbish. The poor get paid whether they work or not, so what's the use of trying to make a profit off this little bit of land? I may just let it all go for sport."

Devon took herself to the other end of the terrace, finding the Colonel's account depressing. She wanted to look at all that land and imagine people living on it, tilling their little fields and gardens. Then a voice close behind her shoulder said, in a lazy, amused tone, "So. He got you, did he?"

Devon started at the words, their content as well as their sudden proximity. She turned to see Polly MacBride's smile, lit with that hint of complicity. Devon looked to see if the two men had heard; but they were still engrossed in their conversation.

The woman took her by the elbow and led Devon toward the steps in the center of the terrace, and she let herself be led, her thoughts a mass of confusion. What did this woman know, and how? Was there something about herself now that looked 'gotten'? Or was that what she'd meant at all? Why this sudden change of attitude – this being, after all, the same woman who had denied Devon the protection of her premises.

They descended the wide steps, the woman's hand still light beneath Devon's arm, her voice casually amused as she said, "Don't worry, it happens to the best of us. The thing to do is to learn how to use it. To make them pay."

With the last words, the voice had sharpened. Devon studied the woman's profile as they walked down the path between two rows of narrow trees, trimmed to stand straight as soldiers, toward a formal garden and the stables beyond.

Devon tried to detect the woman behind the face, this former wife of her beloved Doctor MacBride. It was not a face of classic beauty – not the sort of aristocratic face that would normally match the degree of cool confidence the woman exuded. Beneath the careful makeup, its full cheeks and rounded nose suggested more Devon's little figure of the milkmaid than a fine lady of the aristocracy, or even the gentry. Yet her dress was in impeccable taste, as Devon had been tutored to know it. She recognized its materials and detailing as among the most expensive to be had. And the woman held her head and moved her body with a proud ease that seemed to indicate she had been bested by no one.

"Our Mister Newgate gets to most every pretty girl he spies, sooner or later," Polly MacBride was saying. "He works the men up one side, the women down the other, trying to scrabble his way to the top and enjoy himself to the fullest along the way."

Devon was staring at her, but the woman hadn't turned her face; she seemed to be voicing her thoughts for her own sake as much as for Devon's.

Then she did turn, and looked Devon full in the eye. "He is more dangerous, though, than his transparent charm would indicate. You must keep a step ahead of him and watch your backside."

A shudder passed through Devon; she knew the words rang true. It was a warning that made her think of Sissy, back alone in the house that was actually hers, while her husband was out here, consorting with the gentry, and with intentions for herself that he'd already made clear.

"You know him well then?" Devon asked.

The woman just laughed. "There are few I don't," she said, "such as can do me any good. *Or* ill." And she laughed again, the amusement in her tone weighed down by a sort of heaviness, like the bitter aftertaste of hoarhound candy.

This advice about men, though, Devon thought it best that she understand. "Surely they won't all do you ill though, will they?"

"Not if you don't let them," the woman answered with a harsh laugh.

Considering who her husband had been, Devon had to ask, "Surely not Doctor MacBride."

The woman's face reflected actual sadness then. "No, not him," she said. "The man was as close to a saint as I'll ever get. He deserved better than the likes of me."

Then they had arrived at the stables, and Devon's attention was caught again by the regal beauty of the horses. There was something these creatures possessed, Devon thought, that made them seem proud and free, even confined to a fenced dirt circle as they now were, pawing at the ground in their impatience for release.

She stretched out a hand, but none came to her.

"You need a little sugar in it," Polly MacBride said.

Then the sound of Newgate's quick steps reached them and his voice said, "Listen to the woman, my girl. She is an expert on the attractions of sugar."

Polly MacBride's tone lightened. "I was just imparting to your young friend here," she said, "the art of riding these beasts."

"I'll bet you were," Newgate rejoined, and Devon saw a look pass between them.

"Well then," Newgate said to the woman, "are you going to give me a chance to get even at whist this evening?"

"Any time," she replied, tantalizingly drawing out the words. "Perhaps we could play for somewhat more interesting stakes."

"Any time," Newgate echoed, and they both laughed.

But before that match could take place, Devon had to change into the emerald dress and sit down to an evening feast that struck her as sufficient to stock the larders of all the families she had attended with the doctor. And with each course seemed to come another form of contest.

The first was served on an enormous oval platter that took up most of the center of the long table, some guests having to move their wine glasses to make way for it. The fish upon it was as long as Devon's forearm, and stared through its dead open eye so directly at her that Devon could not touch a bite of it. "I think I'm allergic," she said faintly when the uniformed servant tried to place a chunk of its flesh on her plate.

While the fish was being deboned and served, and the fat carrots and potatoes that lined the platter's rim were scooped onto plates like afterthoughts, the Colonel expounded on his exploits at fishing in England and abroad – stories each man at the table seemed to feel compelled to top. Though it turned out that many, including the Colonel, had not held their lines themselves until the time came for landing the trophy.

During the course of pheasant with mushrooms and partridge pie, the talk turned to guns – which would shoot the quickest, with the least time for reloading; the improvement of caps over flintlock; and which breeds of dogs served best at flushing the prey and leading the way to fallen bodies. A gentleman from Wiltshire, the Colonel reported, had killed eighty-eight pheasants with only one hundred shots – a story many of the men present testified to having heard. And many toasts were made to the absent gentleman.

The fish and pheasants were followed by a fillet of veal lined with limp green stalks someone identified as asparagus; and roasted sweetbreads and tripe. The ladies present congratulated Madame Aliquott on every course, though apparently she had cooked none of it.

During the neck of mutton, which slowed the eating since only so much meat could be separated at one time from the ridge of tiny bones, the ball of conversation was won back by the men, who turned to the topic of politics, about which the women appeared to have ignorance. The most fervent topic seemed to be the need to cut taxes on the rich and stop subsidizing the poor.

It was not until the *piece de resistance* – platters full of red clawed creatures – was underway that the women rejoined the conversation, congratulating both Aliquotts on the recent remodeling of their mansion's façade. The subject sent a ripple of approval around the table.

"It's the new Hindoo style, of course," Colonel Aliquott murmured modestly.

"So intricate!" one woman breathed, as she accepted a little silver instrument from one of the servants and began to poke at the claw before her.

"Most expensive, I should think," Newgate commented, tearing his attention away from the young woman on his left, whose blushes had been giving Devon some hope that she would be spared his attentions for the rest of the visit.

"Quite," responded the Colonel, leaning back in his chair, one hand resting upon his considerable stomach. "I believe I have given employment to every artisan from here to London. Perhaps their first in some time."

"Indeed," said a gentleman near the end of the table. "These yokels cannot expect the same pay as those in London, with all their expenses. I paid less for my stables here than I did for the furnishings alone in my London office."

That seemed a *non sequitur* to Devon – a word she'd just learned in her French lessons from Sissy; but perhaps, she was suspecting, logic played little part in smart conversation.

Devon herself played no part. She was just glad when the feast was over, to be allowed to retire to the bedroom she'd been assigned, her stomach full to bursting though she'd taken only a polite few bites of each course.

She was even gladder to find that the thick bedroom door could be locked from the inside, and turned the key with satisfaction before she stepped out of her gown and hung it carefully in the bedroom's huge wardrobe. She didn't bother putting on the silk nightdress Sissy had packed for her, just stripped to her shift alone and climbed under the fat comforter, her last sensation the extravagant satin sheets against her skin.

Chapter 15

Hunting

Man is simply the most formidable of all the beasts of prey, and, indeed, the only one that preys on its own species.

William James

Devon was wakened by a banging on the door. The fire in the grate had died down and the room was cold.

"Open this door," came the hiss of a familiar voice from the hall, as though the banging hadn't been sufficient to waken everyone within earshot.

Wearily, Devon climbed off the high bed and went to the door.

"Go away," she said, not bothering to whisper.

"You let me in, you bitch," Newgate hissed. "Don't forget who brought you here."

"And who asked you to?" Devon shot back. "Certainly not me." And she returned to the bed and plopped down on her face, pulling the pillow over her head to shut off most of the noise of his continued banging.

Then it stopped, and Devon was quickly to sleep again when a sound startled her and the bed sank with a weight, which was quickly on top of her. Instinctively her body clutched, trying to raise the weight, throw it off her; but his body remained, straddling her back as his knees gripped her ribs.

"That's right," he said, his voice raw. "Buck away. Then it will be my turn." And his hands closed on her arms, pulling them back behind her.

"I will scream till I wake the house," Devon cried, her voice muffled by the pillow.

"Scream away, my girl," he said with a chuckle. "Who do you think gave me the key? These are my friends, and none of yours."

Aren't they Sissy's friends, too? Devon thought. Do they condone such behavior on the part of her husband? Then she remembered the Colonel's leer when they'd arrived together. Apparently at least the men did.

His hands had moved under her now, were sliding from her wrists to the insides of her thighs; and he raised himself slightly to haul her body upwards. "I'll show you how the animals do it," he said. "We're in the country now; best you learn the ways of the other cows."

As he fumbled with her clothing, his hoarse voice kept up a steady rasping litany: "Damned bitches. They may beat me at cards, but *this* is *my* ground."

Devon held very still, her mind racing for a way out of this. He would have to release her, at least momentarily, she reasoned, in order to put himself where he wanted to be. It was then she must make her move.

And when the moment came, Devon launched her body up and back, toppling him off the bed.

He roared with rage and gathered himself to stand, but she was quicker. Rolling from the bed to her feet, she had reached the fireplace before he was upright again, and the poker was in her hands.

His eyes were wild now, in the flickering light that remained of the fire. His body resumed the crouch of the predator about to pounce. "You think this is a game?" His voice had gone so rough, she scarcely recognized it. "Well, I am here to show you it is not. When I am through with you, not even the brothels will have you."

Devon started edging for the door, the poker still aimed at him.

Newgate pivoted, too, in his crouch.

The trouble, Devon thought, her mind as clear as a fire in the darkness now, would be in unlatching the door. She would have to take one hand from the poker to do it, and he might see his opening then.

So she positioned herself, gauging the space her arm would need to reach the latch. Then she lunged at him with the poker, the hooked end catching him in the stomach; and as he bent, she grabbed open the door and bolted into the hallway – straight into the fully dressed figure of Polly MacBride.

The woman laughed as she stopped Devon's momentum and steadied her on her feet.

"Looks like you've taken on too much of a little woman this time, Percy," she said to Newgate as he charged out the door in pursuit. "Again." And her laugh came from deep in her throat, as though drawing upon her whole body for its force.

Still in a crouch, Newgate's lowered face was unreadable, the light from the hallway sconces making wavering shadows of all three of them. Yet Devon was almost certain that she could see Newgate's eyes glow red.

"Why don't you just sleep in my room this night," Polly said to Devon in a casual voice, though still facing Newgate. "I think you might get a better rest there. This one may be roving all the night looking for prey."

The woman turned slowly, then led Devon by the arm down the hall to a door that already stood ajar, and took her in without a backward glance, locking the door behind them.

The room was larger than the one Devon had been given, with a high poster bed and a chair facing the fireplace.

Polly MacBride tossed her a robe from the chair; and only then did Devon realize how violently her body was shaking.

The older woman seemed weary, and moved about the room undressing herself as though she'd forgotten Devon's presence. Huddled in the robe, Devon wondered whether the invitation to remain in this room for the night still stood, or whether that had been said only to ward off Newgate.

Eventually, Polly MacBride sat down heavily at the vanity, still in her corset, the folds of a satin dressing gown hanging loose about her. As Devon watched, the woman reached to unfasten a wig, jet black as was the fashion, its hair tightly curled and wound at the top with a strand of pearls and a dark red rose. Beneath it, her own brown hair was thin and limp, shot through with strands of gray. In the light from the candle on the vanity, the skin of her face looked just as worn, once she'd removed the heavy makeup. It would seem, Devon thought, that Polly MacBride was not nearly as young as she tried to appear.

Then the woman stood and unfastened her corset and let it drop, pulling the dressing gown about her. She was approaching the bed before she seemed to remember that there was another presence in the room.

"Ah yes, a bed for you," she said, and shrugged wearily. "Well, I guess you can share this one if you don't kick. Nothing must keep me from my beauty sleep."

And indeed, before Devon had scarcely settled herself on the far side of the big bed, the rough sounds of snoring were issuing from the form beside her, the smell of whiskey released with each exhale.

For herself, Devon had to concentrate on loosing the tension in each of her limbs in turn before sleep finally came to her again.

It seemed only moments later that Devon was wakened by the high, tinny blasts of horns and the barking of dogs. She sat bolt upright, uncertain where she was and what such noises signified.

Beside her, the body of Polly MacBride had not stirred, and Devon stared at the sleeping face. What on earth could she be doing in this bed, with this woman, now a paler shade of the Mrs. MacBride that had shut her out of her house.

Then there were footsteps in the hall and a knock on the door. "Everyone to the chase," called a man's stiff voice.

That, finally, brought Polly MacBride to life. First her hand shot out to the space beside her, hitting Devon in the hip – which opened the woman's eyes.

"Thank god," she said as her vision focused. "It's only you." And the hand went to her forehead as she groaned. "Lord, who did I drink under the table last night? And why?"

Devon was doing her own stocktaking. What had Newgate said about being beaten at cards? "I believe you must have bested Mister Newgate at that Whist game he challenged you to, if that is a card game," she said to her companion.

Which brought a hearty laugh from the woman's chest. "Ah yes, the tender Mister Newgate." She turned her frank gaze to Devon. "And he ran straight to take it out on you."

Again, Devon marveled at the worn look of the woman's face. What had appeared as smooth as pink china when she'd seen it previously was now creased about the mouth, with dark shadows beneath the eyes.

Apparently, the woman noticed her stare and covered her face with her arm, flopping over onto her stomach in the bed. "You go to the hunt," she said, her voice a low groan. "I've seen enough of them. May they all fall off their horses. My money's on the fox."

Devon moved cautiously going back to her room. But there was no sign of Newgate in the hall, nor in the room, though there were signs that he might have spent the night in that bed. Perhaps to save face, Devon thought, and hoped he'd learned his lesson and there would not be a repeat of his behavior at the close of this day. She briefly considered whether she might lock herself in this room until it was time to return to the city. But then, he'd gotten a key the night before, hadn't he? So she might as well see what these people were up to now.

She did what she could to look presentable in the heavy red skirt and jacket Sissy had said would be "just right for the hunt", and descended the stairs with almost as much curiosity as dread for the day ahead.

Apparently, most of the party had already partaken of the wealth of food set out on the dining table, buffet style. She took a roll and a sausage and crossed the sitting room to look out the French doors to the terrace, and beyond to the stables, where both men and ladies were gathered, among a cluster of restless horses and noisy dogs. All looked in a state of high excitement, and Devon walked out through the doors to join them.

Even this early in the morning, the air was already hot; and the costumes for both men and women were, like her own, of heavy material; but the assembled party hardly seemed to notice, their cheeks flushed and their eyes bright. Those already mounted called out to each other, perched high on their horses as though posing for a picture, the women sitting with both legs to one side of their saddles, twisted around to hold the reins over the horses' necks. Devon wondered how one could possibly stay on a horse that way. The high pitch of their laughter made her suspect they might be wondering the same thing.

The men seemed to be calling wagers to each other:

"A pound for every hedge I clear before you!"

"Forty till we burst the fox!"

"With these hounds? No more than thirty."

The straining, barking dogs were being held at the ends of long ropes by three young boys, who looked to have all they could do to keep them restrained.

A stable boy was just emerging from the darkness of the stables leading a small brown mare and, seeing Devon, headed toward her.

"I've supplied her!" shouted Newgate's voice as the boy was showing Devon how to mount the mare. They both turned to see Newgate, clad in bright red like the others, mounted on a white steed, leading another, smaller, horse by the reins.

The stable boy's brows furrowed. "Glory, sir? But if the miss has never ridden --"

"That will be all," Newgate said, waving the boy away with one hand while he looked steadily at Devon, his eyes dark in the bright sunlight.

He dismounted and held the stirrup of the other horse, as though daring her to put her foot in it.

Devon mounted as she'd been instructed by the boy, unwilling to let her apprehensions make her back down from Newgate's silent dare.

She was just trying to decide what to do with her right leg so it wouldn't get in the way of the reins when

184

Newgate slapped the horse on the rump, shouting, "Away with you then!" and the animal's whole muscled body cut loose beneath her, the saddle becoming a battering ram against her bent leg and buttocks.

Devon gripped the reins with one hand, the saddle with the other, and desperately tried to stay on as the horse hurtled forward. But she heard Newgate's voice shout out "The sport of kings!" just moments before the force of gravity won out over her grip and her body thudded to the ground.

The stable boy caught up to her quickly, saying over and over, "Are you all right, Miss?"

Devon stayed where she was for a few moments, making an assessment of her various parts, before she accepted his hand to raise herself.

Beyond them, the yapping hounds were just cresting the first hill, their shrill cries piercing the air like lightning made sound. And the blood-red riders hurtled after them, approaching and then leaping the first row of hedges, the cries of their voices blending with those of the hounds.

"No, no, I am quite all right," Devon responded to the boy's persistent worries; but she accepted his arm as she tried to make her legs carry her without limping back toward the house.

Well at least, she thought, she would be spared the spectacle of this hunt that had seemed to raise such a blood lust in the spirits of these supposedly genteel gentlemen and ladies. She would just return to the parlor and read a book until she had to deal with them again. If indeed there was a book to be found in this place.

Devon found a book, though one of few and composed mostly of pictures – of architecture and furniture and formal gardens. She had just settled her sore bones onto a lounging couch whose cushions proved not as soft as they looked, when every muscle came back to attention with the sharp sounds of gunfire.

Surely the hunt could not already have reached its conclusion, she thought. Besides, the sounds were too near – somewhere above her, it seemed.

Then they came again: two shots, then a pause, then two others; and Devon was off the couch, straining to track the origin of the sounds.

Again they came, seemingly directly overhead.

But the stairway to the second floor was in the neighboring hallway. Devon moved cautiously to the stairs and started up them. But when her head cleared the landing, there was nothing and no one to be seen in the second-floor hallway. She climbed the rest of the stairs and started down the silent hall.

Again the shots, and still above her. Devon studied the doors on either side. One of them, down the hallway, was slightly ajar. She went to it and peered through the opening. There was no bedroom there, just a metal stairway of narrow steps winding up into darkness. Only when she put her head all the way through the door could she see a small spot of daylight at the top of the shaft.

She listened for the shots again, but there was only the faint sound of voices, one heavy and imperious, the other subdued.

Before she had made a conscious decision, Devon's feet were on the stairs. The tap of her boots on the metal steps was magnified in the narrow enclosure. Devon tried to step silently, her hands seeking a railing but finding only the cold slickness of stone walls on either side. Perhaps, Devon thought, a shiver passing through her as she continued upward, her brother was about to be proved right with his warnings that her curiosity would one day get her into serious trouble. But then, she thought, she was far from the protective walls of her family, and had already encountered so much of what she'd been warned about, how much more trouble could there be?

Then her head came level with the opening, and Devon saw the Colonel with one of his man servants standing on a balcony jutting out from the roof, the Colonel with his feet planted apart, a huge gun with two barrels gripped to his shoulder,

Then a flock of birds rose into the sky from below, and the Colonel jerked the barrel up, then down, then sideways at them. *Boom! Boom! Boom!*

The reports of the gun were followed by no birds falling; and quickly, the manservant took the gun and handed the Colonel another, who fired it again, with – to Devon's great relief – no better results.

"Damn them! They're too quick!" roared the Colonel. "Give me another, damn it!" Then to someone on the ground, "Release them!"

But the birds sailed past his next round with no casualties either, and the Colonel threw the empty gun to the floor of the balcony and sent his oaths after the vanishing birds.

Then he bent to someone below. "Bring the falcon!" he bellowed; then, "And send word to Clapp in the East

Enclosure. Tell him I want to see a stag in my sights, not some bit of fluff that bolts across the sky and is gone."

As Devon watched, a man emerged from an outside stair, a huge glove on his left hand, the talons of a great hooded bird clutching the glove. Its black wings, now folded against its sides, still reached beyond the man's elbow, its head more frightening perhaps in the black hood than it might have been without it. Devon felt a chill rush through her, though whether from the actual behavior of the man or the imagined behavior of this bird would have been hard to choose.

Then the Colonel was pointing to the northeast, beyond the stables. "Here it comes!" he cried. "Look at the points on that buck!"

Devon climbed the rest of the way out onto the balcony to see the form of a stag with enormous antlers emerge from a fenced stretch of woods beyond the fallow field, followed by a man waving his arms to drive it forward.

Still, the stag halted, his head lifted to the wind; and the man had to rush nearer, shouting, before the stag broke into a run across the open field.

"Release him!" the Colonel cried to the man holding the falcon.

The thong binding the bird's foot to the man's wrist was undone and the hood lifted from its high, dark head. The creature appeared to Devon the epitome of evil intent, its eyes glittering, before it spread its great wings and rose effortlessly into the sky.

Devon crept forward, keeping her distance from the guns but as close to the balcony's edge as she dared, until she could see most of the field below, as the stag drew closer. With a mixture of dread and fascination, she watched as the great bird tilted and soared across the sky, then came circling back.

The stag stopped, its head raised to the sky, apparently aware of the falcon now, perhaps judging the distance between them.

Then, as the bird came about and aimed its flight downward, the stag took off running in great leaps across the field.

But the falcon was swifter. Whatever direction the stag chose, the falcon reached before it, wheeling toward it, herding it ever closer to the Colonel's waiting gun.

The Colonel seemed beside himself at the spectacle, bouncing and shouting, until the man who had been handing him the loaded guns took the one from his hands and held it.

Slowly, the circles of the stag and the falcon grew tighter. The stag seemed to seek any direction but that of the house; but he was being turned inexorably toward it, driven nearer and nearer, until Devon could see its body quite clearly, its sides glistening with sweat, heaving with each breath, its great antlers lifting and tossing this way and that as though someone had a bit in its mouth and was jerking on the reins.

Then it stopped still, its black eyes glowing in the bright gray light of the English sky, its head turning from the form of the falcon above it to the turreted mass of the manor house, as though to look directly at those perched there.

Then it reeled and took off down the empty field toward the hedgerows that enclosed it.

"Have at it!" shrieked the Colonel, his stout form bouncing up and down in his high polished boots, his greatcoat flapping against his belly like frantic wings. "The eyes! The eyes!"

And as Devon watched with a growing nausea in the pit of her stomach, the falcon dove again and again at the animal's eyes, its sharp beak driving like a stake to the heart. And the beautiful creature faltered and jerked its head from side to side, to avoid the unavoidable beak of the falcon.

The falcon's handler arrived then; and as the bird hovered above, the stag was turned toward the house again, until the Colonel, having seized the gun back from his servant, was leaning so far forward at the edge of the balcony, looked as though he might topple over the railing. And Devon felt a terrible desire to rush up behind the man and *push*.

Then a shot exploded from the muzzle of the gun and the animal staggered.

"I got him! I got him! Did you see that?" And the Colonel shot the huge gun again.

Devon lost count of the number of times the gun fired; she was no longer looking. She didn't hear the animal fall, but the air was finally still.

"Got you!" the Colonel cried. "And with the head intact. You see that? Not a mark on it. Ah, you will look fine on my wall, you beauty!"

Then the men turned, and the Colonel's gun, tilted downward in the crook of his arm, nearly caught Devon in her churning stomach.

"Ah, watch yourself there, little lady. Did you see that shoot? Thrilling, wasn't it? More so than chasing a fox for hours on end, I can tell you. Besides, it's the hounds that make the kill there. Here, it's just a man and a falcon, a perfect team."

Then he seemed to notice her state of disarray from her earlier fall from the horse. "But you've soiled your dress. Come. We'll find the Missus and get you into something more respectable."

And Devon let herself be led back to the stairwell and down out of the bright gray sky, into the dark bowels of the Temple Aliquott.

Chapter 16

Hemlock

Gently they go, the beautiful, the tender, the kind...
And I am not resigned.
Edna St. Vincent Millay, *Dirge without Music*

On the way back in the carriage, Newgate was in high spirits. Perhaps, Devon thought, his revenge on her had cured his rage. Although it may have been only that his attentions to his dinner partner the night before had borne fruit. In any case, he had not come to her door again.

Regardless, Devon's heart sat heavy in her chest. She felt a great weariness, and wondered if by the time she was Polly MacBride's age, she could bear to be in the company of *anyone* anymore, if this was how 'people of quality' comported themselves. All the beauty of this countryside, and only killing games to celebrate it?

All the talk at dinner the evening before had been of how that legion of mounted hunters and frenzied dogs had triumphed in their hunt. Every effort of the fox at evasion was recounted, and endless toasts were made to the hunters' eventual success. Over one small creature who never did them any harm?!

Throughout it all, the young woman at Newgate's side had looked adoringly upon him; and Devon had seen her slip him something in a handkerchief as they climbed aboard the waiting britzka. Wasn't she – and Devon herself – just another kind of prey?

For most of the way back, Newgate entertained himself with hunting songs and stories, apparently not noticing that he didn't have her rapt attention. Instead, Devon was trying every means at her command to obliterate the vision of that glorious stag in frantic escape, and the dark flapping wings and beak that had pursued it, then the blasts of the shotgun that had ended its life. They had haunted her dreams all night; she thought she would never be able to drive them from her memory.

Is this how all men behaved, Devon asked herself, whether of low birth or privileged? Her father had spoken often of the need for education, such as he had received before his family had lost their enterprise. He seemed to deem it the only way to raise a man above the brutish level so evident outside their door at Eagle and Childe Alley. But weren't the men she'd just seen in action educated? Clearly Newgate had received education to qualify as a barrister, and he was every bit as brutish, if not more. Just in better clothes.

And what of the women? No mention had been made of the women who'd ridden to the hunt. But they, while perhaps more passive, must at least have been supportive. They continued to smile and nod at the endless recounting of the pursuit and killing of a poor small animal.

It was all very depressing; and Devon stared out the coach's window at the many bound fields now lying fallow behind their hedges, too much a bother, with too little profit for their absent owners, apparently, to produce crops. Even these beautiful thick woods apparently held only more prey for their amusement.

Her melancholy, however, was as nothing compared to what awaited her at Wingsbury Hall.

Marianne met them at the back door, her face white blotched with red, as though she'd been crying. "I think she's dead," she blurted out, trembling in the open doorway like a frightened child. "She doesn't answer; she just lays there, her eyes all starey. And she's got so cold."

Devon didn't wait to hear more, but pushed past the girl and ran up the stairs to Sissy's bedroom.

She had only to look at the parchment-white figure in the bed to know that Sissy was gone. Though the unseeing eyes appeared more distracted than blind, as though they were focused more on where she was going than where she'd been. On her chest rested the miniature of the man and young woman in the rowboat, her right hand curled about the little figure of the man. And beyond, on her window sill, stood her sylvan painting of the Temple Aliquott.

Devon fell to her knees beside the bed, the hot tears coming in a rush. Were all the good people destined to die, while the lesser survived? Was everyone she loved going to leave her? Would there be no end to this loss?

Devon became aware then of Newgate's body above her, his hand reaching into her vision to touch his wife's cheek, then close the unseeing eyes. When Devon glanced up, his face was ashen, with a look every bit as frightened as Marianne's.

"How could this have happened?" he whispered.

Devon buried her face in the coverlet.

But she couldn't shut out the sounds of Newgate's boots bounding back down the stairs, his distant shouts at Marianne, or the cracks of the whip on Beauty's back, like bullets from a shotgun, as the phaeton sped out of the mews.

Devon left before people would come to carry away the body. Unable to bear the house another moment without Sissy's spirit in it, she left to pace the perimeter of the square in the incongruous bright sunshine. First she tried to think of the future, then tried not to, as the windows of the houses that surrounded her stared out blindly from behind their useless balconies. Eventually she saw the wagon of the undertaker roll down the square, heading for Wingsbury house.

It was dark when, sitting on a bench in the middle of the square, she saw the phaeton return. The last person she wanted to encounter was Pierce Newgate, but she needed answers, so she followed it, entering through the back door, into an empty kitchen.

Immediately the voices assaulted her ears, coming from the hallway that held Marianne's room.

"Why didn't you fetch a doctor?" Newgate's voice was furious.

"You mean a real doctor? Wouldn't he know?" Marianne bleated through her sobs.

"Fool! That little bit, it's never produced more than weakness before."

Instinctively, Devon ducked into the little cook's room, leaving the door slightly ajar to hear.

"I only give her the same little bit, like always, in the broth," the girl wailed. "But then she seemed stronger, got real hungry, took two bowls and some biscuits."

"Two bowls! You stupid girl, don't you know what you've done?!"

"I only done what you told me." The sullenness was back in her tone. "You're the one give it me, said it'd just put her out of our way nights."

"Stop that blubbering! Where is it?"

"Where's what?"

"The plant, girl! The plant! What have you done with it?"

"It's used up now, i'nt it?"

"All of it?"

"Wa'nt much left." The girl's voice was sulky, had stopped its sobbing. "What gonna happen now? You're not gonna get ridda me, are ya? Take up with that other girl now? I always done what you told me."

"Hush your mouth!" Newgate's voice rasped. "Where is she?"

"Who?"

"The girl!"

"Left just after you did."

"Stay in your room. And say nothing to anyone. I'll deal with you later."

Devon quickly left the cook's room and went back out the door and crouched behind the bushes that bordered the kitchen garden.

She could hear Newgate stomping about in the kitchen, pans clattering, pots banging against the brick behind the stove. She heard his boots crossing and re-crossing the kitchen floor, as though looking for something, all the while muttering a steady string of oaths. Then she heard a knife clatter to the floor and the door banged open.

She shut her eyes as she'd done as a child when playing hide and seek, her child's mind thinking if she couldn't see them, they couldn't see her.

But she needn't have bothered. Newgate wasted no time, just jumped into the phaeton, still waiting there, and shouted orders to Beauty, whose loud snort she heard before he pulled coach and rider back out of the mews and into the street.

She returned to the kitchen. She knew now what to look for. Why hadn't she put it together before? That sprig of green he'd taken from the cutting block the day he'd brought her back here, not as guest but as servant. That day he had left the kitchen laughing, slapping the leaves of that sprig against his cheek.

For a long time now she had suspected something was wrong. But how could she not have *known*? Every time he wanted Sissy out of the way, she had taken sick. After being fed a broth or tea of some sort which was not of Devon's making. Didn't she know by now the evil that some were capable of? And that Newgate was as evil as any of them? Who would know that better than she?

She found it finally. Or what was left of it. In a pail of slops behind the service door. The remains of a root and stem, one limp sprig of leaves left, looking like parsley, smelling like turnip: hemlock. A little would make a body ill; more would kill. She had only seen it in the doctor's book on poisons – but here it was. Or what was left of it.

Devon dropped it in the pocket of her skirt and went to get her cape. The sounds of sobbing from Marianne's room had resumed.

But where could she go? Whom could she entrust with such information? Someone who would also have the power to use it to seek justice. Polly MacBride's warning came to mind; clearly, the woman had known Newgate was dangerous. But she'd not done anything about it, had let him take Devon off with him. No, she thought, Polly MacBride stood first for Polly MacBride.

The only other person she could think of was Mrs. Dofferman. Devon had only the street name of her sister's residence, and had no idea where that street was located. But there was nothing else to do.

Wanting above all to get away from this place as quickly as possible, Devon took what market money there was from the jar, put it into the same pocket as the remnants of the plant, and let herself out the back door, closing it quietly. Though the chances of Marianne hearing anything above the sounds of her own misery were next to none.

Stiles had been given the day off following the trip to the country; at least she wouldn't have to worry about him, whose see-no-evil, hear-no-evil loyalties had been well proven. Still, she hurried out of the mews and turned north at a run, toward Oxford Street. Surely there would be carriages to hire there, with a driver who would know the whereabouts of Crown and Cushion Court.

But Devon found more than carriages on Oxford Street. Having changed out of the fancy clothes she'd been given to wear to the country, into her own modest skirt and blouse rather than the cook's uniform, Devon found her reception on the night streets of the city far different from that of a servant on market day – much less the deference paid her when taken for one of the gentry. Here, bands of laughing young men, heading apparently for an evening's entertainment but ready to entertain any other diversion along the way, stuck their necks out of their carriages and called lewd offers to her. And on the walkways strolled women who appeared to have no destination at all, but hung about singly or in small groups, their attention focused entirely upon the men, on the street or riding by. A few appeared no older than she, and rather well-dressed, only their presence here after nightfall, apparently, a signal that they were making themselves available for such offers as she'd been proposed.

Now and then, one of the carriages would stop to add one or more of the women to its company, shouts and squeals erupting from its dark interior as the carriage took off. And on the street, men passing seemed to assume that she was open to looks and even hands. "How much?" one older gentleman asked hoarsely as he pressed against her side, while a coach of youths singing drinking songs pulled over to the sidewalk.

Devon cut past the coach into the street, heading for an empty carriage. It appeared far too fancy to be for hire, and was past her by the time she reached its path; but Devon ran to catch up, then kept pace by its side until she could grab the door latch and, swinging it open, leap into the carriage's interior, only her hold on the door frame keeping her from toppling back out again.

The driver turned and scowled at her. "Hey, you there," he called over the sound of the horses' hooves. "Just what do you think you're about?"

She thought her actions self-evident, but said, "I am in urgent need of reaching Crown and Cushion Court. Do you know it?"

The man craned his head further around, to get a full look at her. "This ain't no public coach, Miss," he said, sounding as offended as if she'd walked into a house unbidden.

"I have a most desperate need to get to Crown and Cushion Court," Devon repeated, deciding not to argue the appropriateness of her methods.

"Well, there's coaches for hire for that," he grumbled.

"But I can't find one, and it's really most urgent. I see you are driving no one at present. Couldn't you take me there quickly?"

"Makes no matter. This is His Lordship's carriage, and no one rides in it but him."

"But he's not here," Devon pressed her argument, "and I am. I'm sure it won't take long. Couldn't you just take me? I have…" She pulled coins and pound notes from her pocket to count them.

"I don't care what you have," the driver said, but paused as though awaiting the results of her count.

"Two pounds, six shillings, four-pence."

"Still," the man said, "it's not for me to say. His Lordship's at the theater; he'll be needin' his carriage in another hour. And from the looks of you" – he took another look – "I'd say he'd be none too pleased to find a girl so young havin' put herself in it. Plenty more suitable ladies at the Drury Lane."

"Crown and Cushion Court," she persisted. "Do you know it?"

"Seems as I've heard it," the driver said grudgingly. "'Round Smithfield somewhere."

"The market?" Devon knew that name. Sometimes, when the wind blew from the east, the smell of cattle being driven up the New Road to Smithfield Market reached St. Andrew's parish, and the mournful sounds of their bawling could be heard in the still hours before dawn.

Devon leaned forward and handed the man the money she held in her palm. "It's all I have. Please. It's so important, or I wouldn't ask."

The man grumbled, but took the money and slapped the reins against the horses' rumps, quickening their pace.

Devon let herself relax for a moment in the dim interior of the carriage, which smelled of tobacco and cologne. Smithfield Market: they had passed through it, when she was five years old and her father had taken her and Boyle on her first and only big outing, to St. Bartholomew's Fair. She remembered looking down from his shoulders at the press of sheep and cattle being driven through the streets by shouting boys, the crush so dense and the pace so reckless, she had marveled that they could move at all among them. But she remembered no fear. She had trusted her father completely to get them through that or any other peril. Now she made a silent plea that he would be with her on this journey also, where the dangers might be considerably greater.

And to what purpose, really? Newgate was a man of standing, of influence, however he had arrived at it. And herself? Why would anyone in authority see her as anything but an impertinent girl, making such charges, and on the basis of what? A rotted plant.

Just get to Mrs. Dofferman, Devon told herself. That formidable woman will know what to do.

She stared out the carriage window, realizing how seldom she had been out at night, and never alone. The streets, cloaked in an eerie darkness lit only by the wavering flames of infrequent street lamps, could be any streets, in any part of the city. What if this man took her somewhere else? And for some frightening purpose?

Sternly, Devon reined in such fears. This was not the time to let imagination run away with her composure. She must keep her mind clear and her eyes open.

When they reached Holborn Circus, at its juncture with Shoe Lane, Devon felt sure they were traveling in the right direction. Though after Farringdon Street, where the carriage turned left, then right, she lost her bearings again. Until the streets began to stink noticeably of animals and their wastes, an occasional small herd of sheep or oxen blocking their way until, with sticks and shouts, their handlers moved them along.

"Where you want t' be let out?" the driver asked as they drew closer to the smell, the mounting sound of voices added to it.

"Crown and Cushion Court?" Devon repeated hopefully.

"Told you, don't know it, not t' get there," the driver said. "I'll drop you at the market, best I can do. Somebody there prob'ly be able to direct you. I got to get this carriage back 'fore it's missed."

"Yes," Devon said, not wanting to seem unappreciative. "That will be fine. I'm most grateful."

But as the carriage reached the vast expanse of Smithfield Market, filled solid with what seemed to be meat on the hoof, crowded flank to flank into pens and bellowing into the night, Devon began to have doubts about finding anything at all around such a place. Her mind raced for some other way to proceed, but had found nothing by the time the carriage stopped and the driver said, "This as far as I can get. You'll have to go on from here."

Devon opened the carriage door, and despite misgivings, climbed down.

With the chill night air came the stench as well, magnified many times now that she was out of the coach, and she turned to it again. But the horses were already wheeling about, and with a slap of the reins, headed back more quickly than they had come.

Devon huddled her cloak about her, gazing up at the solid mass of tenements that lined the square, looming above their gas lamps like shadowy ghosts of buildings that had long since ceased to exist. Hovering above them in the mist was a hazy cross, and beyond it, the faint outline of St. Paul's. Whatever foul corner of this city she found herself in, Devon thought, that same dome seemed to be there in the background. But whether watching over or only *lording* over the inhabitants, was by no means clear to her now. She knew little of religion, but questioned anything that claimed to be in charge while the innocent died and those with blood on their hands seemed to prosper.

"A bit early for marketing, isn't it, Miss?" a voice said, so close to her that Devon jumped and spun around.

At first she couldn't even locate the face that had spoken. Then a glimmer of teeth and eyes made her realize that the face itself was so dark it could scarcely be seen in the gloom.

It was also very high above her. The tall form, as it moved, she could see held a stringed instrument in one hand and what looked like two bones in the other, their light shapes clearer than his own.

"I'm looking for Crown and Cushion Court," Devon said. "Do you know it, sir?"

"That be a ways off," the man's deep voice said.

Devon's hopes dropped closer to despair.

"I must find it," she said, "I must. If you could just point me in the right direction."

The man pointed to the corner of the square behind her. "That be the direction," he said. Though when Devon turned back, she could see that he was grinning.

"Thank you," she managed with some dignity, and began walking in the direction he'd indicated.

The sound of laughter behind her was followed by footsteps, and the man fell into step beside her, ambling along with one long stride for her every three.

"You got people there?" the man asked amiably.

Devon hesitated. Not speaking to strange men was the most unbreakable rule she'd gro up with. And it had only been reinforced since by those she'd met, in or out of 'society.' But this man seemed less threatening somehow.

"Yes," she said finally, but no more.

"Not the best place for a lady to be wandering in the dark," he said.

Devon wondered what about her marked her as a "lady" – a term, like "gentleman", she'd come to reject, worth seeming to have very little to do with either one. Or was it only that Devon's speech carried no Cockney accent? All the Quail children had been drilled in their father's "proper English". But then, she thought, this man's speech seemed just as 'proper', though lilting with an inflection she had not heard before.

"I must find someone," she said finally. "It's very important."

He nodded. "Must be," he said.

She could make out his features better now that her eyes had adjusted to the dim light about them. They walked along without speaking for a while, speech being difficult in any case with the cries of animals and stock boys not far distant behind them.

Finally, though, Devon's curiosity got the better of her caution. "And what are you doing here, if you don't mind my asking?"

Then immediately, Devon regretted her words, lest they imply that he did not belong. She had seen few individuals of his dark coloring on her rounds with the doctor, and those only in one area near the docks.

He seemed to take no offense though. "I make my music here," he said, and raised his instrument and the bones. "On market days here, at other times in other places."

Devon had seen ballad singers or banjo players on street corners, playing rollicking songs for the most part, like *Buffalo Girls* or *Oh Susannah*; but sometimes there were songs sadder than any others she had heard, sung by people of varying shades of darkness. "Negro spirituals" the doctor had called them when she asked.

"Are you a Negro then?" she asked politely, and was startled when the question produced a boisterous laugh. "I am Ethiopian," he said then, with no loss of geniality. "From Africa. With a few detours along the way."

"But you live here now?"

"For the time being. And you?"

"Oh, I don't live anywhere, really," she replied, "anymore. I grew up in St. Andrews parish. But that was…" She tried to think how long ago and couldn't immediately come up with a measure of time; it seemed forever since then.

"You go to school? You speak well."

"Oh no. I was needed to raise my brothers and sisters. But our father had books. He was educated before the family lost their business."

"Ah yes," he said, as though he knew such situations well.

"And you?"

His deep laugh again. "My father worked in the Big House in the West Indies. I was a 'field nigger' myself, but I managed to pick up a few things."

Devon wanted to ask him what a "field nigger" was; but he'd spoken the words in such a way that she sensed it wasn't something he wanted to say more about.

They had arrived at the far corner of the square toward which he'd pointed. But he continued beyond it, into an alley between two of the tall tenements. Devon knew nothing else to do but follow.

The alley was so dark, the man took her hand to keep her with him, and they moved forward in silence, he walking ahead, the space too narrow to walk side by side.

Devon's hand felt dwarfed in his big one, but it gave her a feeling of safety that she hadn't felt in some time. She wanted to ask him about the "West Indies" he'd mentioned, and his "Ethiopian" homeland; but the darkness and the strange surroundings kept her still, as though any sound might bring down hostility upon them.

As they moved farther back through the alleyway, the stench of animals lessened, but was replaced by that stench that festered in neighborhoods such as those she'd visited with the doctor, where people lived jammed as closely together as the animals were in their pens. The memory of the doctor beside her, and her feeling of purpose when she was with him, made Devon feel all the more keenly her present aloneness, and she was glad to have this kind stranger with her.

They wound through several such alleys before her guide announced one short street as Crown and Cushion Court. Few lamps burned at the doors, and fewer numbers were marked on them; but counting from two down, Devon determined that one tidy two-story must be Number 24. Fearing suddenly that Mrs. Dofferman might not still be here, or her sister either, a panic seized her, and Devon asked the man if he would come with her to the door.

By way of answer, he climbed the steps and rapped sharply on the door himself.

The woman who answered was not Mrs. Dofferman, and stared at the man through the barely cracked and chained door.

Devon joined him on the step. "I'm looking for Mrs. Dofferman," she said. "Are you her sister?"

"I am," the woman replied, her gaze shifting from the man to Devon and back again, losing none of its wariness along the way.

"Is she here? It's terribly important that I speak with her."

"And who might you be?"

Devon's answer was forestalled by the appearance of Mrs. Dofferman on the stairway behind her sister. "What is it, child?" she said. And the sister stood reluctantly aside to let Devon pass, though she might have closed the door on her companion had Devon not had hold of his sleeve and pulled him in with her.

"He has killed his wife," Devon blurted out to the stout, familiar figure. Then she burst into tears. It had been so long since she'd had someone to unburden her heart to; and with all that had happened since she'd last seen this woman and been under her care, the tears poured from her quite out of control.

Soon all four of them were seated in the spare little parlor, and Devon had produced the plant she suspected of poisoning Sissy. After the two women had turned the remnant over in their hands, the sister saying "it might be a wild carrot only, looks to me," the man took it, examined it briefly, and pronounced it to be hemlock.

"I thought so as well," Devon said. "And that could poison a person, could it not?"

"Quick or slow," the man said, "depending on the portions."

"And who are you, pray?" Mrs. Dofferman finally asked.

Devon realized then that she'd made no introductions, didn't even know the gentleman's name.

"Marcus Woldemariam," the man said, a sly smile on his generous mouth. "Musician, magician, free man."

"Excuse my manners," Devon said to him. "My mind has been so distracted. I am Devon Quail." They formally shook hands.

"And this is Mrs. Dofferman, the housekeeper to the doctor I lived with when my family died. And her sister," she said, gesturing to the other woman, who still did not offer her name, only asked Mr. Woldemariam, "And which do you use them bones for, the 'musician' or the 'magician'?"

"Both actually," the man said, grinning broadly now, as though he found the company most amusing.

Devon returned to her central concern. "You are sure then, Mr. Woldemariam, that it's hemlock?"

"Quite sure. When was she given it?"

"I don't know for sure. Over a long period, I think. Two occasions in these past weeks. Small doses most likely, then more the last day."

"And she died."

"Yes." Devon's voice nearly broke on the word. She turned to Mrs. Dofferman. "We were to go to the country, but she took sick the day before. The same thing happened before the ball. Both times, I had to go with him alone."

"Which was his intent," Mrs. Dofferman said. "I should have paid better attention right from the first. I should have seen the true nature of the man. The Doctor would never forgive me if he knew." And her eyes filled with tears.

Devon moved to put her hand over the woman's large, rough one. "You had plenty else to worry about at the time. And I should have suspected earlier myself. The illness was unnatural to her, came on so quickly each time…" And her own tears threatened again.

She turned to Mr. Woldemariam. "When we got back from the country, she was dead. I believe the girl – Marianne, the maid – must have given her too much by mistake. I heard them arguing about it."

"Why would the maid be trying to poison her mistress?" the sister asked.

"Probably was diddling the mister," Mrs. Dofferman said shortly.

Devon nodded. The term 'diddling' was not known to her, but she could guess its meaning. "I could hear them at night. I couldn't understand why Sissy didn't hear them."

"A woman hears what she wants to hear. And nothing she doesn't," the sister stated.

"At least that kept him off you more," Mrs. Dofferman said, setting her other hand over Devon's.

Devon lowered her head, confirming what she could see the woman had already guessed. "Only the once though," she said then, her head coming up again, her face hot with anger. "Since then I have held him off."

"Good girl," said Mrs. Dofferman, squeezing her hand.

"Strange to say," Devon added, "Polly MacBride helped me in that respect, when we were in the country."

Then she regretted the remark, as she saw Mrs. Dofferman's face close over. "Probably intending to use him herself," she said roughly. "He's likely worth a bit of money now."

Devon did not try to set her straight. She knew how the housekeeper felt about Polly MacBride, because of how she felt about the doctor. Life was so complicated; how would she ever figure it out on her own now?

The talk turned then to what should be done with this measure of evidence that Newgate had at least some complicity in his wife's death.

"Don't see there's nothing to do," the sister said stoutly. "Servants don't get involved in such things, if they know what's good for them."

Devon looked to Mr. Woldemariam, who shrugged. "That's the rule where I come from."

"But Sissy was a good person," Devon insisted. "A *wonderful* person. She deserved to be loved and protected by everyone around her."

A surprising sadness overtook the man's features. "Few of the good people get what they deserve," he said. "*And* few of the bad."

Devon didn't want to believe that.

"I suppose it would be the magistrate of that parish would be responsible," Mrs. Dofferman said thoughtfully. "Don't know how a body would get to him though."

"And what would you say if you got to him?" the sister argued. "Do you think they'd take the word of a servant – and a girl at that – over a gentleman's?"

"He does seem to have influence," Devon conceded. "At least an audience with powerful people." To herself, she recalled the sight of the Colonel on the roof shooting at a blinded stag, and wondered how such people had come to be known as *powerful.* In a world of their own making, she guessed.

"Well, there's nothing more can be done tonight," Mrs. Dofferman said, standing. "Best make some kind of bed for you here, let you get some rest. We'll take a look at this trouble again in the daylight."

Mr. Woldemariam took his leave of them then, and Devon thanked him with deep feeling for coming to her aid in the market. It was something she had seen few do since she'd been out in this bitter world beyond St. Andrew's parish, where the rule seemed to be each for himself.

"It was my pleasure," he said, with that flash of a smile. "Always glad to help a lady." He grinned again. "There being so few." And he bent low, the way she'd seen courtiers do in books. "Perhaps our paths will cross again. If it be in the stars."

Devon remembered the last time she had seen stars, from the speeding phaeton, on the way to the inn that awful night. Would the night ever feel safe to her again?

As though reading her mind, Mr. Woldemariam said, "I see fine things in the stars for you, Miss Devon Quail. Not easy, but fine. For you. And through you, for others." And with another sly smile, he disappeared into the night.

Chapter 17

The Pillory

Law is merely the expression of the will of the strongest for the time being.

Henry Adams, *The Law of Civilization and Decay*

Devon didn't know what woke her; she only woke suddenly to a feeling of danger. And there above her head, as she lay wrapped in a blanket on the parlor floor, was Pierce Newgate's face, pressed to the glass of the single window. In the pale morning light, through the ripple of imperfect glass, the face looked twisted, inhuman, the very incarnation of evil.

Inadvertently, her gaze shot to the remnant of hemlock lying on the parlor table. And when she looked back, there was a gleam of victory in the apparition's eyes.

Then he was at the door, pounding to wake the dead. Mrs. Dofferman and her sister came rushing down the stairs, one after the other, wrapping their shawls around them as they came.

"It's Newgate," Devon told them, huddling the blanket around her, standing back from the old oak door in fear that it might break under his onslaught.

"The back way," Mrs. Dofferman said.

Devon bent for her shoes, but the woman said, "No time," and scooped the root off the table, thrusting it into the pocket of Devon's skirt. "Head for the market," she said. "Somewhere there's a crowd. It's the day f'r it. If there's no magistrate about, look for a runner."

She was pulling Devon through the kitchen as she said it, and unbolted a door that opened to the alley. Mrs. Dofferman pulled away the blanket Devon still clutched to her and wrapped her own shawl about the girl's shoulders, then thrust her through the door. *"Run, girl,"* she said huskily. *"Run like the fox."*

And Devon ran – down the dark alley, debris slapping against her thin-stockinged legs like switches against a bare back. Everywhere, the narrow passage was littered with refuse – heaps of garbage, pails of slops, and the reeking contents of chamber pots. In the chill dawn air, steam rose from the stinking piles; and here and there one came to life as she passed, a figure startled to alertness from under its pile of rags.

But she did not stop, not even to try to get her bearings, darting from one alleyway to another, racing on sheer instinct in what she hoped was the direction from which they'd wound their circuitous way the night before. Only occasionally did she look behind her to see if she were being followed, half expecting to see Newgate's leering face suspended, floating in disembodied pursuit.

It could have been hours or only minutes that she ran, scarcely feeling the chill beyond her sweating body, or the cuts to her feet from the broken bottles and splintered wood over which she raced – until the sounds of animals that had been faint on the morning air grew louder, along with the rumble of voices, broken by angry shouts and the hawking of wares.

She headed straight for the noise, the households on either side stirring with their own sounds now, her path crossed by an occasional cart or wagon heading in the same direction, bearing jugs of milk or pigs being taken to sale or slaughter.

"Watch it there!" an old man yelled as she barely missed toppling him and his armload of brooms. She opened her mouth for apology but found no breath left for it.

Then she burst onto the open square and stopped, the sudden brightness seeming a solid thing, as impenetrable as a wall of glass. Until a mass of animals being driven to pen closed about her, taking her in like one of their own.

Devon tried to hold ground, looking behind her and in all directions, feeling exposed now in this wide-open space. The square was bigger than it had seemed at night, and was filling fast with bodies. From her left came the cries of an auctioneer, calling out bids on a parade of animals stretching in a long line behind him. On either side stood the booths of the sellers, offering everything from penny loaves to whiskey punch. But higher than them all, in the center of the market square, stood a platform on which the bodies of four persons were bent toward the crowd, their necks and wrists clamped into the frames of the pillory.

It was a sight Devon had seen only twice before – from a distance, as she'd ridden with the doctor past a square in the city and in one outlying parish – "Some poor soul," he'd told her, who'd found disfavor with authority, being exhibited to the crowd for whatever abuse they cared to heap upon him. "Barbaric custom," the doctor had called it. "Either hang the wretch or leave him be."

A magistrate might be in such a place, Devon thought, and headed for it, the crowd thicker the closer she came to the platform.

To her right, a woman selling "pence oranges" was jostled by another and fell against Devon's shoulder, the oranges tumbling from her basket under the feet of the crowd. Devon stooped to help the woman retrieve them, glancing about as she did so for some sight of Newgate, but seeing only a mob of strangers.

Turning back, Devon found herself face to breast with the orange seller, the woman's full bosom straining at its low-cut bodice, until the woman's reach for a far orange caused one breast to pop out of its constraints.

Instead of blushing with embarrassment, the woman laughed and, cupping the errant breast in one hand, unloosed her bodice until it fell below them both. She stood and retightened the bodice so that it raised both bare breasts to full view. "I think I just upped me price," she said; and taking the oranges Devon had gathered, said, "Thank you, dearie," and turned back to the crowd.

"Tuppence oranges," she cried in a lusty voice. "Come an' get 'em!"

Devon struggled on through the crowd, and came at last to the base of the platform on which the prisoners were being exhibited. Two men and two women, their heads bent so low through the holes in the stocks that their eyes could not rise to the height of their accusers. All around, people were shouting taunts, full of words like "whores" and "rotters" and "mollies."

"Let's see you do your dirty work!" one man shouted, and let fly an egg that hit one of the men on the side of his head. "Filthy molly!" the thrower screamed; and those around him took up the cry, following the egg with rotten apples and hunks of dirt.

"What have they done?" Devon asked a woman near her.

"They lie with each other, the vermin," she sneered, and stooped to pick up an animal's turd, and hurled it at the bent figures, giving no apparent aim to her missile.

It hit the skirt of one of the women.

"All of them?" Devon said.

"Most likely," the woman replied, and threw a rock this time.

Devon turned away, sickened by the spectacle, searching for some figure of authority she might approach.

At the far side of the platform stood a young man in a uniform of sorts, leaning back against the side of the coach the prisoners in the stocks had apparently been brought in, his eyes closed, his face uplifted as though to the sun – which had yet to arrive. The collar of his red coat was open, its front missing several of its gold buttons.

Without great confidence, but not knowing what else to do, Devon began making her way around the platform toward him, her hand closed over the bit of plant in her pocket, knowing that in a crowd this size, one's pockets could at any moment be stripped of whatever they contained.

By the time she reached the coach, the platform behind her was overflowing with rotten vegetables and refuse. The prisoners' legs were buried in them; and one of the women, who had begun shouting epithets back at the crowd, had apparently been hit by a rock and rendered unconscious. Her hands drooped limp from their holes in the stocks, and blood dripped from a cut at her hairline. The ache in Devon's chest from her long run was joined by pity for these four, whose only crime apparently had been their affection for each other.

"Pardon me, sir," Devon said to the young soldier.

She said it twice before there was any sign that he'd heard. His head lowered slowly to fix bleary eyes upon her – whether clouded by drowsiness or liquor was impossible to tell.

"Could you tell me whom I should speak to about a crime that's been committed?" she said, raising her voice to be heard above the crowd, and perhaps to penetrate his apparent stupor. "A murder," she said. "There's been a murder."

The man stared at her blankly – for so long, in fact, that Devon thought he must not have heard her, and was about to repeat herself when he spoke up in a voice as bleary as his eyes.

"Who are you?" he said.

"I'm – I was part of the household," she said. "The woman murdered was the lady of the house."

"And somebody killed her?"

"Yes. Her husband. With the help of the maid. Though I think their intent was only to make her ill. They had been giving her the poison for some time, I believe."

"'You believe.' And were you party to this crime?" The monotone of the man's speech had taken on an edge.

Devon was not sure she understood the question. "I saw it happening, but did not realize at the time that it was the poison that was making her ill."

At this point Devon produced the remnants of the hemlock from her pocket. "This is what they used. It's hemlock. They fed it to her in broth and tea."

The young man looked at it without expression. "You of this parish?"

"I – I'm from St. Andrews' originally. But the household in question –"

"Not this jurisdiction. You pay taxes?"

"I haven't really received any wages yet."

"You apprenticing?"

"No." Devon wasn't sure where all these questions were leading, but suspected it was no closer to her goal. "Could you just tell me —"

"Gotta serve at least a year in the parish 'fore you're entitled to bring a complaint," his voice droned on.

"Just please, could you not tell me –"

But the words were wrenched from her as she was seized from behind, one arm clamping about her waist while the other closed on her throat.

"Now I've got you, you little bitch!" The voice was harsh, guttural. Newgate's.

Devon struggled for breath as her feet were fully lifted from the ground, her back bent by the force of his grasp.

"Thank you, young man," Newgate was saying. "You've caught a right evil one this time." The arm tightened about her neck, robbing her of breath, as he mounted the platform, dragging her body with him.

"Here's another for you!" Newgate shouted to the crowd. "A murderous whore she is, too, as I have witnessed to my sorrow."

The arm left her neck to seize the bit of hemlock she still clutched in her hand. "*Hemlock,* my friends! She has poisoned her mistress with it, my own dear wife. Loved her like a daughter, we did, and this is how she has repaid us!"

"Whore!" Devon heard someone in the crowd shout. Then it was taken up by others.

"She tried to charm and deceive her way into my bed!" Newgate shouted, sounding as though he were just warming to his subject, his voice rising and falling in the cadences of the evangelical preachers Devon had heard sometimes of a Sunday in Eagle and Childe Alley.

"And when that didn't work, she turned to poison. Corrupted the poor maid into her scheme."

Devon felt something hard hit her right breast, then another against her skirt.

"What should I do with a whore such as this?" Newgate cried to the crowd, his voice sounding strained with emotion. "My innocent wife is dead, and this witch lives! The blood is still on her hands, yet she lives!"

The young officer had moved up onto the platform now; Devon could see him at Newgate's side, his face looking nervous and uncertain, his hands twitching at his sides. She tried to wrench herself free from Newgate's grasp, but his arm was like steel around her waist, the other holding the hemlock aloft.

"Here it is!" he cried. "The fatal weed! The one that took my poor wife from me! What should I do? It is too late for my wife, alas, but *how* can I avenge her *now*?!"

His hand dropped the hemlock into the refuse building at Devon's feet and closed on the bodice of her blouse, ripping it downward, stripping her to the waist before the crowd.

"This is the body, my friends," he howled, "that she used to deceive me. This is what she used to undo us all!"

The scene before Devon's angled vision – of sky and faces, fists and mouths – spun, the soldier's voice seeming to come from a great distance as more missiles pelted her head and chest.

"Shall I take her now, sir?" the uncertain voice asked.

"No," Newgate answered. "I will handle this. I am a barrister and can deliver her into the hands of the law myself. Which you can be assured I will do with all proper dispatch."

Then Newgate pulled her down off the platform, his arms like iron bars over her throat and waist, and dragged her in the dirt to where the britzka was waiting. From her dizzying angle, she could see Stiles atop the driver's seat, his face as stiffly unreadable as ever.

Then they were rolling out of the square, Devon's body bent as he had pushed it into the carriage, seeing only the muddy floor and the pointed tip of Newgate's boot. His hand gripped her hair and pulled her head back to see the triumphant gleam of his grin as he said, "Did you really imagine you could set yourself against me and win? Stupid little bitch. The world is a place you know nothing about. Nothing. Law follows power, and that is something you will never have. You're lucky I didn't give you over to the mob completely; they'd have made short work of you."

Then his hand thrust beneath her skirt to grip her in the soft place between her legs. "I will make much longer work of you myself."

Chapter 18
Embarkation

My native land – good night.

Lord George Byron, *Childe Harold's Pilgrimage*

I'm bound for the promised land
On the other side of Jordan,
Bound for the promised land.

Harriet Tubman's variation

on an old spiritual.

Devon tried to hold onto the oblivion that had finally overtaken her that morning. In the blank darkness, there was no pain, no humiliation, no overwhelming anger. But the sun coming through the one high window in the room beat down upon her like an angry eye, prodding her to action.

Every inch of her burned, inside and out, and there was no relief in the heat of the little room, which Devon could not identify from any of its contents. She only knew, before she tried the latch, that the door would be locked.

There was little left of her clothing, but she tried to piece together what she could, dabbing at her wounds with the soft cloth of her skirt. She could hear no sounds of movement in the house, and tried to tell from the direction of the shadows in the room which part of it she must be in, remembering only the back door and the back stairs from hours before, and Newgate's strident, triumphant voice as the floor had come up to hit her again and again.

Devon moved unsteadily to the window. Below, at a sheer two-story drop, was the mews. Through the open doors, Devon could see the britzka and the two mares in their stalls; but Beauty and the phaeton were gone. Doesn't the man, she wondered oddly, ever have to sleep? He must have come after her immediately upon his return, when he'd found her gone. Perhaps he too had thought of the slop bucket and found it disturbed. And he must have remembered, as she had, the street name and number Mrs. Dofferman had shouted to her as he carried her away to Wingsbury. Now, with the sun scarcely past high noon, he had apparently left again. The Colonel's story about the gambling legislator came to mind. Perhaps such men, looking upon life as a game that went to the swift, just kept moving.

With a numb abstraction, Devon wondered as well about the fate of the poor weak Marianne. The house was very quiet; perhaps she, too, had been dispatched by now, her knowledge making her too dangerous to leave among the living. Or more likely, he would keep them both alive until, like a tomcat with a mouse, he was through playing with them and would finish them off.

Devon made herself move to the door and pulled on it again; but both door and lock seemed too strong to be broken, even if she had her former strength about her. There were no other openings in the room; and even the window was protected by an iron grate. She saw nothing about her that could serve as a ramrod to force the door or be used as a weapon. There was only a pile of frayed linens in one corner and some canvasses in another, their faces to the wall. Devon stared at them, wondering if they might be more of Sissy's paintings, and whether it would hurt more to see them, to be reminded of that fragile snuffed spirit, or to leave them unobserved and uncherished.

At last, she felt compelled to see them, and crawled across the room to kneel before the canvasses. The first she turned to face her was a painting of Newgate – her Percy, as Sissy called him. Though the image looked more like the Prince Charming he went as to the masque. His features were idealized, the very image of an aristocratic gentleman. Devon let out a grunt of disgust that he had maintained that disguise to her for so long.

But then, she thought, the painting was here in this storeroom, and its face had been turned to the wall. Could Sissy have removed it from her sight when something happened to make her no longer see him this way? Did she know his true nature in the end? Devon didn't know whether she would prefer that to have happened, or whether she hoped Sissy had held onto her deluded love, it being all she had, really, in her sequestered life.

Then she was startled when the house's silence was broken by a sharp rap of the front door knocker, followed by a loud pounding on the door itself. After a pause, it came again, and continued until Devon heard Marianne's voice say timidly, "Who is it?"

"It's the sheriff!" a voice very like Mrs. Dofferman's, but lower, came booming through the door. And Devon heard the bolt being slid back and the door creak open slightly, then slam against the wall, followed by a mismatched dialogue between whimpers and Mrs. Dofferman's voice bellowing, "You'd *better* know, girl, or it *will* be the sheriff with me when I come again this hour!"

Then footsteps mounted the stairs and Marianne's scared voice was saying, "I think she's been put there, but I don't have the key. Truly."

"Girl?" Mrs. Dofferman called through the heavy door.

"I'm here," Devon answered, her voice coming rough out of the soreness of her throat where Newgate's arm had gripped her.

"Stand back from the door!"

Devon did; and there followed a thud, then another, until Devon could see the wood around the lock begin to splinter, until finally the door came slamming open.

"Good God," was Mrs. Dofferman's only comment when she saw Devon's condition. "Can ye walk?"

Devon nodded, but was glad that the woman's formidable frame was ahead of her going down the steps, in case her legs made good on their threat to fold under her.

"Y'r clothes?" the woman asked when they reached the bottom.

"In the room off the kitchen."

"Get something sturdy and a change. Put on one and tie the other with a blanket in a bundle. And be quick about it: we don't know how long the snake will be gone and I don't want to have to bust him, too; me shoulder's had enough for one day."

Devon moved without regard for the pain in her limbs, the clarity in her head seeming to come from the strength of the woman's voice and her powerful frame. She did not think about where they might be going or how they could ever get beyond Newgate's reach; she only went about the preparations as directed, as though the very acts themselves would be enough to save her.

Devon heard Mrs. Dofferman bustling about the kitchen, and looked to see Marianne leaning her weight against the bolted back door, fear plain on her features, though whether fearful of the women or of Newgate was anyone's guess. Probably both. Devon almost felt sorry for her. Until she recalled the sight of the girl spooning poisoned broth into Sissy's mouth as she lay already ill.

When Devon rejoined Mrs. Dofferman on the front steps, the woman was pacing nervously, gazing up and down the street as though she expected something to materialize at any moment and do battle. But when the hired coach finally arrived and they climbed into it, the proud old square was still as silent as ever. And as they pulled away, the only sound came from Marianne, who rushed down the street following the coach, crying, "Take me, too. He'll take this out on me, he will. He'll kill me, he will."

By the time they reached the docks, Mrs. Dofferman had explained to Devon the simple details of her plan. Devon would sign herself onto a ship bound for America, her passage to be paid at the other end by someone purchasing her services, for as many years as it took to repay the price. Then she would be free to start a new life.

The enormity of this step unreal to her still, Devon asked shakily, "And this America, will it be different, do you think? Better than here?"

Mrs. Dofferman's short reply: "Could it be worse?"

The woman had packed her a basket, with sausages and bread, cheese and two flasks, one large, of boiled water, a smaller of vinegar. "To fight infection," Mrs. Dofferman explained. "Now husband the water, mind. It may be the last you'll have until you reach the other shore."

Passengers were not provided water? Devon wondered, but didn't ask.

Then the coach pulled into a long line of other carriages strung out along the waterfront, where crowds of people – young, old, elegant and ragged – jostled one another with bags and baskets, all facing the sea.

The scene before her seemed to Devon as intangible as a dream. She stood on the coach's runner, reluctant to take that last step down; until there rose before her the tall shabby figure of a man in a long dark coat, his upraised hand holding a whole bouquet of the little windmills – red and green and yellow – like the one her father had bought for her at the St. Bartholomew's Fair, a prized possession she had had to leave behind in Eagle and Childe Alley.

Unthinking, Devon reached out for one, as though if she could only hold it in her hand again, all that had gone between would be undone and she would be a child again in her father's house, all safe and pure and loved.

But it was Mrs. Dofferman who grasped the hand, pulling her unceremoniously off the step into the teeming mass of humanity, all heading for America.

With the older woman setting the pace, they squeezed through the crowd, being jostled and jogged, Devon clutching her bundle of clothes in one arm, her other in Mrs. Dofferman's firm grip, until suddenly her vision cleared the row of square buildings that lined the wharf and there loomed before her the giant profile of a ship standing at the dock ahead.

Devon stopped dead at the sight.

This was nothing like the dirty barges she had seen before, loading their human cargo with the rest of their wares, headed for that other English prison, New South Wales. Even with its sails down, the three tall masts of this vessel stood straight as church spires against the late summer sky, its curving prow lifted above the water as proudly as those chairs set aside for royalty at Covent Garden. Huge below and bulging at both sides, the hull of this ship looked like a great gray face with cheeks filled to bursting, ready to expel its air and propel its bulk all the way to America.

The mass of people pressing forward from the crowd filled the platform of the dock and up the gangplank to the deck of the ship. Several men, with jaunty wide-brimmed caps and scarves that fluttered about their necks, circled the edges of the crowd, trying to keep them all directed toward the plank and away from the other end of the ship, where a few well-dressed men and ladies strolled leisurely up their own incline, followed by their people in servants' livery carrying their baggage. At the top, they stood and waved and called to others on the ground, their bright clothing catching the light like facets of gemstones glittering above the water.

Mrs. Dofferman had to keep tugging on Devon's arm to keep her moving, so spellbound was she by the entire scene. Ahead of them, the great mismatched crowd moved in noisy surges up the gangplank at its end of the ship. At its apex, perched on the railing of the deck, sat a man dressed like the other sailors but with a heavier dark cap and jacket, studded with gleaming white buttons. He sat out of reach of the crush of passengers and the jumble of their parcels, his voice traveling through the hot air like a whistle. Devon couldn't make out what he was saying, but he reached his hand toward the crowd each time he said it, as though extending a benediction.

On the deck at the other end of the great ship, above the smaller, tidier crowd, stood a tall, broad-shouldered man, all in white, with gold braid on his cuffs and shoulders. He stood straight but not stiff, with a prideful sort of ease, as though he were indeed master of all he surveyed. That, Devon thought, must be the captain. And the people he was smiling on, with a word to the men, a bow to the ladies as they boarded, must be the first-class passengers.

Pushing her way through the crowd and pulling Devon after her, Mrs. Dofferman brought them as near as they could squeeze to the bottom of the gangplank, where the press of bodies was even tighter. Blocked finally from all movement, they stood, the hard corner of a metal box pressing into Devon's bruised ribs on one side and the bulk of Mrs. Dofferman's frame hard up against the other. But she could see and hear the man above them better now. He would take something from the person at the head of the line and call out a name in rhyme; then that individual or family crossed the deck, down a ladder and out of sight.

"It's the family Dale with us will sail."

"Step forward, Dawes, into the jaws."

The crowd was laughing with the rhymes, even as unflattering as some of them were.

"Edly Hummel. Must be seventy 'r more. Let's see if he makes it to th'other shore."

But every second or third call was for someone who didn't pass to the ladder, but moved back toward the bow, forming a thickening gathering about the mast and rigging.

"Then step aside, friend Will-i-um," the man intoned, "and let the paying lady in."

Devon soon gathered that the people being put aside were, like herself, seeking an indebted passage, to be paid for at the other end by someone hiring their labor.

"And this Miss Finney will fetch a pretty penny," the man on the rail said, reaching down to cup his hand beneath the woman's chin. Instead of directing her toward the bow, he tucked her beneath him at the rail, where a small group of young women already stood.

A very large man followed the woman, and the voice called out, "Observe this fellow, may be a pounder of iron. We'll see how fat a price *he*'ll earn."

The man on the rail didn't make a rhyme for all the passengers. Either he couldn't think of one, Devon supposed, or he found the subject of too little interest. And as they drew closer, Devon began to wonder, almost with anxiety, what he might say about her, whether he would pronounce her of value or not worth mentioning.

Until then, Devon had been too distracted to think of Newgate; but now she turned, trying to peer back through the crowd to the place where the carriages were still pulling up. If he had traced her to Smithfield, Devon reasoned, he could follow her here. Marianne might have heard Mrs. Dofferman's directions to the coachman, and surely would tell Newgate anything to divert his wrath for letting his prey escape.

But the crowd was too thick to see the carriages themselves, only the drivers of the larger ones on their high seats. And Stiles's scarlet coat was not among them. Still, Newgate would more likely come in the phaeton. From the dread that filled her at the thought, Devon knew Mrs. Dofferman had been right: she could face nothing worse. And it would take an entire ocean to put her safely away from that man.

"Ah, Daisy, is it?" the voice above her was saying in a slow, insinuating drawl. And Devon turned back to see the man bend low over a pretty young woman, his long black curls bobbing beneath his cap as he kissed her hand. "Daisy, Daisy," he chanted, "But can she mix? If so, she may get a visit from this Mister Wicks." And he made room for her in the all-female group just below him.

Devon felt a chill run through her, though the sun was hot.

Then all at once, the man paused, straightened, his neck stiff. He glanced over toward the captain at the other end of the ship, whose own head was cocked slightly, as though listening for something.

Then a slight nod passed between them, and Mr. Wicks returned to his task with quite a different manner. "Move smartly now," he called, as though the line had been dawdling. "Have your tickets ready. Or if you're here to sign on for redemption, step aside, let the others pass; we'll make room for you in due time. It's a west wind coming, and we mean to catch her as she blows."

He lifted a sheet and called out a series of names, telling them to "Step up and present your tickets."

For the first time, Devon saw that there was another man below him on the deck, who held a long roll of paper and was checking off the names as someone arrived with a ticket. He wore a white jacket with a bright yellow sun on its back, the same symbol that rippled on the white flag from the ship's highest mast. Beneath the sun were printed the words *Carolina Lines.*

All around her now, people in the line were pressing forward, holding little squares of paper aloft. And the sailors along the edges of the crowd were pushing harder, pressing the bodies in and up the gangplank, saying, "Git lively along. We'll be sailin' with y' 'r without y'."

Devon looked to Mrs. Dofferman with alarm, but the woman kept steering her firmly forward with the others.

Then they were pressed up the gangplank. "I'll go with ye till I see ye safely aboard," Mrs. Dofferman said. "Or as safe as can be. If they question y'r age, I'll speak as y'r kin. Just remember: ye'r sixteen years. No, seventeen it better be: I don't know how many years it takes to make a grown woman in that land."

Panic filled Devon's throat at the sight of the mob above her – and behind – and on either side. Her breath was coming harder, her heart pounding in her chest. Was she really going to do this, sail away inside this enormous vessel, away from everything she'd ever known, safety as well as pain? It was almost beyond comprehension.

Devon craned her neck to see all the way to the top of the ship's arching prow, where the figure of a great gilded eagle reached, its wings spread wide, its talons gripping the ship. A white flag reading *The Eagle's Nest* in great black letters fluttered above the tufted head of the bird, its curved beak angling sharply down upon the crowd milling about the docks, as though deciding which of them to make its prey. Even in the heat of bodies, Devon shivered and clutched her blanketed bundle closer to her chest.

The crowd was moving erratically now, in bumps and spurts. As they neared the man on the rail, those with the little squares of paper waved them wildly, as though they were small sails themselves that would carry them across the ocean. Over the shoulder of the woman in front of her, Devon tried to read the one clutched in her hand. It was mostly in print, like a formal document, with names and dates and figures filled in by hand. Devon dearly wished she had one of those; such an official document might add credibility to the whole situation, convince her that she would be among the ones to descend that ladder and disappear into the ship's embrace. Instead, she knew she would have to join the growing crowd pushed back against the rail, waiting perhaps for something that would not come. And when the wind took this ship out to sea, out of the reach of Newgate, Devon would be left behind. To do what? Go where? No matter how deep or dark a hole she could find in this city, Devon knew that Newgate would sniff her out, like the Colonel's dogs, and take her back to use her and use her again, until he had used her up, body and soul.

No, she had to go. Devon looked up at the man on the rail with a kind of desperation. He was moving them through faster now, taking the tickets and handing them to the official below without even a glance. "Easy there, you lot," he called to the churning mass before him. "Take it from Mister Wicks: all the able-bodied will get on. We can hold four hundred souls 'tween decks, and there's no more than two have paid their passage. Nobody will be turned away who's a mind to sell their services in the New World."

Still, Devon was trembling by the time she finally neared the head of the line, and felt that all her youth, her inexperience, must show. She tried to stiffen her carriage, raise her chin; but the slight smile that played about Mr. Wicks's mouth as she stepped forward gave her reason to fear that his sharp black eyes were used to seeing through disguises.

"Sixteen," Devon heard herself say, without being asked.

"Seventeen she is, sir," Mrs. Dofferman spoke up behind her. "I saw her born to me sister, God rest her soul, these seventeen years past."

But the man seemed more interested in the surface than the age of Devon's body. "Pretty banged up there, isn't she?" he said. "You beat the girl?"

"My heavens no," Mrs. Dofferman said, clearly surprised by the question. "She – she fell, sir. Falls a lot actually. A clumsy girl she is." And she wrapped her shawl more tightly around Devon's shoulders as though to hide the damage.

The man frowned. "Clumsy doesn't fetch too high a price. But I suppose," he said, looking Devon over from top to bottom, "she's got enough other…charms to recommend her." And he motioned for her to step aside with the others in the group of women below him, calling to them, "Move on back there. Y'all 'll get on, y've got Wicks's word on it. The Carolinas need all the white hands they can get, no matter how soiled." And he grinned broadly, as though he'd made a great joke.

It seemed an eternity, packed in the suffocating crowd, until all the ticket holders had passed below. Then Wicks raised his hand to those gathered under him and around the forward mast. "All right, you lot," he yelled above the din. "Go! Get you below and grab y'r spot. And make it a good 'un, because y'll be in it—"

But his voice was drowned out by the pounding of feet across the echoing deck. Devon did not so much walk as she was carried by the momentum of the crowd, across the slick blond boards, with Mrs. Dofferman rushing behind. Devon scarcely had a chance to return the woman's stiff hug and grab the proffered basket, which would have fallen had there been space to fall.

Some of the contents did spill over as Devon was being jolted down the ladder; but only a sausage escaped completely, a hefty woman snatching it up and tucking it quickly into the blanket roll wrapped about her waist.

Then the crowd pivoted and continued its trajectory to another, ruder, drop into darkness.

At first Devon could see nothing. In contrast to the glare of the sky they'd just left, the vast interior below-decks had all the rank, dark barrenness of a dungeon, lit only by the feeble flames of two lanterns, one at either end, which bumped wildly against the heads of those stumbling about them.

Before her eyes could accustom themselves to the gloom, another group of entrants surged from behind, and Devon was knocked sideways against an upright structure, and nearly pitched into the blacker space beyond.

Grabbing the post to keep from falling, Devon just managed to rescue her basket from under the parade of feet tramping past. Then, her arm with the bundle wrapped tight to the post, her other hand clutching the basket, Devon steadied herself, her feet planted widely apart, and leaned to peer about her, trying to make sense of the shadows careening in the lantern light.

She appeared to be standing between two of a whole series of double-tiered bunks that lined both sides of the gloomy space, four to a run. The bunks themselves, about six feet long and little more than half that wide, were of rough wood, the thick platform between them at a level just above her waist. Since the roof of the space – the same rough planking as the floor – was no more than six feet high, there was scarcely room for anyone taller than a small child to sit up in either the lower or the upper bunks. And from the shapes Devon could make out, people were huddled four and five to a bunk. Plus their bags and boxes. These were the people with tickets, Devon thought, those who could pay. But it surely hadn't bought them much.

Everywhere there was noise – calls, crying, the shuffle of feet and thumps of baggage filling the space as densely as the bodies.

Then Devon was bumped again, this time hitting the end of the narrow space between the bunks and dropping to the floor. A heavy bedroll slammed against her shins and another body dropped into the space she'd just left. "Beg pardon, Miss," a man's deep voice said from beyond the bedroll. She couldn't see his face.

Devon felt along the clammy flooring for her basket, then scooted back as far as she could, setting the basket in her lap. It was probably better, she reasoned, to stay down and back, where there was nowhere left to fall.

Then Mr. Wicks's voice called above the crowd, "Settle down there. There's a place for all," and Devon peered through the bunks to see Wicks standing on the ladder with another man in a uniform that matched the *Carolina Lines* flag, holding a long scroll of paper.

The second man seemed to be counting the crowd, which could not have been easy in the dimness and crush of bodies. "Seems like an awful lot," he said at one point, consulting the list again and surveying the crowd with a frown.

But in the end he shrugged, made a mark on the list and handed it to Wicks, who followed the man back up the ladder. Then the hatch at its top banged shut, cutting off that last shaft of light.

A certain hush fell over the crowd; the only voices raised spoke in whispers; even the cries of the children were subdued. Until, as though to fill the emptiness, there was a great creaking and clanking from the ship's bowels around them, accompanied by calls and shouts from above.

A rush of panic coursed through Devon's body. Wildly, she looked about her. At her back, a succession of great ribs of wood curved above and below, cut off both top and bottom by thick planks of flooring. 'Tween decks': the term had meaning for her now. Combined with the rancid smell of sea water rising from below, thickening the darkness, Devon felt as though she'd just been swallowed by a whale. Although unlike Jonah, she had walked right into its mouth. Now she would be shut up here for weeks, maybe more, among this crush of strangers.

The baby in the bunk above her began wailing, and Devon wanted to cry out, too, that she was only a child herself still, after all; she didn't really know what she was doing, where she was going, what might happen to her there – worse, worse maybe even than here.

Frantically, Devon groped about her for one of the uprights with which to raise herself. Then into the general confusion of sound from above, a certain tone cut through.

"But she's my daughter, you see. And I have reason to believe she might…"

Newgate.

Then another voice: "Sir, at least two hundred…"

Fear throbbed through her head, muffling the voices. Devon stiffened where she crouched.

"Quail." His voice had risen. "She probably gave her surname as Quail. My wife's maiden name, you understand. She uses it to spite me. You know how—"

"Mister Newgate." The other voice had risen as well. "This ship is about to sail. And if you do not intend to sail with her, I suggest you get ashore."

"Captain, I don't believe you've heard me. I say—"

"And *I* say that there is no one on this ship who has not boarded of her own free will."

"But she's a minor, she cannot—"

Then the baby's wail was joined by another two bunks down. And out in the room a fistfight had broken out; a shaft of bodies collapsed like a row of dominoes down the aisle. By the time the hubbub had lessened, Devon was standing, both hands against the plank above, straining to catch the voices again.

"—even if I had the time or the disposition to try."

"Then you had better change your disposition, sir. This is England, and there is such a thing as the rule of law here."

"No sir, that's where you're wrong. This is an American ship; you are as good as on American soil. And believe it or not, we have our laws as well. And one of them is trespassing."

"Is that so!" Newgate's voice had swelled with the same exaggerated overtones as on the stage of the pillory.

"Well, perhaps my friend Judge Winston would contest that premise, sir."

Devon felt her clenched fingernails sink into the rotted wood. She slumped against the dank smelly ribs of the hold, hating the way she was feeling, the fear prickling her skin like fingers, hating the fear. And the hate. Hating the hate most of all.

The voices were barely audible now, and receding. "You can get a 'writ' of anything you like, sir. But this ship is sailing. And if you don't want to pay up your pounds for a ticket to America, I suggest you get off. *Now*."

Then a clanking set the whole vessel vibrating, and a groan rose from the bowels of the ship. There was a jolt, then another, and Devon sank back to the floor. It was too late for any turning back; she was on her way. And probably Mrs. Dofferman was right: whatever that 'New World' might hold, it would have to be better than this old one she was leaving behind.

Chapter 19

In the Eagle's Nest

There is a well-worn adage that those who set out upon a great enterprise would do well to count the cost. I am not sure that this is true. I think that some of the greatest enterprises in this world have been carried out successfully simply because the people who undertook them did not count the cost.

Thomas Henry Huxley

The next hour was a mix of trepidation and excitement, as the great ship shook and rattled, clanked and heaved. People and belongings were tossed about the dark space of the hold like dice from a fist, the two kerosene lanterns swinging wildly above them, sending eerie lights and shadows skittering like ghosts of former occupants of the tightly compacted space.

Then the heavings slowly turned to a rocking motion that the body had to resist if it was not to be rocked side to side, in perpetual motion, for the duration of the voyage. Which would be – how long? Devon realized she had no real information about how far it was across the sea to this

'New World' she was headed for, or how long it would take to get there. She looked around for someone to ask.

In the stand on her left, an entire family seemed to be squeezed into the upper bunk, bent below the low ceiling. The man, woman and two small boys were bundled in woolen coats and scarves even in the steamy heat of the hold. An enormous basket was set in the middle of the row they made, feet tucked under, knees jutting outward like the spokes of a wheel. They seemed such a self-contained unit that Devon didn't want to intrude, looked about for someone alone like herself.

In the bunk below sat a woman – still young, Devon guessed, though it was hard to tell from her pale, thin face and shapeless dress. Women aged quickly on the streets or in a factory; Devon had learned that much in her travels with the doctor. They could look like matrons by the time they were twenty. But the woman did not look up as Devon gazed at her, all her attention going to the baby suckling at her breast.

Ahead of Devon was the large bedroll and even larger man who had dropped into that spot earlier. The man's back was to her, hunched over though there was nothing close above his head, the rough red thatch of his hair jutting out in all directions above a grimy collar. Devon decided it would be wise to get a sense of the nature of this giant before she intruded on his solitude.

She turned to survey the right-hand bunk and found several faces peering down from the bunk above – a man and two boys, or rather one boy and another whose sex she could not be sure of, all three wearing woolen caps pulled low over their foreheads, nearly to their eyebrows. Their stares had a curious quality, neither threatening nor benign, more like animals staring out of their lair to assess the danger.

On the lower bunk, next to the basket Devon had squeezed in beside her, an old woman lay flat, her eyes open but staring straight up at the slats of the bunk above. Her skin was creased with wrinkles and dark as leather from the sun. Her hands, lying cupped at her sides as though waiting for something to drop into them, were as gnarled as the joints of trees. She did not look particularly open to conversation either, but Devon thought her the likeliest person to know about their destination.

"Pardon me," Devon said to her.

Getting no response, she said it again, a little louder.

Only the woman's eyes moved, their pupils rotating toward her.

"I wonder," Devon said, "whether you know where we are going exactly, and how long it will take to get there."

The old woman smiled, her lips curling as slowly as her eyes had moved. But her head turned toward Devon. "It'll be The New Country," she said, as though it were a title. "A brand new world, with new land and new people on it. And there will be animals you've never seen, just running free..." Her voice moved in a singsong rhythm, as though she were only half awake, dreaming about an imaginary paradise.

"What will you do there?" Devon asked. "Will you become a servant there?" Then, because it seemed too impertinent a question to ask a stranger, Devon added, "That's how I'm going, I guess, to be purchased for my services when I arrive."

245

"I paid my fare," the woman said, still vaguely but with satisfaction. "Worked fifty years in the fields. Now I just want to see it, just once—"

There was a sudden jolt, and the rhythm of the ship's sounds and motion changed. They were slowing again. The specter of Newgate re-entered Devon's mind. But surely he could not have gotten the ship stopped, not once they were already underway.

A commotion broke out on deck, a flurry of activity joined by the growing hum of voices, until the hatch at the top of the steps opened again and Wicks's voice rose above the others. "Just give me your names and step on down. We don't want to be here any longer than we have to. We've got room for you all, so just have your passage ready. Ten pounds-five each soul; give it to Mister Truitt there."

They were taking on more people? When the uniformed man, probably an inspector of some sort, had clearly suspected there might already be too many in the hold?

Then footsteps sounded on the ladder, people starting to descend as they gave their names, Wicks repeating them as they passed: "Heinz. Burwell. Dabney. Nelson. Esterly. Crandall. Fitzhugh…"

There were scores of them; Devon couldn't imagine how they would all fit in. But they kept coming, the press of them moving back those who had lodged themselves in the aisles, the already crowded spaces becoming more compressed as more bodies were fed into the darkness. The lanterns swayed around their heads and tempers flared as one body bumped into another in the rocking darkness.

In the bunk on Devon's left, two men shoved in next to the woman with the baby, who shrank back into its corner, looking terrified.

Another tried to climb into the upper bunk; but the family's row proved impenetrable and he moved on.

Most of the newcomers, though, appeared to be women. Their cries cut through the damp air of the hold as they were pushed from behind and pressed into whatever spaces they could find.

Three young women made their way laughingly past the giant in front of Devon and into the lower bunk on her right where the old woman had been lying, forcing her to draw herself up to its head, her back against the wet ribs of the ship against which Devon was pressed, her own legs now drawn up nearly to her chin.

Finally, long past the time it seemed the shallow cavern of the ship's belly couldn't hold another body, the hatch above was closed again, plunging them once more into near-darkness. Shouts from above were followed by another jolting lurch of the ship into motion.

The jostling for position continued for a while, as the ship creaked and groaned and began to gain momentum again. But there was no more violence among this group of passengers. Surprising in fact, Devon thought. It was as though their actions were hushed by the dim light. Or maybe by the air of uncertainty that seemed to pervade the huge space. About where they were going? How they would get there under these conditions? Many of the faces she could see registered a kind of shock. It served to reinforce her own misgivings.

Then Wicks reappeared. His jaunty figure descended the ladder, followed by the man in the pressed white uniform whom Devon had assumed to be the ship's captain.

Wicks stopped on the bottom step, the captain a step above him.

Mr. Wicks spoke first. "All right, listen up, you lot, The Captain" – the title spoken with respect – "has something to say."

The captain's voice was as cultured as his British counterparts in uniform. "Welcome aboard *The Eagle's Nest*," he said. "I am Captain Bancroft. You are in luck to have gained passage on this ship: she's a three-master, five hundred tons of burden, yet the fastest packet on the seas between the English shores and the grand land of America. Charleston, South Carolina, is our destination, and it's thirty days we'll bring her in. Sometimes less depending on the winds, never more. So relax and enjoy the voyage. I know it's a bit crowded down here, so many wanting to come to our fair land. But those who haven't paid have brought food for your trip, I'm sure. And those who've paid for a measure from the Carolina Lines will get it, never fear. Fresh meat from beasts, eggs and vegetables: we have plenty above. And water for everyone," he closed expansively.

Devon was dearly wishing she'd had the means to pay for some of that food. Already she was feeling hungry. And thirty days? That was a month! What she had wouldn't last more than a few days. Was it possible to indenture herself more for some food along the way?

"Those who are making the journey to be redeemed at the other end," the captain was saying, "are in my custody and will be furnished with fresh clothing for the auction when we dock. Meanwhile, please be sure to partake of the limes that will be passed among you daily: I want no scurvy on my ship."

There it was: she would survive on limes?

Devon knew something of scurvy; she had seen it often among the poor on the doctor's route. From a lack of nourishing food. It produced weakness, and swelling. It's why her family's first profits always went to fresh fruits and vegetables. Devon hoped the promised limes would be enough to hold the scurvy at bay for all.

She was somewhat encouraged, though, by the aspect of this captain. He stood tall and spoke easily, engendering confidence. And hadn't he kept Newgate from taking her off the ship? Perhaps she should thank him, she thought. But then she remembered her experiences at the Temple Aliquott. Men tended to stick together in these things. Whatever the captain's reasons for turning Newgate away, they probably had more to do with his authority on this ship than with any concern for her safety. He was, after all, standing there in his spotless uniform, while she crouched in the ship's belly. And she would be getting no fresh food. Class, she suspected, would likely be as present in the New World as it was in the Old.

"We have a number of first-class passengers aboard," the Captain was saying. "Their staterooms are on the upper deck. So I'll ask you not to wander the ship, please, to avoid any confusion. The hatch will be battened down. But Mr. Wicks and his assistants will be visiting you regularly to see to your needs and distribute the limes. The ship's doctor will be apprised of any troubles, should

249

they arise. But I am sure we will have none, and all will enjoy a happy passage to the promised land of America."

There was no sign of Mr. Wicks or his "assistants" for the rest of that day. Day, however, had to be estimated. Its passage into night could only be guessed at by the decrease in activity above them, there being no windows in the thick hull. The flickering light of the lanterns swayed unchanged from one hour to the next.

Devon dozed eventually, shifting sideways to ease the cramps in her drawn-up legs. The cuts and bruises inflicted by Newgate seemed to blend to create a general ache throughout her body that almost welcomed the restriction of activity. Perhaps, she thought, if she could just stay like this, curled like a babe-to-be in its mother's womb, the time would pass as evenly, unmindfully, as it must pass for such a being, until it would be time to emerge into the new world they spoke of.

But by the time she woke fully again, Devon had to struggle to her feet to ease the pain in her calves. And though the dank underside of the deck above was just inches from her face, she chose to stand that way for hours, finding a little better air up nearer the top of the crowded space.

Devon waited as long as possible before taking a few bites of the sausage and bread, and a mouthful of the boiled water Mrs. Dofferman had given her. Somehow, this little bit of food in the basket would have to last her a whole month.

But that was an impossibility she did not yet want to confront.

Chapter 20

The Passage of Hope

Hope in itself is happiness, and its frustrations, however frequent, are yet less dreadful than its extinction.

Samuel Johnson, *The Idler*

At first Devon tried to keep track of the passage of days and nights, focusing on the sounds above to tell her when one passed into another. She made a mark with her fingernail in the rotted wood behind her to track their progression. But there were fewer than a score of marks when she lost track, the rocking of the ship so mesmerizing that time seemed to lose all meaning, no coming and going of daylight to define it, no changes in one's own activity to characterize the hours. Time became one long continuum of waiting, even the object of the waiting becoming indistinct as the senses blurred. They had all come to this place for a purpose; but now, that purpose seemed almost irrelevant to their ultimate fate, which had been taken out of their hands once they descended into this forbidding dungeon.

Those first days, Devon tried to make contact with some of those around her – especially the young women, whom she hoped might prove companionable for the long trip. But the only person who seemed to want to talk was Loretta, the old woman, who less conversed than rambled on in monologue about her life in the Sussex countryside, milking the cows and goats, planting the seed and harvesting the crops. Her stories were peopled more with animals and trees than with humans, whom she mentioned more as events than persons – the son who "passed at Easter, when the dogwood bloomed," or her daughter Anna, who "left to go to London. Probably a scullery maid in somebody's kitchen now," the woman said without rancor. "Or a whore."

That remark had brought from the three women on her bunk their first reaction, having stayed very much to themselves since they'd plopped down, bag and baggage, that first day.

"Don't go callin' names now, ducky," one said, though without particular heat. "We all does what we has to, don' we?" And she turned back to the bread and cheese they were carefully dividing among themselves.

"My mister was enough of men for me," the old woman continued, as though no one had spoken. "When he run off, with the money for that last piece of land, I didn't much miss him. Was more peaceful in that little hut without 'im. And the milk money went longer." Then, without giving its relevance, she added, "Never heard no chimney sweeps to live past seven."

Only by overhearing their conversations among themselves, generally held in low tones punctuated by peals of laughter, did Devon gather that the three young women had all worked together in something called The Dog and Duck, on the waterfront. That had apparently been the ship's stop that first day, to take on more steerage passengers – a practice she gathered from their talk was illegal but quite regular, as it enhanced the profitability of the voyage.

The Dog and Duck was apparently more than just a tavern, and the women more than serving girls, as the one they called Tilly had suggested in her remark to the old woman. They tended bar for room and board; but for any extra – their "spending money", which had been saved for this trip – they were expected to give extra service to the customers. They even referred to the tavern owner, a Mr. Swanwick, as "the old ponce."

It was an arrangement Devon had already learned was far from unusual. More than once, Newgate had warned her that a refusal of his "protection" would only pitch her to the same fate. "A girl who doesn't know a good offer when she gets it will end up in the gutter, going to any bidder," he had said furiously, transporting her to Wingsbury the day after the masque.

The term "bidder" had put Devon in mind of the animals she'd seen being auctioned off at markets – a vision now made all the more ominous by the Captain's use of the word "auction" to signify the future of the indentured at the end of this voyage. For the men, it might be only their labor that would be up for bid; but for the women? Was their fate to be no different from those women she'd seen being shipped off to New South Wales?

Devon would have liked to ask these young women about it, and what their plans might be for the New

World. But the three, whose names she finally gathered were Hope and Bridget and Tilly, seemed to have formed a closed group that did not invite outsiders. Instead, Devon's sleep was regularly invaded now by scenes of herself, stripped to the waist as Newgate had done at the pillory in Smithfield Market, being sold to the highest bidder. If it happened to people from Africa, even the self-assured Mr. Woldemariam, couldn't it just as likely happen to her?

When Mr. Wicks and his 'assistant' sailors began coming down with the limes, Devon saw first-hand how such a barter was conducted. And the "needs" the captain had referred to that the sailors would "see to" proved clearly more their own needs than any other's.

The first day, the limes were given to everyone in the hold, man, woman and child. Nursing mothers, like the silent woman on her left, even got two of the small green fruits.

Wicks played his little rhyming game as part of the ceremony of distribution. "Limes for the limeys," he said, and handed a pail-full to each of his assistants, whom he sent off to the far corners of the hold, while he distributed the third portion himself, beginning with the bunk housing the three Dog and Duck women.

"A little green for the colleen," he said to Bridget that first day.

She took it with a knowing sort of smile, as though it were a game she knew well.

He made similar rhymes to the other two women, and to the old woman now crouched at the head of the bunk. "Even a crone can have one."

Then he got to Devon, leaning past the huge man in front of her, to whom he'd given two. "One more for the boar," he'd said.

"And for the sweet sixteen," he said to her now. "Or is it seventeen, my little queen?" And he laughed heartily.

Devon then responded in a way she couldn't have explained at the time. Instead of reaching out to accept the fruit, she just stared at the man quite blankly, as though she understood neither his words nor his actions. Meeting with no response, Wicks frowned slightly and tossed the lime into her lap and moved on.

As the days progressed, one melding into another until they seemed to form one long flat plank of time, Wicks and his companions came less often, and began distributing the limes only to those he identified as having paid for their passage. And to his favorites among the women, who appeared willing to exchange a flirtatious word or touch with him as part of the bargain.

Luckily, by then Devon had found a good friend in Gordon, the huge man in front of her. He had tried to hide his face from her at first, but finally revealed it as he passed her one of his limes as they got scarce. It was greatly deformed, but the eyes were kind, and she had smiled as she thanked him. After that, he insisted on sharing with her the contents of the huge pail of food he'd brought. At first she'd said no, but he'd said "Yes, please," with such urgency that she'd accepted a modest amount daily, greatly relieved that she might survive the trip now with the extra food.

Then came the storm.

Devon had been dozing, in the little nest she'd made of the extra clothing Mrs. Dofferman had told her to bring, the thick wool of the skirt affording a measure of protection from the dampness that penetrated the ribs of the ship behind her. Curled there, her head upon her now-empty basket, wrapped like her body in the blanket, Devon had learned to let the rocking of the ship carry her off to a semiconscious state that was alert to trouble from the outside but restful within. She thought of it as storing up her energy for whatever awaited her at the other end of this interminable voyage.

Then the rhythm of the ship roughened and accelerated, and suddenly a weight dropped into the curve of her body, spouting noise.

Instinctively, Devon drew away. Then she realized it was the baby of the woman above that had fallen from the bunk. Devon quickly scooped it up and examined its tiny limbs for injury.

Above her, the woman's face looked anxiously down, her arms reaching, an extended "Nooo" coming from deep in her throat; until Devon handed the apparently unharmed baby back to her, its cries soon losing their tone of panic.

"Lily, Lily," the woman kept saying soothingly. "My sweet Lily."

"I think she's all right," Devon said, accustomed to those baby sounds that signified pain.

Thereafter, from even those brief moments of holding the squirming body of the baby Lily, Devon was feeling its absence. All those years of cradling Annalee, and Dunny before her – even Carrie and Cavan – holding them through fevers and new teeth coming, through the nameless aches and pains that babies seemed to experience when they were new, Devon's body ached with an emptiness she'd almost forgotten.

But the storm that then landed upon them with such force did not prove merely one of those sudden squalls that had hit the ship before, tossing it and its contents about for a bit, then letting it rest and put itself back together as it moved forward. This one seized the huge vessel as though it were one of Sissy's miniatures, and tumbled it, first one way, then another, until Devon could hear large objects rolling about on the deck above – heavier than their own bags and baskets that got knocked about when the ship was seized with one of these fits.

Devon could hear the frightened bellows of animals above, being carried, the captain had said, to supply fresh meat and milk and eggs for the first-class passengers. And for those who'd paid below, he'd said, though little of that had been brought down. She'd heard the men complain to Wicks about not receiving their full measure of the promised provisions. But Wicks had just laughed, then spoke more roughly to them. "Best take what you can get while you can get it, mates. You know how it goes: first to those who've paid the most, then the rest to the rest."

The storm lasted for hours on end, over at least one night, before the tumult settled. The silence afterwards seemed enormous. No more bleating of animals; no more crashing of furniture and alarmed voices of the passengers above. Now even the babies below were still, exhausted like the rest of them, Devon supposed, by the ordeal.

People began to quietly put their tiny spaces back in order, having clutched whatever was left of their food as tightly as they held to family members or the nearest object of support. At one point, Devon had feared even the massive timbers of the bunks would give way, as much creaking and groaning as they gave off. But when it was finally calm again, they settled back, into the shapes of looming scaffolding that had formed the framework of Devon's own small space.

But after the storm, things changed. The regular delivery of provisions from above stopped altogether, and only three of the sailors came below now: Wicks and the two he called Iddings and Cry. And their attitude was a lot less jovial. What little provisions of bread and limes they brought were the subjects of serious bargaining.

For the women, that meant more than a casual touch. Devon turned her head from the sounds that came from the bunk of the Dog and Duck women. The rough grunts of the men put her right back into the room Newgate had locked her in that last day in London. She had hoped never to hear that again, but realized how foolish a hope that had been. She had better accustom herself to "how it goes" as Wicks had termed it. And just keep it away from herself.

So when the day came that Wicks leered down at her from the bunk where he'd just been groaning over Bridget, Devon on instinct began shaking her head from side to side, keening in a high voice she'd never used, and letting out barking coughs like no animal she'd ever heard.

The women looked down at her with much the same expressions of surprise as appeared on Wicks's face. And Gordon turned to assess her with great alarm.

Wicks left quickly then, and Devon stopped her wild behavior, smoothing back the hair she'd torn at while in the throes of her mock frenzy. The three women shook with suppressed laughter. "Well done, girl," Tilly said. "I'll remember that the next time."

Devon hoped she would not; any imitation would only tip the sailors to her duplicity. And indeed, Tilly did not. But the three women became much friendlier with Devon after that.

Then the favors of food or limes became strictly for profit. Wicks and Iddings and Cry conducted hushed conferences with certain passengers in the hold, and coins were palmed before any further provisions were handed over. Until there were no more deliveries at any price. All the chickens and sheep and one of the cows had been washed overboard, Wicks reported, so there was scarcely enough meat or milk left for the first-class passengers, who had "paid well f'r 'em." Everybody's dried fruits and vegetables were gone below, and the prized limes were kept above-decks exclusively.

It was clear that the baby Lily had begun to feel real pain. Her cries would erupt suddenly, as though some portion of her tiny body were being attacked. Devon recognized the signs as the colic other mothers had often spoken about with her own mother, who had always prescribed bananas as a cure. But there'd been few bananas available in the hold at any price, and now there were none. Lily's mother, whom Devon now knew as Margaret, had gone with Wicks a few times for limes. But now with none left, she kept her baby at her breast almost continuously, though Devon doubted there was much milk left, as Margaret too had grown thin and weak.

Devon often offered to hold and rock the baby now when Lily would cry helplessly; and Margaret began to talk to Devon about how she'd come to be aboard this ship and what she hoped for at the end of her journey.

She had worked in the Lancashire mines, she said, hauling coal through the narrow underground passages. The men dug it out of the walls and put it in carts, she explained. Then the women and children, some as young as six, were harnessed to the carts with ropes about their waists, and crawled on all fours hauling the coal through the low shafts, there to be drawn to the surface by horse or machine. They worked, Margaret told her, for as long as twelve hours at a time without food or rest.

"You get so bone weary," Margaret said, "you hope for the roof to cave in to end it once and for all." In fact, she told Devon, she had lost her mother when one wall of the passage had fallen in on her and several others. Her father had died in an explosion in the mine two years later, caused by a spark from the wheels in the cloud of all that coal dust.

"We were all mine workers, my brothers and I, and my sister when she turned six. She didn't last long though."

The woman's voice trailed off as she stared at the swaying shadows from the lanterns. "I swore that my Lily would never go down in those mines. Her father was married, so he couldn't claim her. But he gave us some money to leave, enough for the train to London and the passage and food for the voyage."

Devon had noticed several chickens in her basket at the beginning. But they'd been eaten in the first few days, since they'd have spoiled thereafter. The oranges were gone almost as quickly. Once the limes from the sailors were withdrawn, there'd been only jerky and molding bread. And now Margaret's basket was as empty as Devon's.

"What will you do there?" Devon asked her now.

"In America?" The young woman smiled – as serene a smile as Devon had seen. "I will work on a farm," she said. "That's why I chose this ship: it's headed for a place called Charles Town – Charles, like the name of Lily's daddy. They have big farms there, called plantations. I always wanted to work on a farm, out in the sun all day, where the earth is green and the air is sweet. And no mines, Charles said. My daughter will never have to work in a mine. Never."

Margaret's pale face nearly glowed as she said it, its pallor probably due to a lifetime underground, as she was underwater now in the hold of this ship. But there was a patient air about her that Devon hoped she would develop in time, her own nature burning somewhat hotter, wanting things always to move faster than they did.

Especially this passage from an Old World to a New. Especially that.

Chapter 21

School of Survival

Life shrinks or expands in proportion
to one's courage.

Anais Nin

Help from without is often enfeebling in its effects, but help
from within invariably invigorates.

Samuel Smiles, 1859

The pace did pick up that last hard stretch of the journey. But not necessarily as Devon would have wished. As people's provisions ran out and no more were forthcoming from above, even for the paying passengers, tempers ran high and often broke out into violence. There was stealing of food and whatever else could be pilfered when a lull indicated most were asleep.

The sailors grew more aggressive as well, Cry and Iddings having been joined by several more 'assistants'. The troughs of water that had stood here and there in the hold were empty now, and the hoses to refill them turned off from above. Drinking water now was the top prize from above to be paid for below. A guinea a cup, or legs spread then and there for the bearer of the life-sustaining fluid. For a mutton joint – even one that had most of its meat already boiled away – a female 'purchaser' had to disappear with the whole lot of them for a prolonged period of time.

The three women from The Dog and Duck paid their fees as casually – more so – than they divided the remainder of their stores. First one, then another, merely leaned back and opened her knees, the benefactor mercifully hidden from Devon's sight by the spread of the woman's skirts, though the sounds the men made were harder to block out. Devon would bury her head in her arms and sing a tune to herself as muffler.

In her childhood, when Devon had heard sounds in that rhythm rising through the night from her parents' mattress below, Devon had imagined a whole family of spirits – elves, like in the shoemaker's tale her father had read them – busy below, doing the work of the family so they might have a day of rest come Sunday.

When Devon had grown old enough to raise the question, her mother had told her that her father and mother were "love dancing." She had spoken the words with such a sparkle in her eyes that Devon had pictured them privately frolicking like the family sometimes did around the stove of an evening, when they heard a minstrel's pipe playing a merry tune out in Eagle and Childe Alley. Sometimes, when the tune was lively enough, Mary Quail performed a jig so quick her feet became impossible to follow, her arms raised above her head, tossing her hair like a young girl. Then she would laugh breathlessly as her husband hugged her. Devon had asked her mother to teach her those steps, but she'd said there were more necessary uses for her energies.

Now Newgate and his successors in the stinking belly of this ship had taken away all the imagined joys Devon had had of "love dancing" and replaced them with a brutal debasement. Even in the earlier days of the voyage, when Devon had heard couples engaged in that rhythm in the darkness, she had covered her ears, as she had done to keep out the sounds of Newgate and Marianne downstairs gasping and groaning and shrilling in Sissy's house. Now, she shut her eyes as well, wondering if this was all men and women did anymore, a base sort of barter with no exchange of feeling. Perhaps her parents had been the last man and woman in this world who had ever really loved each other.

Devon continued to play the madwoman when the sailors were about, so they kept their distance. And she suspected if they did not, Gordon would see to it that they never reached her behind his broad back. He shared the last of his food and water with Devon and Margaret and the baby, but seemed to not even hear the laughing offers from the Dog and Duck women to trade their favors for a share as well. He told Devon he had been with a traveling fair most of his life, being exhibited as a freak. Devon had wanted to ask him how his parents could have given him over to such people; but she was afraid the answer might be hurtful to him, so kept her tongue for once. She understood, though, why the man kept his distance from the other passengers.

Once when Devon was shrieking and tearing her hair to keep the sailors from her, Iddings said, by god, I think it's possessed. It must be that freak's offspring."

"Stay back, lads," said Wicks. "Its bite's likely pure poison."

Tilly had leaned over her bunk when they left and regarded Devon with frank admiration. "I gotta hand it to y', duck, I was right scared of y' myself for a minute there. Where'd y' learn that from?"

It was a question Devon had no answer to. But Bridget turned to her friend and said, "Same place we all have, dearie: at the Little Ladies School of Survival."

But Devon's talents for survival were to be tested beyond her wildest imagination before the voyage was over.

As everyone's food and water had run out, the lethargy produced by the monotony of the ship's rhythms had turned to restlessness, then anger. And now, with even the paying passengers in the hold deprived of their promised provisions, and the few to be offered priced higher and higher, the angry mutters became clearer calls for action.

The voices of some of the men, meeting back among the slop buckets when the privy became unusable, could be heard all the way up to Devon's spot. They spoke of charging up *en masse* on deck to demand food and water and time above for air, that of the packed hull now too foul to breathe and exhausted of all life.

"We don't have to take this!" Mr. Truitt, the apparent leader of the group, kept saying. "We're human beings, not animals!"

Finally, the group came to appeal to Gordon. They suggested he might overpower the sailors. "Take their guns," said Mr. Truitt. "Then we could make any demands we wish." All the sailors had begun carrying guns since the mood below had turned more hostile. And none came down alone anymore.

"Or we could hold them hostage," said another of the men. "All those come down. Get their guns and demand food and water for the remainder of the trip."

Gordon – now called Gordon the Great by the Dog and Duck women – listened silently to the men. They had not spoken twenty words, if that, to Gordon throughout the voyage, and had not included him in their discussions. But they spoke to him now with every appearance of respect.

"You want me to be the one to do this for you," Gordon said finally, his voice like a great rumble in his chest.

"Yes, exactly," said Truitt. "You are probably the strongest among us, physically, so you'd have a better chance of overpowering them."

Truitt himself was quite small. Tilly'd told Devon that Truitt had been a foreman in a textile mill in Liverpool, and had propositioned her several times with a bill or two from his money clip when she'd first ventured back alone to the privy.

"Or you could go up yourself with the gun and bring down provisions," Truitt suggested. "You'd have the best chance of getting through them."

"Or getting killed," Bridget said hotly from her bunk. There had been no women in their little planners' group, but Bridget was never shy to put a word in.

"Expendable," Hope added.

Truitt frowned at them. "We don't need comments from the baggage," he said. "We're putting together a serious plan here."

"Then why don't ye do it y'rself?" Tilly shot back. "Afraid of getting y'r own wee pecker shot off?" And the three erupted in laughter, joined behind hands by some of the men in the group.

"Shut up, slut," Truitt snapped. "Unless you have a better plan to offer, just keep your trashy talk to yourself."

"Perhaps I do," Bridget said slowly. "Instead of sending up the biggest, most noticeable among us, maybe better to send someone smaller, somebody who might slip about quieter like and attract no notice."

Truitt's smaller stature might have been behind the scowl he leveled at her.

"Like y'rself maybe?" one of the other men said to her, no small amount of admiration in his tone.

"Nah," Bridget said. "I can get what *I* need."

"We noticed," said another of the men.

"I was thinkin' about her," Bridget said.

It was a moment before Devon realized the young woman was pointing at her.

"Me?" Devon said. The amazement came before the fear.

"Right enough. She's quick with her wits," Tilly said. "And probably quick on her feet as well."

Devon didn't know about the first part, but was sure the latter could no longer be true. She wasn't even sure her legs would still carry her to the end of this room. As her food had run out, so had her energy. Her periods of making herself stand and walk in place had become shorter and less frequent.

"That slip of a girl?" one of the men said contemptuously. "This is a job for a man."

"Perhaps not," Truitt said. His pinched face was looking sober, and not a little relieved. "They may have something here. A girl could move quickly, less danger of being spotted."

"We c'd dress her in one of their uniforms," Hope said. "Cry's breeches'd about fit a girl. His gun, too." She laughed at a private joke. "I c'd take 'em from 'im next time he's down."

Gordon spoke up then. "I'll go before I let a girl do it," he said.

But Devon shook her head. She could hardly believe the next words that came out of her mouth. "I think the women are right. I might be less noticed."

Gordon turned to her. "Are you sure? I could go with you as guard."

Devon shook her head again. "Two would be of more notice than one."

His deformed brow wrinkled. "I'd stand guard for you then at the hatch, and come if you needed me."

That seemed to seal it for everyone. And despite the growing queasiness in her empty stomach at the prospect, Devon was thinking that in going to the upper deck, she could get a look at how the other passengers were living on this voyage. And she might actually get herself a lungful of fresh air in the bargain.

So the next time the sailors came down, Hope wooed Cry off into a dark corner and detained him long enough that the others left before him. Then the other two Dog and Duck women moved in and took his gun and his clothes, gagging him with Tilly's garter.

"Wear it in good health, ducky," Tilly said to the bound Cry. "Though I must say it looks better on me than you."

Devon had more than a few qualms about what she was supposed to do on this mission, but she refused to carry the gun. From what she'd seen of the victims of guns, she wanted none of them. Gordon took it instead, saying he would listen at the hatch, and come armed at the first sound of trouble.

So behind the screen of Bridget and Hope, Devon let Tilly take her skirt and put the sailor's trousers on her, and the jacket over her shirtwaist. As she took her first steps in the pants, she was surprised at how natural they felt, how easy it was to move in them, without the bulk of skirts hobbling her legs.

Once the plan was in motion, however, trousers were the least of the things on Devon's mind. She found her energies rising with just the prospect of *doing* something about their condition. And others seemed to feel it, too. People who had never left their bunks all crowded around, as one of their own was preparing to break the barrier between themselves and what they believed was their due. The children picked up the mood and began chasing each other about again, though in slower motion. Whines turned to whoops, and they had to be quieted, lest they be heard from above.

The hardest was the waiting once she was ready. It was agreed that no move would be made until all activity above had stilled. That rhythm had been studied by those below the way Devon had come to realize servants studied the habits of their masters in order to avoid their wrath or turn the knowledge to their own advantage. Now, all movement below had stopped, as the great mass of tight-packed bodies waited – for what exactly, perhaps no one could say. Perhaps only change. Any change.

Then at last it was time to go. Devon stood, unsure whether her legs shook from inaction or fear. But with Margaret and Hope and Bridget and Tilly – and even the old peasant woman, who had for the moment emerged from her dreamlike state – all urging her on, along with the rest of the passengers in the gloomy hold, Devon was virtually propelled up the ladder by their energies.

As Gordon on the step above her strained to heave up the hatch, Devon wondered what her parents would think of her now, gotten up in men's clothing, about to break all the rules under which she was being held. This was not the way she'd been brought up. And if her father had feared for her setting foot alone in Eagle and Childe Alley, how much greater were the likely dangers that awaited her at the top of this 'eagle's nest'.

But she didn't for a moment consider turning back. Those below were depending on her now.

They'd been told that the hatch would be battened down in some way. And as Gordon put his shoulder to it, the creaks and strains seemed the cries of a living thing, until a splintering sound signaled release; and the breaths of her companions below seemed to release as well, with an audible sigh.

Through the opened crack, Devon got her first glimpse of sky in weeks. There were actual stars studding the velvet of the night; and a sliver of moon hung like an ornament among them. Neither Gordon nor Devon moved for some moments, straining to catch any signs of reaction to the sounds they'd just made. But there was nothing.

Then finally, Gordon turned his body sideways and reached down for Devon, and she felt herself being lifted up past the ladder's top, into the air beyond.

Air! That's what there was up here: endless volumes of living *air* all around her, a stiff breeze washing over her face and body. Devon reached for the nearest post to steady herself as, eyes closed, head tipped back, her head swam in the immensity of the air, gulping it in great mouthfuls into her starving lungs.

When her eyes opened again, there was another breathtaking sight: the immense white sheets of the sails billowed above her, spread against the sky, filled with this tangy crisp air to balance the great solid vessel below her feet. How, she thought in that moment, had it ever occurred to somebody that mere cloth and wind could do such a thing as carry a huge ship across a vast sea?

Then she remembered why she was there and looked quickly about her. But she saw no one, and heard only the creaking of the great poles holding the sheets of the sails.

She looked back down at Gordon, who merely nodded his encouragement.

Which direction should she try first? "Look for the dining room," Mr. Truitt had said. "The kitchen should be right behind."

"The galley it's called," Tilly had corrected him, earning another scowl.

There seemed to be only deck to her left, so Devon went right. She found herself crouching as though to become smaller as she crept along the polished floor boards, the wood nearly as slick and glossy as that under the huge dome of the Pantheon that night of the masque. Devon shuddered at the memory, and was glad at least that she was outside under this canopy of sky and stars rather than the false glitter of that pleasure palace.

Devon straightened, feeling that if she were going to be discovered, it would not be in a cowering position like some common criminal. Those below deserved to live every bit as much as those above; and if this is what it took to get them what they needed to survive, then this is what she would do.

Ahead of her, a narrow staircase angled up to yet another deck; and under it, an archway opened to a passage carpeted in darkest red. There seemed to be nothing for it but to go down that path, so Devon set one small booted foot after another on the carpet, moving silently forward until she was through the archway into a quite splendid space beyond.

To her right, lit by a whole row of gas lanterns fastened to the wall and turned low like hushed voices, stretched a room as long as the entire space below, with tables of rich rose-colored wood running down its center, delicate chairs of the same wood on either side, all glowing in the soft light as though awaiting the attendance of a royal party. How many passengers were there up here, Devon wondered, to deserve such luxuries? She'd seen so few standing at the other end of the ship when she'd boarded.

Across the garnet carpet from the dining room gleamed another row of doors, each in a different patterned wood, their smooth brass knobs inviting to the hand. These must be the resting places, Devon supposed, of those who would fill the chairs in the morning and dine upon the gracious tables. She would have liked to peek into each one, but clearly she could not.

Beyond the tables there were louvered doors, next to a polished bar. But that seemed too shallow a space to hold any kind of kitchen. And if it was food she was after, Devon figured she had better find where the food was stored and cooked as directly as possible.

Then footsteps from ahead, beyond a double door at the far archway, made her look quickly for somewhere to hide, and she ducked into the dark triangle of space beneath the stairs.

The figure that came through the swinging doors was dressed in a uniform jacket like the one she was wearing, except for a white collar and cuffs. He walked as though he were in charge of this place, making his rounds at night like the London watchmen.

But he did not pass through; instead, he crossed to the bar at the far side of the dining room.

Other than a few tinklings of glassware being moved about – the low notes of heavy glass against the thin notes of lighter – there were no sounds to indicate what the man was doing or how long he might be doing it. Devon raised herself higher beneath the sloping staircase, until her eyes came level with the gleaming surface of the table across the passageway, and she saw reflected in it the image of the man's back and crooked elbow, raising and lowering a glass to his mouth.

From the way his body leaned against the brass rail of the bar in front of him, Devon guessed the man might be there for some time, so she began to look for ways to leave her hiding place undetected.

Ahead, the doors that had swung apart at his entrance did not reach from floor to ceiling, but were raised to swing free, a space of several feet above and below them. Devon tried to measure the height below against the thickness of her body if it crawled belly-down, the way Margaret must have done in the mines. It seemed possible at least, and perhaps her only chance of getting on with her mission before still another person might come along and she would be trapped where she was until discovered.

She decided to chance it; and with her gaze darting between the man's reflection in the table's surface and the opposite archway, Devon crawled like a lizard along the rich red carpet toward the doors.

Occupied though her mind was on making no sound and willing the man at the bar not to turn; it still occurred to Devon how easy it was to maneuver in these trousers that were divided between one leg and the other. This freedom of movement would never be possible in a skirt. Could that be, she wondered briefly, why women were made to wear skirts?

Then she was at the doors and bent her head sideways to slide beneath them. Flattening her chest on the carpet, Devon felt the buttons of the sailor's coat catch against the soft nap of the carpet; but she pushed with her feet and her shoulders slid clear, until her hips hit the doors, held a moment, then released.

She drew her legs through and waited at the other side to hear if her movements had been detected. But there was only the sound of a bottle being picked up and set down again, then a belch. She gathered herself to stand.

The wind had picked up a little since she'd first emerged from the hatch: the masts creaked with the weight of their sails now in an erratic rhythm. That was good, she thought: any sounds she made would be less noticeable with the ship sending out its own restless noises.

She looked about. Yes, there it was on her right: an open room with a vast brick hearth. The fire in it was still burning; and over it, the fat iron kettle looked big enough to hold food sufficient for every passenger on the ship, above and below decks. Even from this distance, she could smell it, and the fragrance nearly made her swoon: mutton stew, her nose told her. Actual mutton stew – her favorite. She wanted to rush over and stick her head right in that pot and chew her way clear to the bottom, until her stomach would be finally full again.

But she proceeded with a wiser caution. The handle of a giant ladle lay curled over the rim of the pot, jiggling slightly from the simmering contents, telling Devon that the pot wouldn't be left unattended long. She had to hurry.

She looked about for colder, drier provisions that might better fit in the knapsack she'd been given. They would have to be light enough to carry and dense enough to nourish many bodies. Once she'd located such provisions, the thinking went, others could go back up for more later. Getting water on this trip had been ruled out as too heavy for one person to carry. Secretly, Devon hoped she would find both and take them to Gordon, then go back for more. But first she had to find them.

Along the wall to the left of the pot were shelves with rows of plates and bowls and cups and serving pieces, all in a matching pattern of white and gold, with gilt rims. Even the pattern of the utensils matched.

Devon turned to the right-hand wall, where piles of boxes filled several shelves. One whole stack had *Hardtack* printed on the sides, and she quickly unwrapped the knapsack from around her waist and began stuffing in the narrow boxes, then some marked *Johnny's Jerky* from a lower shelf.

Fruit. There must be fruit somewhere, which could provide moisture for their thirst as well as the kind of nourishment needed by people cut off from the sun.

Devon pushed into a smaller room between the rows of shelves. It was dark, and she didn't want to risk a light that would signal her presence, even if she could find a lantern; so she felt along the wall until her hand touched the large bowed sides of a barrel.

Her fingers reached in, hoping to feel the luscious globes of oranges and limes, the rough texture of their rinds. But instead they found a barrelful of sticky substances. Dried fruit: not what her mouth was thirsting for, but at least it was lighter; she could carry more of it. Good.

Devon filled the rest of the pack with the fruit, cramming it down between the boxes until the pack would hold no more.

Then footsteps from the dining room caused her to freeze. A creak of hinges signaled the parting of the swinging doors, and Devon held her breath, hoping to hear the footsteps continue down the deck.

But they did not. Instead, the slightly off-balance steps turned her way and paused. "Cooky?" a low voice called.

Devon shrank back against the barrel. Through the crack in the doorway, in a sliver of light, she could make out the form of the man who'd been at the bar. He turned his head slowly to the left, then the right, as though his brain weren't functioning at full speed.

Then he moved to the bubbling pot, and Devon caught her breath at the fragrance as the man lifted the ladle to his mouth. Then he uttered an oath and dropped the ladle and stumbled out of the room.

Devon smiled to herself: he'd burned his mouth.

She remained still until she could no longer hear the man's retreating footsteps, then crept out and past the hearth.

But the raising of the ladle had released such heavenly smells into the warm room that Devon thought not even life itself would be worth having if she didn't get just one bite of that flavorful stew into her shrunken stomach.

She ducked back to the pot. Holding the laden knapsack in her left arm, her right lifted the ladle. The very sight of the chunks of meat and vegetables made her faint with hunger. And the smell! Her lips trembled as she blew at the steam. But soon the urge to ingest was too great, and she tipped the contents into her mouth and chewed frantically, then gulped it all down her throat.

Never had pain tasted so good. As soon as the first bite reached her stomach, Devon tipped another ladleful into her mouth and, turning back to the hallway with full cheeks and both arms wrapped around the knapsack, Devon left the lovely pot and headed back toward the hatch.

Clearly, there was no way she could slip and slide under doors so burdened, so Devon told herself that she just had to hope she would encounter no one else on her way. And with her teeth and tongue still busy with the mouthful of mutton stew, savoring it as long as she could, Devon pushed through the doors and started down the garnet carpet.

She was halfway along when one of the shiny doors on her right opened suddenly to discharge a portly old gentleman into her path. Clad in a green striped robe with a gold sash and slippers, the man looked quite as startled as she to encounter her.

Devon quickly raised the knapsack to cover her face, resisting the impulse to just run.

"Ah," the gentleman said. "Just looking for the commode. Could you direct me, sir? They seem to keep moving it, I swear." Then he fumbled in the pocket of his robe and drew out a cigar, which he studied as though unsure whether to put it in his mouth or offer it to her.

Devon swallowed the hot contents of her mouth in one gulp, which helped to make her voice husky as she said, "That way?" and pointed behind her.

Her voice must have passed the test, because the old gentleman tipped a nonexistent hat and said, "Thank ye, matey," and scuffed his way down the carpet toward the swinging doors.

Devon all but ran in the opposite direction, toward the hatch, which raised at the sound of her footsteps on the deck.

Gordon's head was surely one of the best sights of her life; and Devon dumped the knapsack onto his reaching arm and slipped past him, almost falling as her first foot missed the ladder's rung. But Gordon's other arm gripped and held her as, one way or another, they made it to the floor of the hold.

Her relicf was short-lived. All that glorious fresh air from above was gone, replaced by the putrid stench of the hold, so devoid of oxygen that Devon could not seem to catch her breath.

When she became aware again, she was lying on a bunk, surrounded by faces that kept asking if she was all right.

Devon cautiously propped herself on one elbow, tried to breathe, then tried to expel the awful stuff, rubbing a bump on her forehead she didn't know how she'd come by, while people clapped her on the shoulders and effused their appreciation.

Meanwhile, Truitt was shouting orders about the division of the spoils, until Gordon plucked the knapsack from his hand and began quietly telling the surrounding crowd how the food would be divided – by age and health and need.

The last thing Devon remembered before a great drowsy darkness claimed her was the tart taste of apricot in her mouth, thick and rich and utterly delicious.

Chapter 22

The Face of Death

I had a dream which was not all a dream.

Lord Byron, Darkness

To live is like to love – all reason is against it, and all healthy instinct for it.

Samuel Butler

After the first trip, some of the men grew braver, and there was a successful foray for water, then another, with two men going, for more food and water. Until Truitt conceded it was his turn and was caught. The hatch was reinforced and battened down for good.

But now there were further reasons given for their isolation from those above. A Mr. Winkles, whom Devon recognized as one of the sailors who'd been coming down to trade food for favors, presented himself to tell them that Mr. Wicks was ailing, and was sure he'd caught whatever he had from them.

"It's these here fleas and mites and lice," he said. "They all causes fevers, an' we got fevers now above, prob'ly from you lot comin' up an' stealin' our food an' water. We hung the varmint we caught, an' if we find out who else's involved, we'll hang them too. The doc says it might be typhus an' we should seal off the source. So there's nobody gonna leave this pit till we docks in Charles Town. An' that includes whoever try t' trick us down here."

That was the first allusion made to the time Cry had spent bound and gagged in the hold, while his uniform ventured above. Tilly had shrugged off any consequences for that part of the scheme with the observation, "Won't no man admit being bested by a woman, much less gagged by a garter." And apparently she'd been right.

That had, at least, stopped the sailors' visits, and that was a relief. If there was typhus above, everybody hoped it would stay there. While half the population below had respiratory distress, there were no fevers high enough to indicate a more serious disease.

Until Margaret took sick. Not one to complain, she'd said nothing at the outset. Her silence, in fact, was one of the first signs to Devon that the young woman was ill – beyond the hunger and thirst they all shared. Because she'd grown quite talkative once that first barrier between them had been broken. Especially about Lily's father. It was as though she had kept the secret of their affair for so long, she now had a need to unburden herself, and would talk in low, wistful tones of her love for the man and her desolation that she would never see him again.

"He was a full manager, so he put himself in danger for me. Once I found I was pregnant, he made work for me above, never allowed me to go down into the mines the whole time. His wife couldn't have children, so he said mine would be special for him. And he'd give me whatever I needed to keep the baby healthy. Wouldn't even send it into the mines with the other children. He'd find some job for it above – at least until it was full old enough for that kind 'a work. But then his wife found out and we had to leave."

That didn't sound entirely caring or generous to Devon, but of course she said nothing. Margaret needed all the positive feelings she could find within herself to get through the voyage alive. They all did.

But now Margaret lay silent on the bunk, Lily tucked into the curve of her belly. It wasn't until Devon noticed the film of sweat on her face and its uncharacteristically high color that she realized the young woman's illness must be serious.

There was, at least, plenty of cold water for compresses; bilge water had begun to rise out of the cracks in the deck below ever since the storm, until it was now ankle-deep and stinking of rot and refuse. Those, like Devon, who had sat on the bare planks of flooring now perched on their empty packs or baskets. And some moved up into the bunks, with or without invitation, adding to the crowding. Yet Devon noticed that there was little of the fighting that had plagued the group before they'd begun to send members up to get what they needed. Something about taking matters into their own hands had seemed to bond and strengthen them in some fundamental way.

But Margaret's condition went quickly from bad to worse; and the rashes that had broken out on her face and arms began appearing on the skin of others as the fever spread. Devon suspected that Wicks himself was the source of the disease; and that Margaret's eventual submission to him for food had infected her – and now, it seemed, might infect all those below as well.

Devon feared for Margaret, but for Lily even more. The babe lay in her mother's arms quite silent now, her blue eyes opening seldom, and then with a kind of emptiness, as though seeing nothing. Then the fever seized her small body also, and Devon kept soaked cloths wrapped about her like swaddling clothes.

But she could save neither. Margaret went first, the gaze she kept fixed on her baby becoming blank and lifeless. Devon closed the eyes and hugged Lily's body more tightly to her. But its labored breathing was soon stilled as well, and Devon had to let them both be taken by Gordon, placing the baby in her mother's arms as he carried them up to be delivered to the sea. The hatch was opened now only to a special knock to signal that another body was ready to be disposed of.

By then, the fever was in Devon as well; her whole head felt as though it were being pelted from the inside by the angry missiles of the pillory. She buried her head on her arms, and was only dimly aware when Gordon lifted her onto the bunk above, in Margaret's place.

The next stretch of black time was filled with lurid images – of Newgate's leering face above her at the inn; the gaping mouths shouting obscenities at her stripped body at the pillory; the stricken eyes of the stag and the merciless gleam in those of the falcon; and a seemingly endless parade of those she'd loved who had died, marching through her head with heavy feet.

Only when something cool was laid on her forehead did the images still for a moment. Then, she would open her eyes to see Gordon's face hovering over hers as he settled the cloth; and Devon would reach to touch his cheek, swollen in its deformity, and Gordon would lay his huge hand over hers.

Then there was only a long sinking into darkness. At one point Devon even thought she saw the face of death – not victorious such as the faces of the living who took the life of one of their fellow creatures, but calm, benign, a presence that offered relief. Later, when she returned to consciousness, Devon wondered why she had not accepted that welcoming offer. She thought she even remembered seeing the faces of her mother and father, her whole family, smiling at her from some shining place just over the border from the fevered turbulence that gripped her.

Yet in the end, she had pulled back, had felt a sort of tug from the opposite opening of that long dark tunnel, toward another light, one that sparked her curiosity, leading toward marvels she had yet to experience. She remembered it as a kind of turn, like that she might have experienced in the womb as an infant, restless to be out and about in the world beyond that dark protected space.

All the images fell away, like puppets being lowered behind the stage after their performance at the St. Bartholomew's Fair so long ago. And Devon sank into a deeper, more peaceful darkness, from which she finally emerged weak and pale but curiously rested, as though

she had gone to some magical place and had returned
from it refreshed.

Chapter 23

Welcome to America

Land of the West, we rush to thee!

Home of the brave, soil of the free,

Huzza! She rises o'er the sea. An Owenite song

By the time The Eagle's Nest reached its destination, the cargo of souls it carried in its hold had been reduced by half. When Devon had regained consciousness, she found to her dismay that Gordon himself had joined Margaret and Lily in their watery grave. Loretta had hung on amazingly long for her age, but had finally succumbed to the illness as well, and Bridget had died soon after.

Devon did what she could to ease the others when her strength returned enough to move about. But there was little to be done, except to share whatever blankets and provisions remained, some belonging to the dead, and to cool the foreheads of those still in the grip of the disease.

Again, Devon wondered why some died and some did not, why she had been spared when so many had been taken – all worthy of life, she was sure, if worthiness were the measure, and if indeed any actual Being were doing the measuring. At times like these, she was tempted to wish she had some religious doctrine to hold onto, something that would tell her the how and why of events. Perhaps, she thought, she just wanted someone to blame – or to thank, for that matter, for her own repeated salvation. But she had to admit, from what of life she'd seen already, there just didn't seem to be any such Being in charge. Or if there were, that Being was far from just. Who prospered and who fell; how many of the former were evil and the latter good: she could see no justice in any of it.

For herself, Devon was left feeling that she had only her family looking over her, those who'd gone to death before her. And that would have to be enough – that and whatever strength she could develop in her own mind and spirit. She hoped that hers would be equal to the challenges that would be presented to her in this new land. The good, Devon thought, probably had to make their own justice, and she hoped she would be up to that task.

It was Mr. Wicks who finally came below to take a head count and to issue clothing to those who would be auctioned off for their services. He had survived, Devon thought bitterly, while so many more worthy had not. What more proof was needed of the absence of any kind of divine justice?

For at least an hour, the sounds above had signaled they might at last be nearing their destination, and a flurry of excitement had run through those below. But Mr. Wicks was all business again. He didn't even glance at Margaret's bunk, Devon noted, as he descended the ladder, his face half covered by a kerchief against the stench.

"We are nearing port," he announced briskly, his voice somewhat muffled by the cloth across his nose and mouth. "The Captain's made it in forty days and forty nights, typhus and typhoon notwithstanding. So you have that to thank him for, that more weren't lost, as surely there would have been if we'd been longer at sea."

He consulted a paper. "When I call off your name, speak up," he said, "so we know that you're still among the living. Those who've paid their passage, move to the rear and the doctor will come to take a look at you, see if you're fit to leave the ship. Those who've come indentured to the Captain, move up to the front here so's you can be issued presentable clothing. The mates will be bringing it down, along with soap and water to cleanse yourselves. Buyers are put off by soiled goods. So step lively: the auction will begin at eight sharp tomorrow morning, and we mean to get a fair price."

After that, bedlam reigned in the hold, as the promise of relief seemed near. People began gathering their meager belongings and rearranging their positions depending on whether they'd been able to pay for their passage or were now indebted for service – to whom and for how long were yet to be known.

Devon suspected that question was uppermost in the minds of all who'd come indentured, as it was in hers, though she'd heard no one speak of it. One lesson this ordeal may have taught them was that in difficult circumstances, only each moment could be dealt with at a time; to look beyond might bring on despair.

When the ship's doctor finally descended, wearing a white mask over his own nose and mouth, he ordered those still ill to separate from the others into a stand of bunks on one side. Then he moved among them, making cursory examinations and ministrations. The sailors, also masked, passed among those at the front, distributing clean clothing. Soap and water were brought to another section, designated for bathing and dressing, to be ready for the morning. Ironically, the suffocating shallow space of the hold was made almost spacious by the deaths of so many. And the living could finally wash themselves and begin to feel human again.

Devon washed as best she could and put on the clean clothing she'd been given. There was no division of men from women for their preparations, but no one seemed to care. Devon suspected they all had but one thing in mind: their final release from this hell hole.

As Devon dressed in the white shirtwaist and plain gray skirt, that typical maid's costume reminded her of Marianne, and she wondered whether Newgate might have actually killed her as she'd feared, in his temper at finding himself powerless to remove Devon from the ship before it sailed.

Hope and Tilly, who had grown quiet with Bridget's illness, and had held each other all night when she'd died, now broke into their more characteristic laughter at the clothing Devon and the other future female servants had been provided with.

"Glad I didn't come a pauper," Tilly said. "Rather earn my living on my back than put this fine body into them straight-laced goods."

Devon was trying to button all the tiny buttons that traveled up her back, and Tilly gave her a hand, doing the same for the barrel cuffs at her wrists. "You do look the proper virgin," she said, giving Devon a last hug as she and Hope prepared to leave. "Just try to stay that way. These gents want more than their tea served to 'em, I can guarantee you that. So keep your guard up and your wits about you, girl."

It was advice that Devon found profoundly depressing, only confirming her fear that this new land might hold as many predators as the old; and that she still would be considered fit prey.

By the time all the paying passengers who were well enough had been released, and those to be sold were washed and dressed, most of those left in the hold stretched out on the emptied bunks, storing up sleep now that the end of their journey was near and the unknown future was yet to come.

But Devon was restless. She had spent too many days and nights already in this underground dungeon, and her lungs couldn't stand another moment of the airless space. She had not heard the bars being slid back over the hatch when the doctor had left the hold; and the snatch of sky she'd glimpsed when it had been opened for him had recalled the vast expanse of the heavens that had greeted her on her one clandestine trip above for food.

So before she could let reason dissuade her, Devon made her way quietly up the ladder, noting how much easier the climb had been in the stolen sailor's trousers than in this tight skirt. She had to hoist the skirt with one hand and hold tight to the steep ladder with the other to keep herself from tumbling back down it.

But indeed the hatch lifted without resistance, and she was released again into a heavenly world of sweet, fresh air. Devon stood on the deck, breathing it in. She could never get enough of it again, of that she was certain.

The stars above were as bright as those she remembered at sea. And now, there was also a glitter of lights from the dock and the buildings beyond it. There were tables in an open market, though no one was selling at this hour. The houses she could see on the street beyond looked quite grand, though smaller than their counterparts in Regent Square.

Habitation reminded her, however, to find some sort of concealment, lest she be discovered above before her designated time. She made her way to the ship's rail and slid behind a lifeboat hung on its side.

Below, she was surprised to see another ship – entirely dark, with no flag and untethered to the dock. It was barely half the size of *The Eagle's Nest*, its hull and masts painted black. But while the ship she was on seemed to be waiting for morning, the dark ship teemed with activity, though all of it near silent.

Those on deck, clad in dark uniforms, spoke to each other in hushed tones. The ship's sails were down, but no gangplank connected it to the dock. Then, as Devon watched, a hatch in the middle of the deck was raised, and bodies so black they were almost invisible in the night began rising from the depths of the ship, while the sailors turned hoses on them, knocking many down with the force of the water.

Devon had seen animals less crudely cleansed for market. But these were naked bodies, both male and female, some of them children; and Devon watched in horror as the smaller stumbled and fell, those who were herding them striking their bare skin with lashes or clubbing the downed bodies with stout sticks.

As her eyes grew more accustomed to the night, Devon could see chains glistening on the wrists and ankles of those being hauled from the hold, each body chained to the next like so many sausages hanging in a butcher's stall.

So riveted was she by the sight that she did not hear footsteps approaching until a voice close behind her said, "And what might you be doing here?"

She turned sharply to see the uniformed figure of Mr. Wicks.

His eyes narrowed as he took her in. "Wait a minute, I know you. You're Sweet Sixteen. Or is it the freak's kid?"

He took a step toward her. "But you're not loony at all, are you? In fact, you're quite the plum."

His hand was as quick as her jump to avoid it, catching her by the wrist and bending her arm behind her, bringing her body hard up against his. "Well, you won't escape me this time, my pretty, I can promise you that."

Keep your wits about you, Tilly had said.

Devon forced her muscles to relax, her voice to become as wheedlingly soft as Bridget's when she was 'bartering' for what she needed.

"I knew I'd never fool a smart man like you," she told him, in what she hoped was a seductive tone. "It was those others I wanted to avoid. But I've had my eye on you from the beginning."

Confusion stilled his features for a moment; then a wary smile stretched his small mouth. "Have y' now? And just what did y' have in mind?" But he gave her arm another yank upward, as though to remind her that he still had the upper hand.

Devon reached to steady herself, and felt the curved bottom of the boat lashed to the rail. "Actually," she said, "I was hoping to go for a little boat ride. A sort of advance look at the city." She forced her body to move against his. "But what I need is a sailor."

She saw doubt warring with vanity in his features. "Say no more, my little whore," he said, producing his rhymes again. "My cabin's just down the way here. We can have a little fun. Then in the morning…"

"Oh," Devon said quickly, "but I like it by moonlight. Out on the water. Wouldn't that be romantic?" She felt mortified and ridiculous saying such things, and hoped he wouldn't notice that in fact there was only a sliver of moon showing.

"Do y' now?" he said again.

Devon wriggled from his loosening grip and turned to the boat. "I was just trying to see how to get one of these free. But I can't figure out the knots."

"Mmm, I don't know about that," the sailor said. "These are lifeboats, not pleasure boats."

"Oh, but I'll bet you could *make* it a pleasure boat." The giggle Devon tried to produce to go with the words came out sounding more like a gag.

"If I wanted," Wicks said, still sounding reluctant. But he hoisted himself up to stand on the lower rail to get a better look at the ropes that bound the boat. "I don't really fool with these things much myself," he said. "That's for ordinary sailors." He backed up another rail. "As the First Mate, I'm more like the assistant to the Captain."

Devon decided this was as high as she was going to get him; it was now or never. Gathering all of her strength, she leaped at him, shoving the man's legs up with all her might, toppling his body up and over the rail.

Her momentum was such that she almost went over with him, but grabbed a rail just in time to stop herself. As he hit the water, she heard a voice she barely recognized as hers scream, "*That's* for Margaret! And for Lily, damn you. And the rest of the dead!"

Then a voice behind her said calmly, "Well. It seems our Mister Wicks will need a life ring."

Devon whirled to see the Captain in his tall white uniform standing there. Her time in this New World, she thought despairingly, might be only as long as it took to find a noose for her neck.

As Wicks's body broke the surface, cursing and sputtering, Devon searched her mind frantically for some compelling explanation for her behavior.

But the Captain appeared far from angry. He stepped up beside her, peering over the rail with a smile on his face. "He's had that coming for a while," he said. And as he unfastened one of the white rings bound to the rail, he added, "The man needed taking down a peg or two. And he is quite down there now, isn't he?"

He tossed the ring over the edge, watched it land near the flailing figure. "Actually, I don't think Sailor Wicks can even swim."

Then he turned, taking in her costume. "I take it you're to be redeemed in the morning."

Devon nodded mutely.

"I believe I might know just the position for you then," the Captain said, cocking his head as he surveyed her. "Archer likes spirit. In moderation, of course."

He made a gesture for her to accompany him, and began walking back toward the dark garnet carpet Devon had ventured down on her mission not many days before.

"I trust you do not always express yourself so forcefully," he said easily, glancing back at her.

"No, sir," Devon managed, hurrying to catch up.

They arrived at one of the doors with the brass knobs Devon had seen that night. The Captain opened it with a large key and ushered her in with a sweep of his arm.

"You can pass a more comfortable night here," he said. "Then in the morning, after the auction, I will take you myself to a post I think might suit you well. You do not speak French, by any chance, do you?"

"A little," Devon said, amazed that she could say it. Sissy's lessons in polite French hardly made her fluent in the language; she hoped she was not misrepresenting herself.

"A little should be quite enough," the Captain said. He looked her over appraisingly in the brighter light of the cabin. "Yes, I think you should do quite nicely."

And he closed the door. Devon heard it lock.

She hardly knew what to feel. Relief? Fear? Anticipation?

She guessed she felt all of that and more. She looked about the stateroom at the fine woods and rich fabrics, lit by a brass oil lamp. She knew better than to think she would be living in this new country in such luxury. She was still to be sold, after all. As a servant. And the door was locked.

But it had never been luxuries she'd wanted, and she'd never seen anyone truly happy who had them.

Freedom. Freedom is what her heart longed for. And freedom she had always pictured as being green. Green hills, green crops, pure air and water, like those she'd always pictured in her mother's Ireland – The Green Isle. Why she would need French in such a setting she couldn't imagine. But she could hope, couldn't she?

She could hope.